CW00702523

LONDON
THE
ROYAL CITY

INTERWORLD
PUBLICATIONS

LONDON
THE
ROYAL CITY

written by
Dr. S. Panteli

assisted by
Anna Lavithis

First Published in 1989
by Interworld Publications Ltd
12 The Fairway
New Barnet, Herts. EN5 1HN
England
Tel: 01-449 5938

ISBN 0 948853 10 7

Credits
The bulk of the photos were taken by
Mr. Renos Lavithis.
— All other contributors have been credited under
the photographs they have supplied.
— Some old photos and prints are from
Mr. Dennis Shilston Collection
— Illustrations by Eddie Brockwell.

— Designed and Produced by
TOPHILL DESIGNS, 12 The Fairway,
New Barnet, Herts. England.
— Typesetting by
Sunset Typesetters — Edmonton, London
— Printed and bound in Cyprus
by PRINTCO LTD.

— *Colour Reproduction by:*
Custance Graphics London EC1

©**Copyright:**
Interworld Publications Ltd 1989.
All rights reserved. No part of this book
or any photographs, may be reproduced
or transmitted in any form in any
country, wothout the permission of the
publishers.

NOTICE
Every precaution has been taken to ensur
accuracy of the information contained in thi
book, but the publishers accept no responsibilit
for errors or omissions as some information ha
been published as supplied to us.

CONTENTS

ACKNOWLEDGEMENTS

For valuable help and advice we wish to thank the following
institutions and individuals:

- London Tourist Board and Convention Bureau
- English Heritage
- National Trust
- British Museum
- London Transport Museum
- Theatre Museum
- Simon Hughes MP
- David Sadler MBE
- Fred William
- Renos Lavithis

and all others too numerous to mention.

FOREWORD

LONDON, the oldest, largest and most cosmopolitan city of the UK is one of the world's great metropolises packed with places to visit and sights to see. We have not given a 100% comprehensive guide (that would certainly have been impossible), of the capital's attractions but we have shown what are worth seeing.

Our text, photographs, plans and maps, guide the visitor a long way. Our fact-finder, index and the selective historical data given, complete the cycle: tourists can then use the available means of transport (the tube, taxi, bus or train) to take them to their chosen destinations.

However, before setting out on a detailed journey to discover historic London the complete newcomer may well want a masterview. He cannot do better than follow the advice of W.E. Gladstone:

> *"The best way to see London"*, declared the great Victorian Prime Minister, *"is from the top of a bus"*.

The Tower of London, Wrens' St. Paul's Cathedral, the Houses of Parliament and Big Ben and that great magnet for tourists, Buckingham Palace, are a must. World-famous landmarks, magnificent historic buildings, colourful pageantry, time-old traditions and modern attractions all contribute to its distinctive character and appeal. Nowhere else on earth can you see a Royal tradition as splendid as in London. For a 1000 years or so, the Kings and Queens of England have set their seal on the capital. Today, their heritage — with its pomp and pageantry, its palaces and parades — lives on as an integral part of London's daily life.

London's greatness is shown by the fact that in 1988 it attracted over 9 million overseas visitors supplemented by thousands of day visitors both from the continent and the rest of the United Kingdom.

The Royal City is proud of its Heritage.

Have a nice stay.

CHAPTER ONE

LOCATION, HISTORY and IMPORTANCE OF LONDON

LONDON lying on the banks of the River Thames, 80km (48 miles) from the North Sea, is situated within a broad depression — known to geographers as the *"London Basin"*. Its geographical position is latitude 51° 31' north and longitude 0°. The London basin is bounded by two ranges of hills, the **Chilterns** to the northwest and the **North Downs** to the south and divided by the **River Thames.** The position of London surrounded by marshes and moorland, from the very first has been that of a town which could grow nothing for its own people hence has had to depend upon outside or distant places for her supplies. Despite this setting, The Royal City grew and grew.

Thomas Alley *(The History and Antiquities of London, 1827, Volume I)* wrote:

"The remote history of this magnificent city, which in wealth or magnitude has never been surpassed, is involved in much obscurity. Some of the early chroniclers even go so far as to claim the Trojans as its founders . . . "

Without getting involved in any historo-archaeological debate we can safely say that human habitation along the banks of the Thames can be traced back to the **STONE AGE.**

London however, only became an important town after the **ROMAN** conquest of the first century AD. The very name London — **Londinium** — is Roman in origin. During these centuries of Roman administration (from AD43 to AD410 when the last legions were finally withdrawn) there was ample time for growth.

The Romans built a bridge (the first London Bridge) at the Thames' lowest bridgeable point and established a protective bridgehead on the northern bank. This developed from a military encampment to an important trading town. Indeed, though not the capital of Roman England, it became its foremost commercial centre; in fact the administrative genius of the Romans helped to develop London as the medieval "capital" of England. It was so important that in the 4th century it was the seat of a bishopric and a mint and held the title of *"Augusta"*. In 61AD London was burnt by **Queen Boadicea** (who led a British rebellion), and when the town was rebuilt it soon spread to the western hill; in fact its massive wall enclosed 330 acres making it one of the largest Roman towns in western Europe.

The departure of the Romans (soon after AD400) was followed by the invasion of the **ANGLO-SAXONS** and led to control of London being in dispute between the adjoining kingdoms of the **ANGLES, SAXONS and JUTES,** and subject to invasion from the Continent. Though its prestige and independence may have weakened for a while, it preserved its identity as a cosmopolitan town. It became the diocese of **Bishop Mellitus** in 604 and the church of St. Paul was built on a dominant site.

In the next century London was described as *"a mart of many peoples",* and subsequent wars and invasions only served to emphasise its importance. Thus in 835 the **DANES** raided England (Sheppey) and sacked London in 836 and in 851 burnt parts of London again. However, Alfred soon conquered London and it became the base of English resistance to the Danes: **ALFRED THE GREAT** became King of England from 871 to 899. He was known as "England's champion against the Danish invaders".

The DANES attacked London again in 1009; in fact there were almost annual attacks on England from 1003 to 1014. Consequently, **CNUT** was recognized as the country's King. When he died in 1035 his kingdoms were divided between his three sons and **HAROLD HAREFOOT** obtained England. When he died in 1040 he was succeeded by **HARDACNUT**, himself being succeeded in 1042 by **EDWARD THE CONFESSOR,** son of Ethelred. He ruled to 1066 (died on 6 January), and among his achievements was the building of the magnificent Westminster Abbey. For a brief period he was succeeded by **HAROLD II** who was then defeated and killed at Hastings on 14 October

THE NORMANS were the next rulers of Britain — from 1066 to 1154, and inaugurating the reign was **WILLIAM THE CONQUEROR** (1066-1087). London's defences were strengthened by three towers and owing to more peaceful times it expanded very rapidly. The famous Tower of London was taking shape (1081-1090) under the watchful eye of Bishop Gundulf.

Medieval London Crayon drawing by Forestier *(The Museum of London Collection)*

Following the Norman invasion the Bishop of Amiens described *"London-town"* — as its people then called it — as *"overflowing with inhabitants and richer in treasures than the rest of the kingdom"*.

When London and the whole country submitted to William the Conqueror, the new King granted a charter to the citizens, written in their native language and confirming the laws and customs they had enjoyed in the time of Edward the Confessor; the charter is still preserved in the Guildhall.

Some general remarks about the early, middle and late **MEDIEVAL PERIOD** will not be out of place:

During the **Peasant's Revolt of 1381,** when the workers of the country rose against their cruel exploitation by the ruling class and marched on London, the apprentices opened their gates to them and many a London tradesman and drunken young squire joined the angry rebels in blockading the young Richard II in the Tower, in murdering several of his ministers, and in parading the head of the Chancellor, Archbishop Sudbury, round the streets on a pike. It was not until 15 June after the rebel leader, **Wat Tyler,** had been pulled down from his horse by the Mayor at a conference at Smithfield and stabbed to death that the revolt in London was brought to an end.

Again briefly, Medieval London became the model of self-government for the other English towns and increased trade led to a population boom within the walls and without, especially towards the west. Londoners concentrated on

9

industry and trade and organized themselves into many guilds. It was also an intellectual centre and even in Norman times there were four schools — *St. Pauls, Holy Trinity, St. Martin-le Grand* and *St. Mary-le-Bow.*

Nevertheless 15th century London despite its spreading suburbs and expanding satellite villages was still essentially a walled town of the middle ages in an open countryside.

TUDOR London (1485-1603) showed no distinct changes. There was the same marked contrast between rich and poor, splendour and squalor; there were the same pageants and processions, water sports and bonfires, quarrels, riots and plagues. Men still drank wine at the *Pope's Head Tavern* in Cornhill at a penny a pint (the bread was free); they still got drunk at *Bartholomew Fair* as they had done since the 12th century and they still flocked to Southwark to enjoy the excitements of the brothel and the bull-ring. Pirates were still hanged in chains downstream from the Tower as they had been since Roman times; the heads of traitors were still displayed on London Bridge until blown into the river on a windy night; hundreds of beggars and footpads still roamed the streets keeping a close watch for simple countrymen and unsuspecting foreigners; the markets (especially Cheapside and Leadenhall), bigger than ever, busy and roudy six days a week, still continued very much as before.

But there were changes and the population of London and the surrounding district increased as follows:

           1563— 90,000 inhabitants
           1583—120,000   ”
           1600—200,000   ”

London continued to expand after the 16th century and it saw a great development in both overseas and inland trade. The years **1665** and **1666** were two of the most eventful in its history. A **PLAGUE** in 1665 was disastrous and soon the streets were deserted and few houses were to be seen without the red cross and the words *"Lord have mercy upon us",* mantled upon them. The plague was scarcely stayed before the whole city was in flames.

The so-called **GREAT FIRE OF LONDON** raged from 2-7 September 1666; it begun when a baker's house in *Pudding Lane* caught fire. Of the 98 or so parish churches within the walls 85 were burnt down, including St. Pauls; also Guildhall, the Royal Exchange and the Customs House and around 13,200 homes suffered the same fate. In all, perhaps 80,000 became homeless. London was soon rebuilt.

As in other parts of the country and the world at large, the 16th and 17th centuries brought many changes. By the 18th century London saw a great development. The expansion of

The Great Fire of London — Detail from a contemporary engraving.

British colonisation and commerce and the **industrial revolution** which had extended over to the following century meant that the whole character of London had changed. As early as 1802 **William Wordsworth** saw the *"mighty heart"* of the metropolis from Westminster Bridge as follows:

"Silent, bare,
Ships, towers, domes, theatres and temples lie,
Open unto the fields, and to the sky;
All bright and glittering in the smokeless air."

By **1820,** London's population increased to more than 1,100,000 — socially, commercially and financially it was the hub of the kingdom and of the British Empire.

VICTORIAN ENGLAND. First there was simply the wealth, vigour and inventiveness of Victorian England, a dynamic State in an age of excitement: capital looking for markets, vitality looking for opportunity, success looking for new fields. Then, there was further growth abroad. The PAX BRITANNICA was not a boastful fraud. On the whole Britain's supremacy in the oceans and along the shores of the globe was used on the side of peace, goodwill and freedom —the world certainly enjoyed one of its most tranquil periods. The growth of the Empire resulted in the primacy of London as a financial centre. Beyond the 1870s the capital also witnessed rapid improvements in sanitation, lighting, locomotion, public libraries and baths, and to some extent in housing. The death-

11

Above: 18th century engraving of St. Jame's Square, one of London's most fashionable places of the 18th century. *Below:* "Early London Transport" — street scene.

rate rapidly declined, town life was made increasingly tolerable on its purely material side, and primary education became universal.

Nevertheless, it was in many respects a dreary heritage to pass to the 20th century. There was no town planning, unscrupulous property developers almost reigned supreme: in vast areas of London there were no open spaces within reach of the children, whose only playground outside the school yard was the hard and ugly street. To millions the divorce from nature was absolute.

THE GREAT WARS

The 20th century with its 2 World Wars (1914-18 and 1939-45) brought the greatest setback in the history of modern London. The German air raids resulted in around 2,632 casualities in the capital alone and the gearing up of the economy to war production dented the growth of London —the main target. The years 1939-45 were to prove catastrophic. A brief chronology of the raids is as follows:

July 1940 (following the fall of France), the Germans intensified their air attacks on British cities, communications and shipping.

15 August, around 1,000 German planes ranged as far north as Scotland. The British retaliated with heavy raids on Berlin Düsseldolf, Essen and other German cities.

7 September, intensified bombing of London raised the casualties to 300-600 a day and 1000-3000 injured.

10 October, resuming the air assault with full intensity the German Lüftwaffe, with some Italian air squadrons, raided London heavily. The German **"Blitzkrieg"** severely shattered many British cities and 14,000 civilians had been killed in London alone.

May 1941, intensified German attacks, facilitated by long days and clearer skies, culminated in a shattering attack on London (10 May).

By *22 June* however, the **"BATTLE OF BRITAIN"** subsided with the opening of the Russian front.

In all, the air attacks killed more than 30,000, injured more than 50,000, damaged most public buildings and in such cases as the area of Stepney, obliterated whole sections of the street system. Westminster Abbey, the Houses of Parliament, the British Museum were damaged but saved as were St. Pauls and Guildhall in the City.

What of the **IMPORTANCE** of London? Dr. Samuel Johnson, an 18th century eminent scholar, wrote that

> *"when a man is tired of London, he is tired of life, for there is in London all that life can afford . . . "*

Succintly correct then, it is also true today.

Musically, London is equalled by few cities in the world and surpassed by fewer — the concert and theatregoer has ample and varied choices;

The **Gourmet** not only has restaurants offering traditional British cuisine but has a bewildering variety of overseas traditions — Greek, Chinese, Indian, Japanese, Caribbean etc. And there are around 6,000 pubs in London where one can enjoy a drink and, especially at lunchtimes, eat some food.

Those who enjoy **Sport** (football, tennis, rugby, cricket etc.) are liberally catered for;

Those who enjoy **Open Spaces** will find large tracts of open country (Hampstead Heath, Richmond Park etc.) and in the very centre of the metropolis, the five royal parks (St. James', Green Park, Hyde Park, Kensington Gardens and Regents Park) combined with many smaller open spaces, provide citizens and visitors with ample opportunity for fresh air.

London of course, is far more than a centre of **Recreation** and **Entertainment.** Since Greater London houses around $\frac{1}{7}$ of the population of England and Wales and thousands commute into the capital every day, it is therefore by far the largest concentration of **Economic Activity** in the UK. Thus the Port of London is the country's leading port, handling around $\frac{1}{3}$ of the UK's imports and exports; London's two major airports (Heathrow and Gatwick) are among the busiest in the world. The City of London contains an insurance and banking centre of international importance and a host of other financial and commercial enterprises including the nation's principal Stock Exchange. Greater London is also an industrial centre of the first magnitude. And, how about London's rising new 'city' —the Docklands?

Finally, London as the nation's **capital** (moved from Winchester in 1042) is the foremost *political and administrative centre.* The Queen's main residence is Buckingham Palace; the Prime Minister lives at No. 10 Downing Street; Parliament meets at Westminster and Government offices are scattered throughout London with the most important grouped near Parliament especially in the street called *"Whitehall".*

How right Dr. Johnson was in 1773 when he said,
"by seeing London, I have seen as much of life as the world can show".

anoramic view of London from Hampstead Heath.

Above: One of Henry VIII's most famous portraits.
Left: An old engraving of Richard III.

CHAPTER TWO

BRITISH MONARCHS From 1042

THE OLDEST surviving monarchy in the West has been associated with London ever since Edward the Confessor built Westminster Abbey. The Royal line and Dynasties since then are shown below:

SAXON AND DANE

Edward the Confessor....	1042—1066
Harold II	1066

NORMAN

William I	1066—1087
William II...........	1087—1100
Henry I	1100—1135
Stephen	1135—1154

PLANTAGENET

Henry II	1154—1189
Richard I	1189—1199
John	1199—1216
Henry III	1216—1272
Edward I.............	1272—1307
Edward II...........	1307—1327
Edward III..........	1327—1377
Richard II...........	1377—1399

LANCASTER and YORK

Henry IV	1399—1413
Henry V	1413—1422
Henry VI	1422—1461
(and October 1470 to May 1471)	
Edward IV..........	1461—1483
(except as shown above)	
Edward V...................	1483
(April to June)	
Richard III..........	1483—1485

Richard the II.

TUDOR

Henry VII...........	1485—1509
Henry VIII..........	1509—1547
Edward VI..........	1547—1553
Mary I	1553—1558
Elizabeth I	1558—1603

STUART

James I	1603—1625
(VI of Scotland)	
Charles I	1625—1649
(Beheaded)	

17

INTERREGNUM

(or Commonwealth)	1649—1660
Charles II	1660—1685
James II	1685—1688
(VII of Scotland)	
Mary II and William III	1689—1702
Anne	1702—1714

HANOVER

George I	1714—1727
George II	1727—1760
George III	1760—1820
George IV	1820—1830
William IV	1830—1837

SAXE–COBURG

Victoria	1837—190
Edward VII	1901—191

WINDSOR

George V	1910—193
Edward VIII	193
(Abdicated	
George VI	1936—195
Elizabeth II	1952–

Below: From left to right: Queen VICTORIA penny black; King George V, Silver Jubilee; King George VI and Queen Elizabeth now known as the "Queen Mother", Coronation stamp.

The coronation of H.M. Queen Elizabeth II, on 2 June 1953.

CHAPTER THREE

HOW THE U.K.
IS GOVERNED
and the Role of the Monarchy

THE BRITISH Constitution, unlike that of most other countries, is not written ie, contained in any single document. Formed partly by statute, partly by common law and partly by convention, it can be altered by Act of Parliament or by general agreement to create, vary or abolish a convention. The Constitution thus adapts readily to changing political conditions and ideas.

The organs of government are clearly distinguishable although their functions often intermingle and overlap.

THE LEGISLATURE: Parliament is the supreme legislative authority. Its three elements, *the Queen, House of Lords* and the elected *House of Commons,* are outwardly separate, are consituted on different principles and meet together only on occasions of symbolic significance such as the State Opening of Parliament. The main functions of Parliament are:

(i) to pass laws;

(ii) to provide, by voting taxation, the means of carrying on the work of government and,

(iii) to scrutinise government policy and administration particularly proposals for expenditure.

Supreme legislative authority rests with the *Lower House* i.e., the House of Commons which is elected and consists of 650 Members of Parliament (MPs). For electoral purposes the U.K is divided into constituencies, each of which returns one member to the House. In fact the present system relies heavily upon the existence of organised political parties, each laying policies before the electorate for approval. The party which wins most seats, although not necessarily the most votes, at a general election, or which has the support of the majority of members in the House of Commons, usually forms the Government. By tradition, the leader of the majority party is asked by the sovereign to form Her Majesty's Government; the largest minority party becomes the official Opposition with its own leader and shadow cabinet. The

19

House of Lords (Upper or Revising *Chamber)* consisted of 1189 members in mid-1984 of which —

- 26 were **Lords Spiritual** and are the Archbishops of Canterbury and York, the Bishops of London, Durham and Winchester and the 21 diocesan bishops of the Church of England; and
- 1163 **Lords Temporal** of which 763 were hereditary peers who had succeeded to their titles; 31 hereditary peers who had the titles conferred on them (including the Prince of Wales) and 369 life peers of whom 20 were *"law lords"*. The latter assist the House in its judicial duties — as such it is the highest appelate court in the U.K.

The House is presided over by the *Lord Chancellor* (the House of Commons by the *Speaker),* who is a leading Cabinet Minister and also head of the Judiciary. He is ex-officio Speaker and takes his place on the WOOLSACK — the traditional name given to a broad red-covered seat, which is stuffed with wool, in front of the throne. In brief, the woolsack was originally made from wool of English sheep when this was a leading commodity in the country's economy and as such presumably symbolised prosperity. The date of its introduction is uncertain. The modern woolsack is filled for symbolic reasons with wool from several countries of the Commonwealth.

The **EXECUTIVE** consists of —

(i) *The Government:* around 100 Cabinet and other senior and junior ministers, who are responsible for initiating and directing national policy;

(ii) *Government departments,* which are responsible for national administration (eg Home Office, Foreign Office etc.);

(iii) *Local authorities* which administer and manage many local services such as education and housing, and

(iv) *Public corporations,* responsible for operating particular nationalised industries or for example, a social or cultural service, subject to ministerial control in varying degrees.

THE JUDICIARY, determines common law and interprets statues and as such is independent of both legislature and executive.

Accountable government in Britain has two main elements: Ministers are responsible to Parliament in that they cannot govern without the support of an elected majority; and they are responsible for the advice they tender to the Queen, and therefore, for any action she may take. Political decisions are taken by the Ministers, and the Queen performs the functions of an IMPARTIAL HEAD OF STATE

The British people look to the Queen not only as their head of state, but also as the symbol of their nation's unity. The monarchy is the most ancient secular institution in the U.K. During the last 1000 years its continuity has only been broken once (by the establishment of a REPUBLIC under CROMWELL which lasted from 1649 to 1660) and, despite interruptions in the direct line of succession, the hereditary principle upon which it was founded has always been preserved. The Royal title in the U.K. is:

"Elizabeth the Second, by the Grace of God of the UK of G.B. and Northern Ireland and of Her other Realms and Territories Queen, Head of the Commonwealth, Defender of the Faith".

e Houses of Parliament
House of Commons"
*Woodmansterne Picture
brary).*

rd Hailsham
rd Chancellor) leads the
ocession for the State
ening of Parliament.
O.I.)

21

The form of the royal title is varied for the other member nations of the Commonwealth in which the Queen is Head of State to suit the particular circumstances of each: all these forms include however, the phrase *"Head of the Commonwealth"*.

The UK is governed by Her Majesty's Government in the name of the Queen. There are however, many important acts of government which still require the participation of the Queen. The Queen summons, prorogues (discontinues until the next session without dissolving) and dissolves Parliament. Normally she opens the new session with a **SPEECH,** from the throne (in the House of Lords) outlining her Government's programme. This is prepared by the Government and is a straightforward list of the measures which they intend to introduce in that session. When the Queen is unable to be present the Speech is read by the Lord Chancellor. Before a Bill which has passed all its stages in both Houses of Parliament becomes a legal enactment, it must receive the **ROYAL ASSENT** (normally it is always granted), which is announced to both Houses.

As the **FOUNTAIN OF JUSTICE,** the Queen can, on ministerial advice pardon or show mercy to those convicted of crimes. All criminal prosecutions are brought in the name of the Crown. In law the Queen as a private person can do no wrong, nor being immune from civil or criminal proceedings, can she be sued in courts of law. This personal immunity, which does not extend to other members of the Royal Family, was expressly retained in the Crown Proceedings Act 1947, which for the first time allowed the Crown (in effect a government department or minister), to be sued directly in civil proceedings.

As the **FOUNTAIN OF HONOUR,** the Queen confers peerages, knighthoods and other honours: most honours are conferred on the advice of the Prime Minister. As Commander-in-Chief of the Armed Forces she appoints officers, and as Supreme Governor of the Established Church of England, she makes appointments to the bishoprics and other senior offices. In International affairs the Queen (to whom foreign diplomatic representatives in London present their credentials), at least in theory, though not in practice, has the power to conclude treaties, to declare war and to make peace, to recognise foreign states and governments, and to annex and cede territory.

These and similar functions involve exercising the **ROYAL PREROGATIVE** — broadly speaking, the collection of residual powers left in the hands of the Crown. With rare exceptions (as in the appointment of the PM), acts involving the R.P. are nowadays performed by Ministers who are responsible to Parliament and can be questioned about a particular policy. It is not necessary to have Parliament's authority to exercise these powers, although Parliament has the Power to restrict or abolish a prerogative power. The Crown is not bound by an Act of

State Banquet for King Fahd of Saudi Arabia — with Queen Elizabeth II (right); the Duke of Edinburgh and Queen Elizabeth, the Queen Mother (left) — *(C.O.I.).*

Parliament in the absence of any express words to the contrary.

An important function of the Sovereign is appointing the Prime Minister. By convention the leader of the party which commands a majority in the House of Commons is invited by the Sovereign to form a government. If no party has a majority, the Queen has the duty of selecting a PM. In such circumstances she would be free to consult anyone she wished. In fact her closest official contacts are with the PM who has an audience with the Queen on average once a week when the Queen is in London, and, through him or her, with the Cabinet. She sees other ministers as well, generally to discuss the affairs of their departments, and sees all Cabinet papers, the Cabinet agenda in advance, and the minutes of the meetings of the Cabinet and of its committees. She may discuss memoranda with the ministers responsible and, if necessary, seek further information on any topic from departments through her

Private Secretary. The Queen receives copies of all important Foreign and Commonwealth Office telegrams and despatches. She also receives a daily summary of parliamentary proceedings prepared for her by a member of the Government.

The Sovereign succeeds to the throne as soon as his or her predecessor dies and there is no interregnum. The automatic succession is summed up in the phrase

"the king is dead; long live the king!"

The Coronation follows the accession, after an interval, and it does not affect the legal powers of the Crown. The coronation service, customarily conducted by the Archbishop of Canterbury, takes place at Westminster Abbey in the presence of representatives of the peers, the commons and all the great public interests in the UK, the Prime Ministers and leading citizens of the Commonwealth countries, and representatives of other countries. It must be noted that the service used at the coronation of Queen Elizabeth II in 1953 was derived from that used at the coronation of King Edgar at Bath in 973.

As the inheritor of a monarchical tradition which had endured for over 1000 years, the Queen is not just the Head of State, but the living symbol of national unity; she provides the natural focus for popular loyalty. Ceremonial has always been associated with British Royalty and, in spite of the changed outlook of both the Sovereign and the People, many traditional ceremonies and customs are retained. For example, Royal marriages and funerals are still marked by impressive ceremonial and the birthday of the Sovereign is officially celebrated every June by Trooping the Colour on Horse Guards Parade. Royal Processions add significance to such occasions as the Opening of Parliament, when the Queen drives in State from Buckingham Palace to Westminster, and the arrival of visiting Heads of State.

One of the most important duties performed by the Sovereign is to act as host to the Heads of State of Commonwealth and other countries when they visit the UK. When a state visit is involved, guests usually stay at Buckingham Palace or Windsor Castle. Their entertainment includes banquets, receptions, often a special ballet or opera performance and visits to places of particular interest throughout the country.

The contribution by other members of the Royal Family in supplementing the Queen's public functions is of the greatest importance. They too have a heavy schedule of official appearances, both national and international. They help to entertain visiting Heads of State and pay official visits overseas, occasionally representing the Queen, though usually in their own right in connection with an organization or a cause with which they are associated.

They serve as patrons or presidents of many of the most prominent institutions and charities in Britain and are constantly making public appearances.

HISTORIC ROYAL HOMES

· BUILDINGS · DISPLAYS ·
CEREMONIES

NO OTHER area of Britain is as rich in history, traditions and cultural associations as London. Throughout the capital (around 40 kms from north to south and even more from west to east) there are great palaces and mansions, venerable old buildings, quaint houses, unrivalled collections of art treasures, tremendous sweeps of glorious parkland, and colourful ceremonies to suit every possible taste and mood.

Historic Royal Homes and Buildings within easy reach of central London include:

TOWER OF LONDON

(Tower Hill EC3 – ⊖ Tower Hill – Tel: 01-709 0765)

It was built in part by William the Conqueror in the 11th century. Its purpose was to protect and control the City, ie, to guard the river approach to London. Since the end of that century it has been a fortress, palace, mint and prison — the scene of murder execution (e.g. Anne Boleyn), pageantry and years of solitary imprisonment. Edward I completed the outer wall.

The **White Tower** in the centre contains, besides its collection of armoury and execution relics, the finest early-Norman chapel in this country. The **Crown Jewels** are also kept here in the *Waterloo Block*. The Tower of London is also the home of the **Heralds Museum** and **Royal Fusiliers Museum**.

The Tower's total area amounts to 18 acres/7.3 hectares.

The ancient **Ceremony of the Keys** still takes place at the Tower every

Above: The execution of Sir Thomas Strafford (Charles I former adviser) at the Tower in 1641. *Below:* 13-14th cent. plans of the Tower. One of the most formidable defence complexes in Europe.

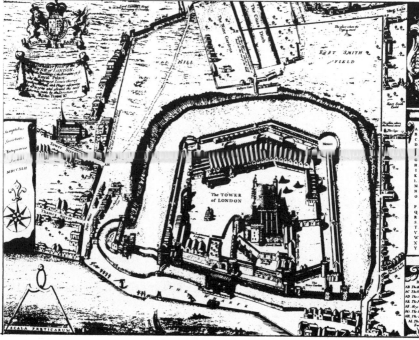

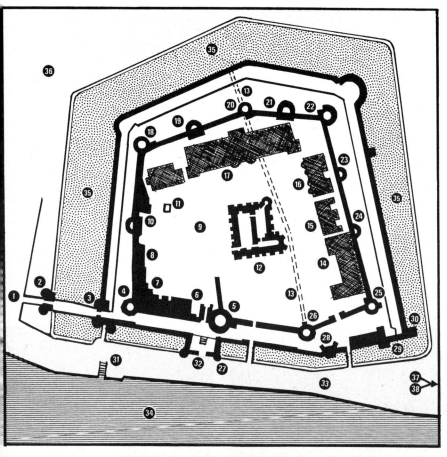

THE TOWER OF LONDON
— General Plan —

(1) ENTRANCE
(2) Middle Tower
(3) Byward Tower
(4) Bell Tower
(5) Wakefield Tower
(6) Bloody Tower
(7) Queen's House
(8) Gentleman Gaoler's
    Lodgings
(9) Tower Green
(10) Beauchamp Tower
(11) Site of Block
(12) WHITE TOWER
(13) Site of Ancient
    Roman Wall

(14) New Armouries
(15) Hospital Block
(16) Royal Fusiliers Museum
(17) Waterloo Barracks
(18) Devereux Tower
(19) Flint Tower
(20) Bowyer Tower
(21) Brick Tower
(22) Martin Tower
(23) Constable Tower
(24) Broad Arrow Tower
(25) Salt Tower
(26) Lanthorn Tower
(27) St. Thomas Tower
(28) Cradle Tower

(29) Well Tower
(30) Develin Tower
(31) Queen's Stairs
(32) Traitor's Gate
(33) Tower Wharf
(34) RIVER THAMES
(35) Dry Moat
(36) Tower Hill
    and Underground
(37) To Tower Bridge
(38) To Katherine's Dock

night from 9.30 to 10pm when the Chief *Yeoman Warder,* in long red cloak and Tudor bonnet, carrying a lantern, marches out toward the Byward Tower with the keys of the fortress in his hand and calls out:

"An escort for the keys".

Four armed soldiers of the garrison fall into step beside him, and march through the gates of the Byward Tower and over the causeway to the entrance gate beyond Middle Tower. The gate is locked; the escort marches back in the darkness towards the towers of the outer ward; the gates of the Byward Tower are locked.

As the Chief Yeoman Warder and his escort approach the *Bloody Tower,* the sentry on guard comes forward with the challenge:

"Halt, who goes there?"
The C.Y.W. replies: *"The keys"*
"Whose keys?"
"Queen Elizabeth's keys".

The sentry presents arms, the C.Y.W. removes his bonnet and calls out

"God preserve Queen Elizabeth"

The whole guard call *"Amen".*

A visit to the Tower of London *(now several Towers)* and Tower Bridge is a highlight on any London itinerary. The Tower attracts millions of visitors annually.

Open (March–October)
Monday to Saturday 9.30am to 5.45pm
Sunday 2pm to 5.45pm
Open (November–February)
Monday to Saturday 9.30am to 4.30pm
Sunday Closed

Above: The Crown Jewels:- "St Edward's Crown".
Left: The colourful ceremony of the keys at the Tower. *(Dept. of Environment).*

An aerial view of the Tower of London and the Tower Bridge.
(Dept. of the Environment).

BANQUETING HOUSE

Banqueting House — General View

(Horse Guards Avenue, Whitehall SW1 – ⊖ Charing Cross or Westminster – Tel: 01-930 4179)
Designed by Inigo Jones for James I in 1619 and completed in 1622, it is the only building left of the Royal Palace of Whitehall destroyed by fire in 1698. The fire marked the end of the ceremonial significance of the Banqueting House and it was then converted by Wren into a *Chapel Royal* — the old chapel had been burnt. In 1963 it was redecorated in its original colours and opened to the public.

A portion of the ground floor was partitioned off in Stuart times to provide a wine-grotto where the king could drink with his immediate friends. The principal apartment, the banqueting hall, on the first floor is 102 feet (33.5 metres) long and 51 feet (16.5 metres) broad and fairly high. This is particularly famous for the 9 allegorical ceiling paintings on canvas by Peter Paul Rubens, completed in Belgium in 1634 and installed the following year. Their themes are the blessing of peace and prosperity conferred on the Union of England and Scotland by the wise rule of James I and the benefits of monarchical rule.

On a more gloomy spirit, Charles I, who commissioned the paintings, passed beneath them on the way to his execution (1649) on a scaffold set up, just in front of the Banqueting House.

Open:
Tuesday to Saturday 10am to 5.30pm.
Sunday 2pm to 5.30pm.

ST. JAME'S PALACE

St. Jame's Palace — General view.

Marlborough Road – SW1)
It was erected in 1532 for Henry VIII on the site of a hospital for leper women. Some of the original buildings remain, but much has been added to this irregular brick building which encloses several courtyards. When Whitehall Palace was burnt down in 1698 St. Jame's became the official residence of the Sovereign and all court functions were held there. Even today Ambassadors are accredited at the *Court of St. Jame's,* although received at Buckingham Palace —the London residence of British Monarchs since 1837.

Today it contains the offices of the Lord Chamberlain and is the head-quarters of the Queens Bodyguard: The *Yeomen of the Guard* instituted in 1485 and the *Gentlemen at Arms,* instituted in 1509.

The Palace was built around 4 courts, of which 3 still exist: Colour Court, Ambassadors Court and *Friary Court.* The latter is the scene of a ceremony enacted in connection with changing the Guard, when the new Colour is lodged in the Guard Room. The proclamation of a new sovereign also takes place from a balcony overlooking the court and Privy Councillors still assemble here for the Accession Council as they did on 8 February 1952 in the entrée room to hear Elizabeth II make her first speech as a Queen.

The superb **Queen's Chapel** (across Marlborough Road) was designed by Inigo Jones in 1623 for Henrietta Maria, wife of Charles I. The interior retains its 17th century fittings. The public are admitted to services.

N.B.: *Apart from the Queens Chapel, St. Jame's Palace is NOT open to the Public.*

31

MARLBOROUGH HOUSE

(Marlborough Road & 66 Pall Mall SW1)

Built for Sarah, Duchess of Marlborough, who obtained a 50-year lease of land adjoining St. Jame's Palace from her friend, Queen Anne. It was built by Wren using red bricks brought back as ballast from Holland after the Duke's military campaigns there. It was completed in 1711 and it is surrounded by a large garden.

Edward VII lived here as Prince of Wales and Queen Mary was the last royal resident — she lived here until 1953; she also died here and there is a memorial plaque to her.

In 1959 the house was donated to the Government for use as a Commonwealth Centre, and was opened as such in 1962. It also houses the Commonwealth Foundation.

The principal room is the saloon which is two storeys high. On its wall are paintings of the *Battle of Blenheim* (1704) by Louis Laguerre. On the ceilings are Gentileschi's Arts and Sciences painted in 1636 for the Queen's House in Greenwich but removed by the Duchess of Marlborough after being granted permission by Queen Anne.

Beyond is the main conference room with two smaller ones on either side. On the staircases to the first floor are more paintings by Laguerre of the *Battles of Ramillies* (1706) and *Malplaquet* (1709). All three Battles were victories for the Duke of Marlborough. There is also Edward VII's smoking-room lined with bogus books.

Marlborough House stands to the east of St. James Palace, between the Mall and Pall Mall.

*Marlborough House is **NOT** open to the public.*

LANCASTER HOUSE

Lancaster House, General View.

(Stable Yard, St. Jame's Palace, SW1)

This is the nearest to Buckingham Palace and was completed in 1827 for the Duke of York (known then as York House but renamed as above after 1912), but later enlarged for the Duke of Sutherland.

Was the home of the London Museum until 1946 and in 1953 the Coronation Banquet for Elizabeth II was held here. It is now used for government receptions and conferences.

The entrance is on the north side from Stable Yard where the imposing entrace portico can be admired. Lancaster House is a sumptuously decorated palace.

Behind it lies **York House** the residence of the Duke and Duchess of Kent.

NB: Neither is open to the public at present.

arence House — General View *(C.O.I.)*

(Stable Yard Road, St. Jame's Palace, SW1)

Close to Lancaster House and Buckingham Palace it was finished in 1828 by Nash and King William IV (on whose lodgings it was reconstructed before he became king) lived here. It was also the home of Princess Elizabeth and the Duke of Edinburgh from 1947 to 1950. Since 1953 it has become the residence of the Queen Mother.

Although twice remodelled and enlarged and restored after bomb damage in the second World War, three storeys remain of Nash's building as well as a number of ceilings and mantelpieces of the same period. It also contains many valuable paintings from the Queen Mother's private collection.

It is interesting to note that a piper plays in the garden every morning at 9am when the Queen Mother is in residence; and at the recent wedding of Prince Andrew and Sarah Ferguson (Wednesday 23 July 1986) the Bride's procession left here with a Bridal Escort of Life Guards.

*N.B. Clarence House is **NOT** open to the public.*

Kensington Palace — General View.

(Kensington Gardens W8 – ⊖ Queensway or Notting Hill Gate – Tel: 01-937 9561).

The estate (Nottingham House) was acquired by William III in 1689 "to escape from the damp air of the Palace of Whitehall".

ing (a former Jacobean Mansion) was improved by Wren and the interior was later embellished by W. Kent. George II was the last monarch to use the palace, though it is still a royal residence.

The Prince and Princess of Wales have their London home here, as does Princess Margaret.

The **State Apartments** were first opened to the public by Queen Victoria who was born and brought up in the Palace.

Visitors will certainly admire the fascinating *Court Dress Collection* depicting the colour and glitter of 200 years of Society. A number of rooms have also been restored including the *Red Saloon* and Queen Victoria's birthplace.

Open: Monday to Saturday 9am to 5pm
Sunday 1pm to 5pm

KEW PALACE

Kew Gardens, Kew, Richmond – Surrey – ⊖ Kew Gardens and British Rail – Tel: 01-940 3321 or 01-940 1171 or Royal Botanic Gardens)

Kew, the smallest of the Royal Palaces (was formerly a Jacobean mansion) was built in 1631 and acquired by the Crown in 1728. Today, after careful restoration it reflects the private lives of George III and Queen Charlotte who used it as their family country retreat from 1802 to 1818.

The present garden behind Kew Palace is named the **'Queen's Garden'** after Queen Elizabeth II, who opened it to the public in May 1969. It is laid out in the style of a 17th century garden with herbal plants of the period, much grey stone, and features such as a *"mount"* with a rotunda on top.

"Queen Charlotte's Cottage", built about 1772 and used by George III and his family for picnics in Kew Gardens, is also open to the public. It is about one mile away from Kew Palace.

Open: 11am to 5.30pm Monday-Saturday (April-September only)

HAMPTON COURT PALACE

(East Molesley, Surrey – British Rail to Hampton Court, approx 28 minutes from Waterloo B.R. Station – Tel: 01-977 8441)

The oldest Tudor Palace in England. The original mansion of Hampton Court was built for Cardinal Wolsey, one of Henry VIII's richest and most powerful subjects, between 1515 and 1520. He presented it to the King in 1526 in an attempt to remain in his favour. At once Henry set about enlarging it and made it into one of the most splendid palaces in the Kingdom.

The **West Front,** the **Clock Court** (with Anne Boleyn's Gateway and the astronomical clock) and the **Great Hall** are Tudor (c.1535). In 1689 William III and Mary commissioned Sir Christopher Wren to rebuild the ageing palace. Large additions were made including the **Fountain Court.**

The palace ceased to be regularly used as a royal residence in 1760. Today it provides *'Grace and Favour'* homes for those who have retired from the service of the Crown.

The famous **State Rooms** consist of two distinct suites; the *King's Side* and the *Queen's Side.* They hold a valuable collection of pictures (Titian, Giorgione, Holbein etc.) 45 fine tapestries covering 4 centuries of history, intricate carvings and painted ceilings.

The **Haunted Gallery** which leads to the **Royal Chapel,** is said to be visited by the ghost of Catherine Howard, one of the six wives of Henry VIII, who lived at Hampton Court. Accused of infidelity and treason, she was later beheaded.

Also of particular interest are the **Great Kitchen,** the **Wine Cellars,** the **Tennis Court** (the oldest in the world); the **Orangery** with the priceless Mantegna Cartoons of the *Triumph of*

Ceasar; the **Banqueting House** and the **Great Vine** planted in 1769 and the **Maze**. The **Knot Garden** is a replica of a 16th century design and in the grounds almost every kind of flowering shrub and tree can be seen. **Home Park** surrounds the Palace.

Open: **Palace:** *1 April-30 September,*
Monday to Saturday 9.30am to 6pm
Sunday 11am to 6pm
1 October-31 March,
Monday to Saturday 9.30am to 5pm
Sunday 2pm to 5pm
The **Maze:** *March to October 10am to 6pm*
Park: *7am till dusk.*

Hampton Court is very popular and requires a day out . . .

WINDSOR CASTLE

(Windsor, Berks – British Rail from Waterloo: 23 miles/37km – Tel: 07538 52010)

The town of Windsor, largely Victorian and probably more *'royal'* than any other in Britain, is dominated by the Castle, founded by William the Conqueror and still used by the Royal Family.

The **Round Tower** was built in the reign of Henry II, while **Horseshoe Cloisters** are of 15th century origin.

St. George's Chapel is an outstanding example of perpendicular architecture with its exquisite and intricate fan vaulting.

The **Choir** contains the stalls and brasses of the *Garter Knights* and is the burial place of royalty.

The fine **State Apartments** can also be visited. Also on view are important drawings from the Royal Collection and the famous **Doll's House** given to Queen Mary.

Other exhibits include presents which have been given to the Queen from people throughout the world and a new display of Royal carriages in the **Royal Mews.**

Drawings by Leonardo Da Vinci, Holbein and other artists are also on view.

Times of Opening (daily):
1 Jan. to 28 Mar. – 10am to 4.15pm
29 Mar. to 30 Apr. – 10am to 5.15pm
1 May to 31 Aug. – 10am to 7.15pm
1 Sept. to 24 Oct. – 10am to 5.15pm
25 Oct. to 31 Dec. – 10am to 4.15pm

Windsor Castle; it fascinates all the visitors.

BUCKINGHAM PALACE

ıckingham Palace in the Spring *(C.O.I.)*

ondon SW1 – ⊖ *St. Jame's Park)*

The Palace has become so well-known as the royal family's residence n London that it may come as a surprise to many that it was completed n 1703 for the Duke of Buckingham. George III purchased it in 1762 as a own dwelling for Queen Charlotte and they occupied it as a private, rather than as a state, residence.

The building of the present palace, started in 1825, was carried out to the designs of the architect John Nash, employed by King George IV. The palace was built in Bath stone (Buckingham House was originally a red brick building) and Nash retained the shell of the earlier house and much of the plan. He designed the building as a three-sided court open on the east, in front of which stood the **Marble Arch** (later removed to its present site at the north-east corner of Hyde Park). In 1847, the east (front) wing of the palace, the most familiar to the public, was built, enclosing the courtyard. The facade of the east wing was refaced in Portland stone in 1913 as part of a scheme that included the erection of the Queen Victoria memorial beyond the forecourt at the front of the palace.

Buckingham Palace has been the London residence of British Kings and Queens since Queen Victoria ascended to the throne in 1837.

The forecourt is nowadays patrolled by sentries of the Household division in full dress uniform. Everyday from April to October and on alternate days during the winter the colourful ceremony of **Changing the Guard** is performed at 11.30 in the morning and a Guard's band play.

When the Queen is in residence, the *Royal Standard,* her personal flag, flies at the Palace's masthead.

With the exception of the Queen's Gallery and the Royal Mews, Buckingham Palace is not open to the public.

The State Apartments in the west wing of the palace, are approached by the *Grand Hall* and *Grand Staircase* with its marble stairway and gilt bronze balustrading. The *Ballroom,* which is the largest of the apartments, was built for Queen Victoria in the 1850s. Lit by six immense chandeliers formed of crystal bowls, it is here that state balls, state banquets and investitures are held.

The *Blue Drawing Room,* was the palace ballroom before 1854. In this room is the *"Table of the Commanders"* made for Napoleon I in 1812 and after his defeat presented to King George IV (then Prince Regent) by King Louis 18th of France. The table

Queen Victoria Memorial in front of the Palace.

is of green and gold Sévres porcelain The *White Drawing Room* is a white and gold room, with delicate yellow upholstery and curtains and a magnificent flowered carpet. Its furniture includes many fine examples of English Regency and French craftsmanship.

The *Throne Room* with a marble frieze depicting the Wars of the Roses of 15th century England is lit by seven cut-glass chandeliers.

The ivory and gold *Music Room* has a domed ceiling and a half-dome over the bow, the elaborately moulded plaster work being richly gilt.

The two huge cut-glass chandeliers are probably the finest in the palace. Queen Victoria and Prince Albert held musical evenings in this room.

Adjacent to the Blue and White Drawing Rooms and the Music Room is the *Picture Gallery* which contains particularly fine collection of 17th century Dutch paintings, including works by Rembrandt, Van Dyke and Rubens.

The **Queens Private Apartments** are in the north wing. The east wing is mainly used as guest rooms on occasions such as state visits. When the east front was added, King George IV's Oriental pavilion at Brighton was sold to contribute to the cost of building the new wing and, therefore, much furniture in the Chinese style was available. From there came the four porcelain pagodas which stand at either end of the principal corridor, whose mirror-glass doors reflect portraits, antique furniture, crimson curtains and carpet, forming a gallery for the display of works of art, as do the long corridors on all floors; and the style of the *Balcony Room* whose walls are hung with six finely embroidered panels of old Chinese silk of imperial yellow. The central window is used by the royal family to step on to the balcony on important occasions when crowds gather before the palace.

The Palace Gardens, covering some 40-45 acres (16-18 hectares) and extending to Hyde Park Corner, were laid out for King George IV by W. T. Aiton. They comprise a lake, lawns and paths and a large variety of flowers and trees, including one of the mulberry trees planted in the early 1600's in an attempt to encourage the silk industry.

In the summer the gardens are the scene of three royal garden parties during which the Queen and the Duke of Edinburgh meet some 22,000-23,000 guests of many nationalities and from different walks of life.

The South Wing of the Palace contains the **Queen's Gallery** *(Tel: 01-930 3007 ext. 430)* open since 1962 for the public display of art treasures from the royal collection. In it a small chapel is screened from public view.

In the **Royal Mews** (or stables) on the south side of the Palace grounds, the coach houses, carriage horses and royal cars and carriages can be viewed by the public twice a week. The carriages include the *Gold State Coach,* built for King George III in 1762 and used at coronations ever since.

The Royal Mews are open Wednesday-Thursday 2pm to 4pm – Tel 01-930 4832 ext. 634)

The Glass Coach in the Royal Mews *(C.O.I.)*

TRADITIONAL EVENTS/DISPLAYS etc.

THE pageantry of the Capital's traditional events can be enjoyed through the year at the Changing of the Guard or Ceremony of the Keys at the Tower of London. Most spectacular of all is perhaps Trooping the Colour which marks the Queen's official Birthday in June. The State Opening of Parliament is another highlight in the ceremonial calendar.

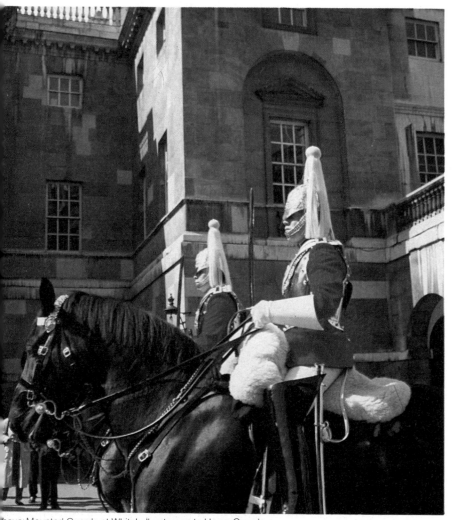

bove: Mounted Guards at Whitehall entrance to Horse Guards.
ft: Trooping the Colour — The Queen takes the salute (the Queen now wears civilian clothing during the lute) *(Woodmansterne)*

GUARD CHANGING CEREMONIES

BUCKINGHAM PALACE: The Queen's Guard is changed at 11.30am. The ceremony which lasts approximately 30 minutes, takes place inside the Palace railings and can be viewed by the public from outside. The Guards, usually accompanied by a Band, leave Wellington Barracks at 11.27am and march via Birdcage Walk to the Palace.

From April to the end of July the ceremony takes place daily, though on alternate days from August to the end of March. There is no Guard change in very wet weather, and times may alter on days when State events take place e.g. Trooping the Colour or Opening of Parliament.

ST. JAME'S PALACE: The St. Jame's Palace Detachment of the Queen's Guard marches to Buckingham Palace at 11.15am and returns at 12.10pm. When there is no ceremony at Buckingham Palace, there is no Guard change at St. Jame's.

HORSE GUARDS, WHITEHALL: The Queen's Life Guard is changed daily throughout the year at 11am Monday to Saturday and at 10am on Sundays. The ceremony lasts around 25 minutes. The Guard leaves Hyde Park Barracks at 10.28am (9.28am on Sundays) and rides via Hyde Park Corner, Constitution Hill and The Mall.

Times may altar on days when State events take place.

TOWER OF LONDON: The Guard is changed at 11.30am only on days when there is a Guard Change at Buckingham Palace.

WINDSOR CASTLE: The Guard is changed at 11am daily in the summer (alternate days in the winter). The Guards, usually accompanied by a band, march through the town of Windsor up to the Castle. When H.M. the Queen is in residence, the Regimental band is also on parade. During the winter months the Guard is changed every 48 hours on an alternate day to the Guard change in London.

GUARD MOUNTING

As a practice for the Queen's Birthday Parade, Trooping the Colour, the ceremony of Guard Mounting is performed on certain days during May on Horse Guards Parade. The dates for 1987 were 11, 12, 13, 15, 18, 20 and 22 May. *Exact dates can be given by the London Tourist Authority.*

CEREMONY OF THE KEYS

As explained earlier the 700 year old ceremonial locking of the main gate of the Tower of London is carried out nightly from 9.30 to 10pm by the Chief Yeoman Warder of the Tower accompanied by an escort of Guards.

GUN SALUTES

Gun salutes take place annually on the following dates:

February 6 . . . . Accession Day
April 21 . . . . Queen's Birthday
June 2 . . . . Coronation Day
June 10 . . . . Prince Phillip's Birthday
August 4 . . Queen Mother's Birthday

No salute is ever fired on a Sunday; if any of the above dates fall on a Sunday, the salute is held over to the next day.

Above: Changing the Guard at Buckingham Palace
Below: Firing Royal Salute in Hyde Park — *(both from Woodmansterne)*

There is always a 41-gun salute in Hyde Park (opposite the Dorchester Hotel) at 12 noon, fired by the King's Troop, Royal Horse Artillery. The soldiers gallop their horses down through the Park pulling the massive gun carriages behind them, set them up, then fire. And a 62-gun salute is fired at the Tower of London at 1pm by the Honourable Artillery Company.

Gun salutes also take place for Trooping the Colour and the State Opening of Parliament as well as some State Visits — times for these salutes vary.

TROOPING THE COLOUR

This ceremony celebrates the Sovereign's official birthday. The Queen (wearing the uniform of the Battalion to be trooped), leaves Buckingham Palace at around 10.40am and goes down The Mall to Horse Guards (a stone building with a central arch surmounted by a low clock tower, built in 1760 on the site of a guard house of 1649, which stood on the old tiltyard of the Palace of Whitehall), arriving at 11am. As the Queen reaches the Saluting Base, the National Anthem is played and a Gun Salute is fired in Hyde Park. She then inspects the parade and on returning to the Saluting Base, the whole spectacle of the Birthday Parade unfolds.

The Queen arrives back at Buckingham Palace at 12.30pm and appears on the balcony for a flypast by the Royal Air Force at 1.00pm when there is also another gun salute at the Tower of London.

Celebrations in Britain of Commonwealth Day are held on the same day and by military units stationed overseas.

Only one Colour can be trooped at a time, and the 5 Regiments *(Grenadier Guards, Coldstream, Scots, Irish and Welsh)* take their turn year by year in strict rotation.

The ceremony therefore, which derives from 2 old military ceremonies *(Trooping the Colour and Mounting the Queen's Guard)* can be divided into the following phases: The arrival of the Queen at the Horse Guards Parade, her inspection of the troops, the actual Trooping, the march past and the Queen's return to Buckingham Palace.

STATE OPENING OF PARLIAMENT

The State Opening is one of the most magnificent and colourful of Britain's ceremonial occasions — only slightly less dramatic than a coronation — and it happens every year as each session of Parliament begins, usually in November.

The Queen in person traditionally opens Parliament by reading the Speech from the throne, which sets out the government's legislative programme for the coming year. For this purpose, both Houses of Parliament are summoned to the Parliament Chamber *(the Debating Chamber of the House of Lords)* and neither House may conduct any business in the new session until the *Speech* (prepared by the government) has been delivered.

The ceremony begins at around 11am with a royal procession from Buckingham Palace to the Houses of Parliament. The Queen rides in the Irish State Coach escorted by a mounted squadron of the Household Cavalry. Once the Queen is inside the House of Lords *(the route: The Mall, Horse Guards Parade, Trafalgar Square, Whitehall, Parliament Square and Old Palace Yard),* the ceremonial begins.

The State Opening of Parliament; H.M. the Queen makes her speech in the Chamber of the House of Lords. (C.O.I.)

At 11.30am the Queen enters the Chamber; the chandeliers are turned up dramatically and the gold leaf, crimson leather benches, scarlet robes, diamonds, emeralds and rubies flow and glitter in one of those great spectacles of British ceremonial which are still unique in the world. The assembly rises, until the Queen, seated upon the Throne and surrounded by her retinue says,

"My Lords, pray be seated"

As soon as the members of the House of Commons arrive and temporary silence prevails the Queen reads the speech. The text is delivered to her at the steps of the Throne by the *Lord Chancellor* (a senior member of the government and speaker of the House of Lords), who carries it in a ceremonial purse, and receives it back from her at the end of the speech — on each occasion retiring backwards down the steps.

The Queen ends the speech with a traditional prayer:

"My Lords and Members of the House of Commons, I pray that the blessing of Almighty God may rest upon your counsels".

The procession then retires; the Sword of State and the Cap of Maintenance are returned to the Tower of London, the Gentlemen of Arms hand in their axes; and a new session of Parliament begins. The Queen and her family return to Buckingham Palace. In a couple of hours, in brilliant and colourful pageantry and with impeccable precision, an essential stage in the democratic process has been completed; the Government's policy has been promulgated, openly and with maximum publicity, by the sovereign in Parliament. The ancient chain which binds the Parliament of today to the *"great councils"* of medieval England has been tested and strengthened. The State Opening underlines each year the fact that Parliament consists not of a Monarch and two Houses of Parliament sitting separately, but of the sovereign on the throne, the Lords Spiritual and Temporal on the benches and the Commons at the bar; all three are indispensible elements of our parliamentary democracy.

So the State Opening of Parliament is not just a tourist attraction; it is a political occasion of profound significance as well.

CHAPTER FIVE

THE ROYAL CITY'S OTHER STAR ATTRACTIONS

YES, historic London has much to offer – the list is truly endless. The following must NOT be missed by any visitor.

ST. PAUL'S CATHEDRAL

Ludgate Hill EC4 – ⊖ St. Paul's – Tel: 01-248 2705
This present building was started in 1675 (finished in 1710) by Wren after the Church (the 4th to be erected on the Ludgate Hill site) was destroyed by the Great London Fire (1666). It is one of the largest Christian monuments in the world — external measurements are height 366 feet (120 metres) and length 518 feet (170 metres).

. Paul's Cathederal as seen from Blackfriars Bridge.

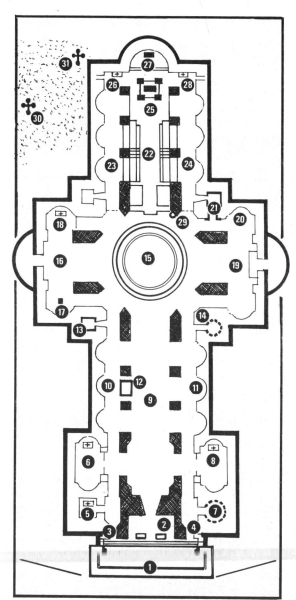

ST. PAUL'S CATHEDRAL
— General Floor Plan —

(1) MAIN ENTRANCE From Ludgate Hill
(2) Great West Door
(3) North West Door
(4) South West Door
(5) Kitchener Memorial & All Soul's Chapel
(6) St. Dunstan Chapel
(7) Gemetrical Staircase
(8) Chapel of St. Michael and St. George
(9) THE NAVE
(10) North Aisle
(11) South Aisle
(12) Wellington Monument
(13) Lord Mayor's Vestry
(14) Stairs to: Wisbering Gallery; Dome; Library
(15) THE DOME
(16) NORTH TRANSEPT
(17) The Font
(18) Chapel in North
(19) SOUTH TRANSEPT
(20) Entrance to Crypt; to O.B.E. Chapel
(21) Dean's Vestry
(22) CHOIR/QUIRE
(23) North Quire Aisle
(24) South Quire Aisle
(25) HIGH ALTAR
(26) Chapel of Modern Martyrs
(27) Jesus Chapel; American Memorial
(28) Lady Chapel
(29) Pulpit
(30) Memorial Cross
(31) Site of St. Paul's Cross

St. Paul's is the seat of the Bishop of London. Major ceremonial functions have been held here, among them the funerals of Nelson, the Duke of Wellington and Sir Winston Churchill. Happier events included the *Silver Jubilee Service* for Queen Elizabeth II (1977), the Queen Mother's 80th birthday thanksgiving (1980) and the Wedding of Prince Charles and Princess Diana (1981).

he interior of the Cathedral is ominated by a massive **Dome** con- sting of an outer wooden frame overed in lead, an inner dome ecorated with 19th century mosaics y *Salviati* and scenes from the life of t. Paul by Thornhill, and a brick one structure wedged between the nner and outer domes to support the eight of the lantern.

o the left of the **Nave** lies the onument to the Duke of Wellington ied 1852).

he *Choir* has the original choir stalls y Gibbons, while the canopy over e main altar is of contemporary ate — 1958.

he **Crypt,** running the full length of e building, has many famous tombs including Christopher Wren's with its famous Latin epitaph (composed by his son) *"Lector, si monumentum requiris circumspice" – "Reader, if you seek his monument, look around you"* and those of Wellington and Nelson. The latter's remains lie in a Renaissance sarcophagus designed by Benedetto da Rovezzano for Cardinal Wolsey.

In the Upper level of the Cathedral are the **South Triforium Gallery** (museum), **Library** and **Trophy Room.** The **West Gallery** offers a spectacular view over the nave. Higher still is the famous **Whispering Gallery,** the **Stone Gallery** outside with its fine view over London, and above the lantern, the **Ball.**

e Chapel of St. Michael and St. George

Services take place every week day at 8am, 10am and 4pm. Since visitors are not allowed to look around during services, it is advisable to plan your visit accordingly. The exterior of the Cathedral is floodlit after dark (from around 4pm during the winter) making it look particularly magnificent.

In fact the Cathedral's famous dome dominates the skyline.

The galleries and the crypt may be visited as follows:

Monday to Friday 10am to 4.15pm
Saturday 11am to 4.15pm
Sunday: Closed.

The Main Entrance from Ludgate Hill — an old photograph.

e Choir and High Altar — St. Paul's *(Woodmansterne)*

HOUSES OF PARLIAMENT

(Parliament Square SW1 – ⊖ West-minster – Tel: 01-219 4272 for admission to Strangers Gallery).

Officially known as the **New Palace of Westminster,** this forest of towers, tarrets and spires rising from a vast honeycomb of courts, corridors and chambers, stands on the site of a palace which was a royal residence from the time of Edward the Confessor until the reign of Henry VIII.

The building which incorporates the ancient Westminster Hall and the crypt and cloisters of St. Stephen's Chapel, was designed by Sir Charles Barry and built 1840-50 (the whole complex was destroyed by fire in 1834), in an imposing Gothic style. Augustus Pugin, an architectural genius in his early twenties provided many of the detailed drawings.

During World War II the House of Commons and adjacent chambers were destroyed by bombs but rebuilt in 1950. Covering 8 acres, it contains the House of Commons in the northern half and the House of Lords in the southern half in addition to the dwellings of various parliamentary officials — including the *Speaker.*

On entering the Houses of Parliament the visitor goes through **St. Stephen's Hall** thence to the **Central Hall** where corridors lead to the **House of Commons** and the **House of Lords.** Beyond the latter are to be found the ceremonial rooms used at the *State Opening of Parliament,* namely the **Robing Room** and the **Royal Gallery** which the *Sovereign* reaches by the Royal Entrance under the **Victoria Tower.** This Tower is the repository for over 3 million parliamentary records. Among them are famous documents, such as the *Bill of Rights* and the *Death Warrant* of *Charles I*

Houses of Parliament and Westminster Bridge to the right.

St. Stephen's Entrance into Westminster Hall.

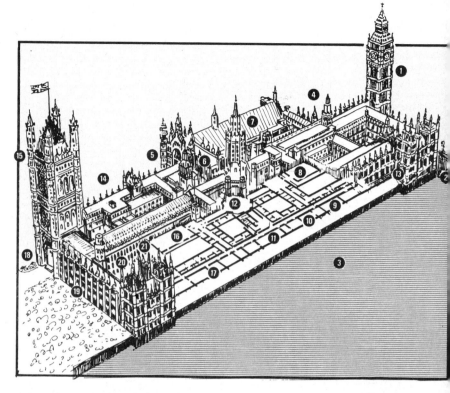

HOUSES OF PARLIAMENT
— General Plan —

(1) CLOCK TOWER
(2) Westminster Bridge
(3) RIVER THAMES
(4) New Palace Yard
(5) St. Stephen's Entrance
(6) St. Stephen's Hall
(7) Westminster Hall
(8) Common's Chambers
(9) Common's Library
(10) Member's Smoking Room
(11) Member's Dining Room
(12) Central Lobby
(13) Speaker's Residence
(14) Old Place Yard
(15) Victoria Tower
(16) Lord's Chambers
(17) Lord's Library
(18) Royal Entrance
(19) Queen's Robing Room
(20) Royal Gallery
(21) Prince's Chamber

They are all available for consultation in the House of Lords records office. At the northern end of the House of Commons is the magnificent gilded **Clock Tower** incorporating the famous bell ($13\frac{1}{2}$ tons), known to all since 1859 and nicknamed **'BIG BEN'** after Sir Benjamin Hall, the First Commissioner of Works. When the **Ayrton Light** shines in the spire above the clock (336 spiralling stairs to the top), it indicates that the Commons are in session.

WESTMINSTER HALL is the most important part of the old Palace of Westminster; others being the **Crypt of St. Stephen** and the **Jewel Tower** (built as treasury and office for the private jewels and plate of King Edward III in 1365-66).

The Hall built by William II in 1097-99 was in its time the largest chamber in Europe. Rebuilt by Richard II in 1394-1402, it is one of the finest and largest timber-roofed buildings in Europe.

From the 13th century it was used as the Chief Courts of Law. Thomas More (1535) the Earl of Essex (1601) and Charles I (1649) were all tried here. Hence it has been the scene of many great moments in British history including the forced abdication of Edward II (1327) the deposition of Richard II (1399) and trial of Guy Fawkes (1606).

N.B. The Houses of Parliament and Westminster Hall are no longer open to visitors except for those attending debates or visiting in an organized party arranged by an MP or a Peer. During sessions admission to the *Stranger's Gallery* in either house by advance application to an MP or a Peer or by queuing at St. Stephen's Entrance.

Above: Victoria Tower
Below: Crypt Chapel *(Woodmansterne)*

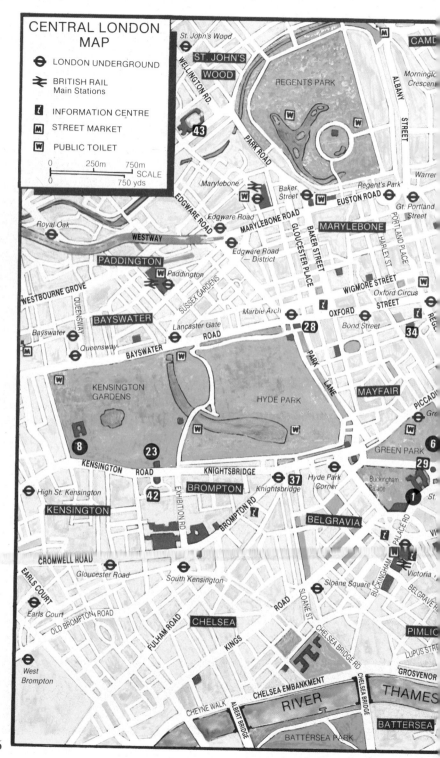

CENTRAL LONDON MAP

LONDON UNDERGROUND

BRITISH RAIL Main Stations

i INFORMATION CENTRE

M STREET MARKET

W PUBLIC TOILET

0   250m   750m
0   750 yds   SCALE

St. John's Wood

ST. JOHN'S WOOD

REGENTS PARK

WELLINGTON RD.

CAMD

Morningic Crescen

ALBANY STREET

Warren

PARK ROAD

43

Marylebone

Baker Street

Regent's Park

EUSTON ROAD

Gt. Portland Street

EDGWARE ROAD

Edgware Road

MARYLEBONE ROAD

MARYLEBONE

GLOUCESTER PLACE

BAKER STREET

HARLEY ST.

PORTLAND PLACE

Edgware Road — District

Royal Oak

WESTWAY

PADDINGTON

Paddington

WIGMORE STREET

Oxford Circus

STREET

REG-

WESTBOURNE GROVE

SUSSEX GARDENS

i OXFORD

Bond Street

34

QUEENSWAY

BAYSWATER

Lancaster Gate

Marble Arch

28

Bayswater

Queensway

BAYSWATER ROAD

MAYFAIR

PICCADI

Gre

KENSINGTON GARDENS

W

HYDE PARK

W

PARK LANE

W

GREEN PARK

6

8

23

29

KENSINGTON ROAD

KNIGHTSBRIDGE

Buckingham Palace

1

St.

High St. Kensington

42

BROMPTON

Knightsbridge

37 Hyde Park Corner

EXHIBITION RD.

i

BELGRAVIA

KENSINGTON

BROMPTON RD.

i

VI

CROMWELL ROAD

Gloucester Road

South Kensington

Sloane Square

Victoria

PALACE RD.

BUCKINGHAM

BELGRAVE R

EARLS COURT

Earls Court

OLD BROMPTON ROAD

FULHAM ROAD

KINGS

SLOANE ST.

CHELSEA

ROAD

PIMLIC

LUPUS STR

West Brompton

CHELSEA

CHELSEA BRIDGE RD.

GROSVENOR

CHEYNE WALK

ALBERT BRIDGE

CHELSEA EMBANKMENT

RIVER

CHELSEA BRIDGE

THAMES

BATTERSEA PARK

BATTERSEA

56

HISTORIC ROYAL HOMES
STAR ATTRACTIONS
Other Important Landmarks

HISTORIC ROYAL HOMES pages 25-40
- (1) Buckingham Palace
- (2) Tower of London
- (3) Banqueting House
- (4) St. Jame's Palace
- (5) Marlborough House
- (6) Lancaster House
- (7) Clarence House
- (8) Kensington Palace

*ROYAL CITY'S OTHER
STAR ATTRACTIONS pages 47-64*
- (9) St. Paul's Cathedral
- (10) Houses of Parliament
- (11) Westminster Abbey
- (12) Westminster Cathedral
- (13) Lambeth Palace
- (47) Southwark Cathedral

*MORE IMPORTANT
LANDMARKS pages 107-117*
- (14) St. Katharine's Dock
- (15) H.M. Belfast
- (16) Parliament Square
- (17) Jewel Tower
- (18) The Cenotaph
- (19) Downing Street
- (20) Trafalgar Square
- (21) St. Martin-in-the-Field
- (22) Piccadilly Circus
- (23) Albert Memorial
- (24) Queen Alexandra Memorial
- (25) Queen Boadicea
- (26) Cleopatra's Needle
- (27) Guards Crimea Memorial
- (28) Marble Arch
- (29) Queen Victoria Memorial
- (30) The Monument
- (31) Inns of Court
- (32) Law Courts
- (33) Central Criminal Court
- (34) London Diamond Centre
- (35) House of St. Barnabas-in-Soho
- (36) Collector's Corner
- (37) David Godfrey's Historical
  Newspaper Shop
- (38) Old Curiosity Shop
- (39) Prince Henry's Room —
  Samuel Pepy's Exhibition
- (40) Guildhall Clock Museum
- (41) Design Centre
- (42) Museum of Instruments
- (43) Cricket Memorial Gallery

WORLD PUBLICATIONS Ltd

57

WESTMINSTER ABBEY

(Parliament Square SW1 - ⊖ West-minster and St. James Park – Tel: 01- 222 5152).
It is located at the south end of Whitehall and facing onto Parliament Square. Seen by over 3 million visitors a year. Tradition holds that there was a church on the site in the 7th century, but the first authentic records are of a *Benedictine Abbey* founded between 730 and 740, dedicated to St. Peter, with the name of **West Minster** *(Western Monastery,* probably from its position as west of the City of London). The Abbey was rebuilt by Edward the Confessor and again later by Henry III. It is an architectural masterpiece. Neither a cathedral nor a parish church, Westminster Abbey is a *"royal pecu-liar"* under the jurisdiction of a Dean and Chapter, subject only to the Sovereign.

The Abbey is famous for its:

HENRY VII CHAPEL: The great glory of this Chapel completed in 1519 is the vaulted roof, an out-standing example of this spectacular Tudor style of architecture. Since 1725 the Chapel has been used as the *Chapel of the Order of the Bath.* Gaily coloured banners, crests and mant-lings of the knights adorn the 16th century wooden stalls, beneath the seats of which are beautifully carved misericords.

Behind the Altar are buried Henry VII and his consort Elizabeth of York. Their monument is by the

Westminster Abbey. Main View with Big Ben in the background *(C.O.I.)*

The High Altar — Westminster Abbey — *(C.O.I.)*

Italian sculptor Torrigiani. Buried in the Norse Aisle of the Chapel is Elizabeth I (died 1603). She lies in the same vault as her half-sister Mary. The monument contains a white marble effigy which is a faithful likeness of the queen.

At the east end is the *RAF Chapel*. The brightly coloured memorial window incorporates the crests of the 68 Fighter Squadrons which, in 1940-41 took part in the Battle of Britain.

THE CHAPEL (or Shrine) OF ST. EDWARD THE CONFESSOR: The Abbey was consecrated on 28 December 1065. Its founder, the saintly king Edward, was too ill to be present and died a few days afterwards. 200 years later Henry III began rebuilding the Abbey to house a shrine worthy of the Saint. It is this building you see today. Buried near the shrine are 5 kings and 4 queens.

CORONATION CHAIR: This oak chair was made for King Edward I by Master Walter of Durham. It was designed to hold the ancient stone of Scone seized from the Scots in 1296.

For coronations the chair is moved to a position in the Sanctuary. Since 1308 it has been used at the coronation of every sovereign.

Only 2 (Edward V and Edward VIII) were never crowned here.

POETS' CORNER: The tomb to which Poets' Corner owes its origin is that of Geoffrey Chaucer, the first great English poet. He was buried in the Abbey with a simple memorial in 1400. The present more imposing tomb was erected in 1556.

The placing here of memorials to poets began in earnest in the 18th century with the full-length statue of Shakespeare, carved over a century after his death. This still continues; Eliot, Auden, Dylan Thomas and 'Lewis Carroll' are among the most recent.

THE SANCTUARY: The focal point of the Abbey's architecture and of its life today is the High Altar, framed by three 13th century tombs, medieval wall paintings and a masterpiece of Italian Renaissance painting.

59

Westminster Abbey.
Northern Entrance

THE NAVE: This is a beautiful Gothic one — the tallest in Britain —with the grave of the *Unknown Warrior* and memorials to many statesmen, scientists and servicemen. A side chapel is always available for private prayer.

THE UNDERCROFT MUSEUM: Following 2 years of major overhaul it was opened to the public on 24 June 1987. Its exhibits include the Abbey's spectacular collection of Royal (e.g. Charles II and Elizabeth I) and other Effigies.

THE CLOISTERS: Rebuilt after the Great Fire of 1298 it is characterised by illuminated panels, depicting various stages in the Abbey's construction and its use as a Church of Coronation. On the left of the East Cloister is the **Chapter House** dating from 1250 which was probably inten-

ded for secular as well as monastic use.

Close by is the **Pyx (or Box) Chamber** which today houses an exciting display of plates of the Abbey and of St. Margaret's Church.

Complete your visit to the Abbey by making a brass rubbing — your own unique souvenir of the visit. In only 25 minutes you can create the memory of a lifetime.

N.B. **Worship and Prayer** still remain the primary function of the Abbey. There are services everyday in which visitors may join and also a brief act of Prayer on every hour during the day.

Steeped in tradition and history, the Abbey is a treasure house of national culture and heritage; architecturally one of the masterpieces of the Middle Ages. It is the most famous Anglican church in the world.

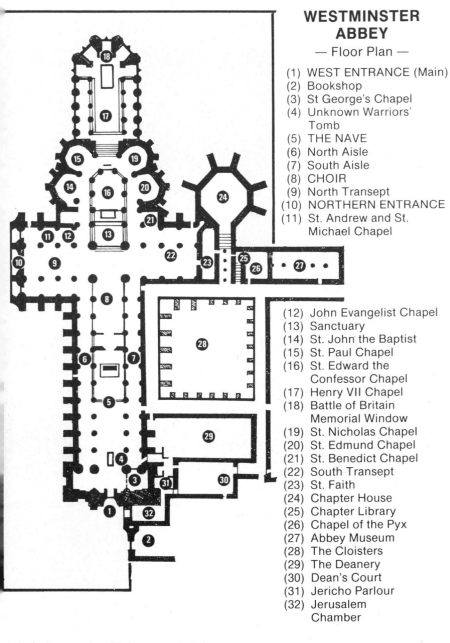

WESTMINSTER ABBEY
— Floor Plan —

(1) WEST ENTRANCE (Main)
(2) Bookshop
(3) St George's Chapel
(4) Unknown Warriors' Tomb
(5) THE NAVE
(6) North Aisle
(7) South Aisle
(8) CHOIR
(9) North Transept
(10) NORTHERN ENTRANCE
(11) St. Andrew and St. Michael Chapel
(12) John Evangelist Chapel
(13) Sanctuary
(14) St. John the Baptist
(15) St. Paul Chapel
(16) St. Edward the Confessor Chapel
(17) Henry VII Chapel
(18) Battle of Britain Memorial Window
(19) St. Nicholas Chapel
(20) St. Edmund Chapel
(21) St. Benedict Chapel
(22) South Transept
(23) St. Faith
(24) Chapter House
(25) Chapter Library
(26) Chapel of the Pyx
(27) Abbey Museum
(28) The Cloisters
(29) The Deanery
(30) Dean's Court
(31) Jericho Parlour
(32) Jerusalem Chamber

Admission to the Cloisters and the Nave is free but there is a charge if one enters the Royal Chapels.

Open Monday to Friday 9am to 4.45pm
Saturday 9am to 2.45pm.

WESTMINSTER CATHEDRAL

Westminster Cathedral — General View

(Ashley Place – Francis Street SW1 ⊖ Victoria – Tel: 01-834 7452)
It is the seat of the Roman Catholic Archbishop of Westminster. It is in neo-Byzantine style, inspired by St. Sophia in Constantinople and St. Mark's in Venice. The fabric of the building was completed in 1903.

The interior of the Cathedral has aisle galleries supported by columns of green marbles from the same quarry which provided material for St. Sophia. The decorations are colourful, especially the mosaics, which depict symbolical and allegorical themes. On the main piers, the bas-reliefs of the Stations of the Cross are by Eric Gill. The body of the martyr St. John Southworth lies in the *"Chapel of St. George and the English Martyrs"* dedicated to those persecuted during the Reformation. The *"Lady Chapel"* has an alabaster statue (c. 15th century) of immense value. A lift serves the *"Campanile"*, which is 284 feet high.

LAMBETH PALACE

A general view of Lambeth Palace

(Lambeth Palace Road SE1 –
⊖ Lambeth North – Tel: 01-928 8282)
The London home (official residence)
of the Archbishops of Canterbury for
some 750 years.

The *"Gateway"* with its twin towers
is an early Tudor construction in
brick c.1490. In the courtyard, on the
west side, is a fig tree (c.1548) said to
have been brought from Rome by
Cardinal Pole. The *"Great Hall"*
rebuilt by Archbishop Juxon (1660),
is of Gothic origin with a fine
hammer beam roof and houses the
"Library" with its valuable collection
of books and illuminated manuscripts.

Although the Chapel itself has been
restored several times, the Crypt is
the oldest part (12th century) of the
palace. To the west is "Lollards
Tower" (15th century) named after
Wycliffe's followers, who had probably been imprisoned there. Next to
it is *"Laud's Tower"* (1635). The
"Guard Chamber" is noted for its
14th century ceiling and portraits of
archbishops — among them Laud,
Warham, Herring and Secker.

ELTHAM PALACE

(Off Court Yard SE9 –
Tel: 01-859 2112)

This was a Royal Manor dating from
the 13th century but largely rebuilt
from the 15th century onwards.
Surviving buildings include the bridge
over the moat and the late 15th
century great hall with its splendid
hammer-beam roof.

SOUTHWARK CATHEDRAL

Southwark Cathedral — General View of Entrance and Tower.

(London Bridge SE1 – ⊖ London Bridge – Tel: 01-407 3708)

It is the largest Gothic edifice in London after Westminster Abbey and it stands on the spot which had been the traditional southern entrance to the City, across London Bridge, since Roman times.

The Cathedral church of *St. Saviour* and *St. Mary Overie* is the 4th church to have been built on this site, the three early ones having been destroyed by fire — the first is said to have been built in the 7th century by wealthy ferrymen.

The Cathedral (1905) is extremely rich in monuments. Among the earliest is an oak effigy of a knight, ankles crossed, one hand on the pommel of his sword, about 1275. Another is the effigy of John Gower, poet and friend of Chaucer, on a tomb-chest, gilded and painted, with the inscription *"Angl. poeta celeberrimus"*. In the south aisle is a memorial to Shakespeare carved in 1912. There is also a Harvard Memorial Chapel in memory of John Harvard the founder of the prestigious American University who was born in Southwark in 1607 and baptised in St. Saviour's.

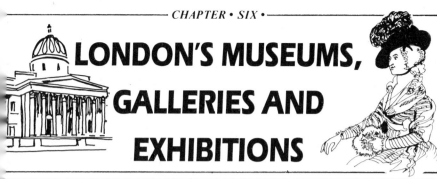

CHAPTER SIX

LONDON'S MUSEUMS, GALLERIES AND EXHIBITIONS

VISITORS TO LONDON

never fail to be impressed by the capital's rich heritage and the variety of its culture and arts. There are countless opportunities to gaze at priceless works of art or unearth history and discover links between the past and the present.

There are approximately **250 Museums and Galleries** in London which must give the city claim to be the *"Museum Capital of the World"*. They range from the massive dignity of the British Museum (BM) and National Gallery to the two-storey privately owned, London Toy and Model Museum in Bayswater.

In recent years London's museums and galleries have seen many changes. They still boast some of the finest collections in the world, covering an amazing list of subjects from Egyptian mummies to early motors and pop-art. But they have shed their old-fashioned show cases and too serious image in favour of exciting displays with push-button controls or walk-through *"settings"* of old workshops and houses, even an Edwardian chemist's shop. Labels and explanations are excellent. Access for disabled visitors has improved and cafes and restaurants have been restyled and enlarged.

Most major museums and galleries are free, some *"ask"* for a voluntary donation and others charge but offer reductions for children, groups and old age pensioners.

THE MUSEUMS

Below we describe some of the more popular Museums and some which are not so well known. Others of course are described in other chapters — please see index.

Please note that some museums have recently started charging entrance fees and others may follow suit in the near future.

BRITISH MUSEUM

(Great Russell Street WC1B 3DG –
⊖ Holborn and Tottenham Court Road
– Tel: 01-636 1555).

The collection which began one of the world's largest and most varied treasure houses was founded in 1753 and since then has grown to include every conceivable kind of artefact from all over the world. Exhibits not to be missed include the superb *Elgin Marbles* from Greece, the mummies and sculpture in the *Egyptian Galleries,* two of the four existing original copies of the *Magna Carta,* the beautiful 17th century *Sutton Hoo Treasure* from a ship burial discovered in Suffolk, the Assyrian lion-hunt reliefs, the Indian sculptures and the Rosetta Stone — the first key to reading hieroglyphs.

The British Museum is one of the great museums of the world, showing the works of man from prehistoric times to the present day. There are permanent displays of antiquities from Egypt, Western Asia, Greece and Rome. Prints, drawings, coins and medals are displayed in a series of temporary exhibitions.

The British Museum also houses the **British Library** (Tel: 01-636 1544). In 1986 it included 15.5 million books and other collections; furthermore around 200,000 to 250,000 items are added to the Library stock every year. The famous *Reading Room* with its 100 feet dome is only accessible to ticket holders or on regular tours.

The British Museum attracts over 2 million visitors annually.

Open Monday to Saturday 10am to 5pm
Sunday 2.30pm to 6pm.

British Museum — Main Entrance *(British Museum)*

bove left: Caryatid from the Akropolis of Athens. *Above Right:* Mummy and coffin from Egypt. *Below:* 'arrior on Horseback from Lucania *(British Museum)*

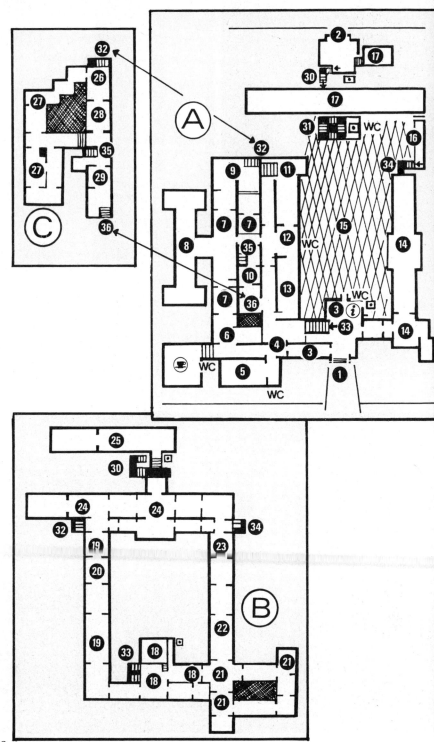

he Mildenhall Treasure: British Museum Collection *(British Museum)*

THE BRITISH MUSEUM
— Floor Plans —

A — GROUND FLOOR

(1) Main Entrance — Great
    Russell Square
(2) North Entrance — Montague Place
(3) Shop
(4) Prehistoric Greece
(5) Special Exhibitions
(6) Archaic Greece
(7) Greek & Roman
(8) Elgin Marbles
(9) Halicarnassus Mausoleum
10) Western Asiatic
11) Ancient Palestine
12) Ancient Egypt
13) Assyrian Sculpture
14) British Library Exhibits
    (books, maps, stamps etc)
15) British Library (members only)
16) Map Gallery
17) Oriental Collection

B — UPPER FLOOR

(18) Prehistoric & Roman Britain
(19) Ancient Greece & Rome
(20) Ancient Cyprus
(21) Medieval and later years
(22) Special Exhibitions
(23) Western Asia (Middle East)
(24) Ancient Egypt
(25) Prints & Drawings

C — BASEMENT

(26) Architecture Gallery
(27) Ancient Greece & Rome
(28) Lecture Theatre
(29) Western Asia (Syria etc)

≡ STAIRS

(30) North Stairs
(31) North Stairs (leading
     downstairs & upstairs to (24))
(32) West Stairs (downstairs to (26)
     and upstairs to (24))
(33) Main Stairs to Upper Floor
(34) East Stairs to Upper Floor

69

THE MUSEUM OF MANKIND

(6 Burlington Gardens W1X 2EX –
⊖ Piccadilly Circus – Tel: 01-437 2224).

The Museum of Mankind is the British Museum's Department of Ethnography (has over 850,000 items) and, apart from a few exhibits, has no permanent display but long-running temporary exhibitions. The Museum in fact presents a series of changing exhibitions which illustrate the variety of non-western societies and cultures. Its collections come from the indigenous peoples of Africa, Australia and the Pacific Islands, North and South America and from certain parts of Asia and Europe, including some ancient as well as recent and contemporary cultures. Exhibitions depict the way of life of particular peoples or focus on specific aspects of their cultures.

Opening and Closing times as British Museum above (closes somewhat later on Sundays).

Mosaic Mask of Tezcatlipoca, Atzec period from Mexico *(British Museum)*

Ivory Salt Celler, Sherbro-Port from Sierra Leone *(British Museum)*

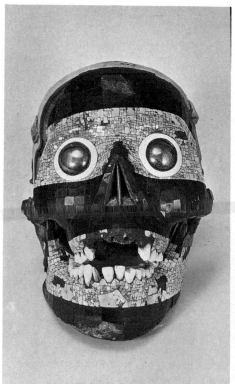

NATURAL HISTORY MUSEUM

Cromwell Road SW7 – ⊖ South Kensington – Tel: 01-589 6323)
Here some 40 million specimens are housed. The main building is Victorian romanesque. Inside, the central part is conceived as the nave of a cathedral, decorated with numerous plant and animal motifs representing the wonders of Creation.
Large displays of fossils, plants, insects and animals are on show, including remains of a dinosaur and other extinct species.
Open Monday to Saturday 10am to 6pm Sunday 2.30pm to 6pm.

GEOLOGICAL MUSEUM

(Exhibition Road SW7 – ⊖ South Kensington – Tel: 01-589 3444).
Among its many attractions are the newly opened permanent exhibitions dedicated to the origins of our planet and its natural resources in its most fascinating *son-et-lumière* technique. The earthquake platform effectively brings home the realities. In fact the *"Story of Earth"* exhibition which traces the 5,000 million year history of our planet is a must for all visitors.
Open Monday to Saturday 10am to 6pm Sunday 2.30pm to 6pm.

General View of the impressive building and entrance of the Natural History Museum (the Geological Museum is to the right — *(Natural History)*

NATURAL HISTORY MUSEUM
— Floor Plan —

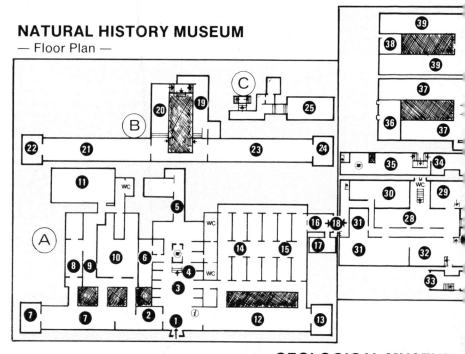

A — GROUND FLOOR

(1) ENTRANCE
(2) Shop
(3) Dinosaurs
(4) Steps to First Floor
(5) Fishes & Reptiles
(6) Spiders
(7) Birds
(8) Insects
(9) Marine Invetebrates
(10) Human Biology
(11) Mammals (Part 1)
(12) Fossil Mammals
(13) Ecology
(14) New Exhibitions of
    Fossils etc.
(15) Temporary Exhibition
    of Fossils
(16) Lasting Impressions
(17) British Geological Centre
(18) Entrance (Museum Link)
    to GEOLOGICAL MUSEUM

B — FIRST FLOOR

(19) Man's Place in Evolution
(20) Mammals
(21) Origin of Species

(22) African Mammals
(23) Minerals, Rocks
    and Gemstones
(24) Meteorites

GEOLOGICAL MUSEUM
— GROUND FLOOR —

(26) Main Entrance — Exhibition F
(27) Shop
(28) Gemstones
(29) Britain Before Man
(30) Treasures of the Earth
(31) Story of the Earth
(18) Museum Link to NATURAL
    HISTORY MUSEUM
(32) Story of the Earth
(33) Story of the Earth
    in Mezzanine
(34) British Fossils in Mezzanine
(35) Temporary Exhibition area

— FIRST FLOOR —

(36) Britain's Offshore Oil & Gas
(37) British Regional Geology

— SECOND FLOOR —

(38) Building Stones
(39) Mineral Deposits of the world.

C — SECOND FLOOR

(25) British Natural
    History Display

bove: Natural History Museum
elow: Human Biology exhibition at the Natural History Museum *(Natural History)*

VICTORIA and ALBERT MUSEUM

(Cromwell Road SW7 – ⊖ South Kensington – Tel: 01-589 6371).

The V&A comprises 11 acres and 7 miles of galleries, housing everything from Renaissance sculpture to needle point — and there is always a special exhibition.

The present building was opened by Queen Victoria in 1899 — its vast number of exhibits is arranged in two parts:

The *"Primary Collections"*, where objects are brought together by age, style or nationality and the *Departmental Collections* which comprise displays of ceramics, metalwork, paintings, textiles etc.

The *Henry Cole Wing* houses the collection of the Department of Prints, Drawings and Photographs and Paintings.

Like the British Museum, the V&A is a day trip in itself. It attracts over 2 million visitors annually.

Open Monday-Thursday and Saturday 10am to 6pm – Sunday 2.30pm to 6pm –Friday closed.

Above: The entrance to the Museum.
Below: The Entrance hall of V & A.

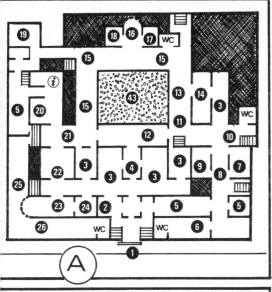

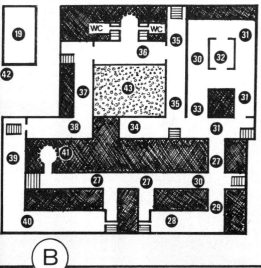

VICTORIA & ALBERT MUSEUM
— Floor Plans —

A — GROUND FLOOR

(1) ENTRANCE
(2) Shop
(3) Eastern & Asiatic Art
(4) Medieval Treasury
(5) Sculptures
(6) Continental — 19th cent.
(7) Italian Cast Court
(8) Fakes & Forgeries
(9) Victorian Cast Court
(10) Carpets
(11) Spanish Art
(12) Gothic Art
(13) North European Renaissance
(14) Medieval Tapestries
(15) Italian Renaissance
(16) Cramble Room
(17) Poynter Room
(18) Morris Room
(19) Photos & Prints
(20) Boilerhouse Project
(21) High Renaissance
(22) Dress Collection
(23) Raphael Cartoons
(24) Woodwork Collection
(25) 17th Cent. Continental
(26) 18th Cent. Continental

B — FIRST FLOOR

(27) Stained Glass
(28) Carving & Bronze
(29) Glass Vessels
(30) Armour & Ironwork
(31) Tapestries
(32) 20th Cent. Collection
(33) Jewellery
(34) Library
(35) Enamel & Metalwork
(36) Silver
(37) Theatre Museum
(38) British Art
(39) English Renaissance
(40) British 1650-1750
(41) Musical Instruments
(42) Henry Cole Wing
(43) Garden

Please Note: At the time of going to press, the Museum is undergoing changes and the floor plans above may alter, if they haven't already. The Museum is trying to project a more up-to-date image of its exhibits.

SCIENCE MUSEUM

(Exhibition Road SW7 – ⊖ South Kensington – Tel: 01-589 3456).

For push-button technology and life-like tableaux, the Science Museum is extremely popular. This large assembly of scientific and technical achievements includes *"Puffing Billy"*, the oldest locomotive in the world (1813), *Stephenson's "Rocket"* (1829) and the *"Apollo 10"* command module used as a dress rehearsal for the landing on the moon.

A new gallery at the S.M. is **Exploration of Space** which shows the historical development of spaceflight from the earliest Chinese gunpowder rocket, dating from about 1000 AD to the age of the manned American and Russian space stations. The display, covering an area of 1,400 square metres, is divided into 8 main sections and includes rocket technology and applications and problems and solutions of living in space.

Also recently given to the S.M. are the *Domesday* video discs, prepared by the BBC as the 1986 equivalent of William the Conqueror's Domesday Book of 1086, when the new King took note of his kingdom's assets.

The **Children's Gallery** with its working models and dioramas is particularly attractive as is the display of *"Glimpses of Medical History"* based on items from the **Wellcome Museum** which, since 1977 has become a part of the Science Museum.

Through a series of well arranged scenes the visitor can appreciate the extraordinary range of activities developed by mankind in trying to understand and treat disease.

Open Monday to Saturday 10am to 6pm
Sunday 2.30pm to 6pm.

The Science Museum — Exhibits by the Main Entrance.

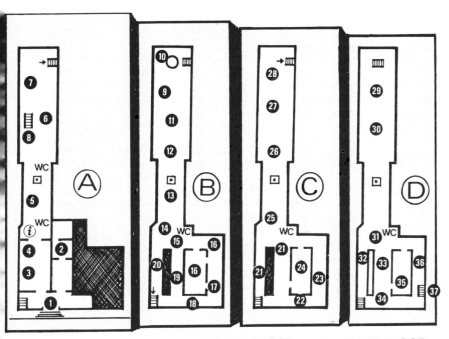

SCIENCE MUSEUM

— Floor Plan —

(1) ENTRANCE
(2) Shop
(3) Motive Power and its development
(4) Gas, Hot Air and Oil Engines
(5) Exploration Items
(6) Transport
(7) Hand & Mechanical Tools
(8) Stairs leading to Natural History Museum

B — FIRST FLOOR

(9) Astronomy
(10) Star Dome
(11) Map Making & Time Measuring
(12) Meteorology
(13) Gas
(14) Agricultural
(15) Plastics
(16) Telecommunications
(17) Textiles
(18) Hand & Machine Tools
(19) Glass
(20) Iron & Steel

C — SECOND FLOOR

(21) Chemistry
(22) Weights, Measures & Lighting
(23) Physics & Nuclear Power
(24) Paper Making & Printing
(25) Computing
(26) Navigation
(27) Sailing & Marine Engineering
(28) Docks & Diving

D — THIRD FLOOR

(29) Aeronautics
(30) Clothes for Work
(31) Oceanography & Geophysics
(32) Heat & Temperature
(33) The King George Collection
(34) Optics
(35) Photography & Cinematography
(36) Magnetism & Electricity
(37) Stairs to "Wellcome" Museum

Science Museum exhibits *(Science Museum)*

THE IMPERIAL WAR MUSEUM

(Lambeth Road SE1 6HZ – Ø Lambeth North – Tel: 01-735 8922).
Founded in 1917 and established by Act of Parliament in 1920, the Museum has been in its present home (formerly Bethlem Royal Hospital or Bedlam), since 1936.

The Imperial War Museum illustrates and records all aspects of the two World Wars and other conflicts involving Britain and the Commonwealth since 1914. The displays in the public galleries include aircraft, armoured fighting vehicles, artillery pieces, small arms, medals, uniforms, paintings, posters and photographs. See a Sopwith Camel, Battle of Britain Spitfire, First World War Tank, midget submarine, one of the Dunkirk 'little ships', escape material from Colditz, the Falklands Surrender Document and much more.

The museum's extensive reference collection of three-dimensional objects, films, books, documents, photographs, works of art and sound recordings are available to the public by appointment. In addition there are regular film shows in the Museum's theatre.

Open Monday to Saturday 10am to 5.50pm Sunday 2pm to 5.50pm.

General View of the Imperial War Museum and entrance *(Imperial War Museum)*

CABINET WAR ROOMS

(Clive Steps, King Charles Street, SW1A 2AQ – ⊖ Westminster – Tels: 01-930 6961 or 01-735 8922).
The Cabinet War Rooms comprise the most important surviving part of the underground emergency accommodation which was provided to protect **Winston Churchill,** the War Cabinet and the Chiefs of Staff of Britain's armed forces against air attacks during the 2nd World War — 1939 to 1945.

Visitors can view a suite of 21 historic rooms, among them the *Cabinet Room,* the *Transatlantic Telephone Room* from which Churchill could speak directly to President Roosevelt in the White House; the *Map Room* where information about operations on all fronts was collected; and the *PM's Room* which served as Churchill's emergency office and bedroom until the end of the War.
Open 7 days a week – 10am to 5.50pm.

The Cabinet Room and Prime Minister's seat in the back *(Imperial War Museum)*

NATIONAL ARMY MUSEUM

(Royal Hospital Road, SW3 – ⊖ Sloane Square – Tel: 01-730 0717)
The NAM tells the history of the Army from Tudor times to 1914

through displays of uniforms, weapons, paintings and personal records.
Open Monday-Saturday 10am to 5.30pm
Sunday 2pm to 5.30pm

(London Wall EC2Y 5HN ⊖ Barbican (closed on Sundays), St. Paul's Moorgate – Tel: 01-600 3699).

The Museum of London was opened in 1976 in the ultra-modern Barbican complex. It was formed by amalgamating the **Guildhall Museum** (founded in 1826) and the **London Museum** (a national museum dating from 1911).

The Museum of London illustrates by means of brilliantly-displayed exhibits, models and audio-visual effects, London's continually evolving and fascinating story.

The Museum is arranged chronologically (Roman, Medieval, Tudor and Stuart, and Modern London), and the exhibits include a relief model showing the archaeological levels of the Thames Valley, a reconstruction of the Great Fire (1666) — complete with realistically crackling flames, and the lavishly decorated *Lord Mayor's State Coach* which was made in 1757. Additionally, there are two archaeological field and research units, which are responsible for excavation within the City of London and Greater London respectively.

A research library which specialises in London's history, is open by appointment only.

Hence, the best place to find out all about London and how it came about is the Museum of London.

Open Tuesday–Saturday 10am to 6pm
Sunday 2pm to 6pm (Closed every Monday)

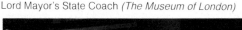

Lord Mayor's State Coach *(The Museum of London)*

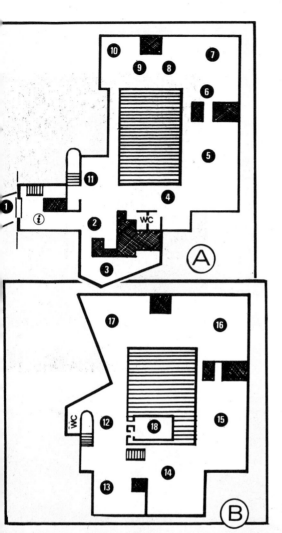

THE MUSEUM OF LONDON
— Floor Plan —

A — UPPER LEVEL

(1) ENTRANCE
(2) Shop
(3) Special Exhibitions
(4) Prehistory of London
(5) Roman London
(6) The Dark Ages
(7) Medieval London
(8) Tudor London
(9) Early Stuart
(10) Great Fire Display
(11) To Lower Level

B — LOWER LEVEL

(12) Lord Mayor's Coach
(13) Late Stuart London
(14) Georgian London
(15) Early 14th Century
(16) The Imperial Capital
(17) 20th Century London
(18) The Treasury

The Great Fire of London exhibition painting Dutch School, painted c.1666. *(The Museum of London)*

THE THEATRE MUSEUM

(Tavistock Street & Russell Street, Covent Garden WC2 – ⊖ Covent Garden – Tel: 01-836 7891).

Opened by Princess Margaret on 23 April 1987 *(on the 423rd anniversary of Shakespeare's death),* it will be the home to the V&A's varied collection of costumes, models, designs, jewellery, props, paintings and playbills.

In addition to a semi-permanent display of the story of the performing arts, arranged in chronological order, a second gallery, named in honour of Sir John Gielgud, will house temporary exhibitions on more specific themes.

The Museum will also have an 85-seat auditorium for lectures, presentations, workshops and performances.

Open Tuesday – Sunday 11am to 7pm

Above right: The Spirit of Gaiety — from the old Gaiety Theatre in the Aldwych.
Below: Part of the main gallery of the Museum *(Theatre Museum)*

THE MUSEUM OF MOVING IMAGE

*South Bank Complex, SE1 –
Tel. 01-928 3535)*

t was opened by Prince Charles in
eptember 1988 and is the world's
argest and most exciting museum
evoted to cinema and TV.
One of the capital's most complex
rchitectural projects it houses a
ermanent display of film and TV
istory. Its exhibits include Fred
staire's tail coat worn in several
lms and Charlie Chaplin's hat and
oat from the 'Gold Rush'. The
Museum has a mock-up Hollywood
tudio and a Foyer of the 1930's
Odeon cinema.
*pen Monday-Saturday 10am-8pm
unday 6pm.*

low: "Metropolis" — The Museum of Moving
age. *(E. Draper, M.O.M.I.)*
low right: London buses on display at the London
ansport Museum.

LONDON TRANSPORT MUSEUM

Centrally located and easily accessible
— within the Covent Garden complex,
the LTM was opened in 1980.
The representative collection of road
vehicles includes a reconstruction of
George Shillibeer's original omnibus
(1829) and more up-to-date motor
buses, trolley buses, trams and
coaches. Among the rail vehicles are
a steam locomotive of 1872, built for
the Duke of Buckingham's private
railway, a locomotive of 1866 used on
the Circle line, and a windowless
coach from the City and South
London Railway, the first 'deep tube'
railway in the world, opened in 1872.
The working displays (many of which
can be operated by visitors) include a
section of an underground tunnel, an
undergrond train controller, and a
signal cabin.

THE GUARDS MUSEUM

(Birdcage Walk, London SW1E 6H – Tel. 01-930 4466)
Was opened in February 1988. The purpose-built building facing ont Wellington Barracks adjacent to th Guard's Chapel, houses a collectio of uniforms, colours and artefac spanning over 300 years history c the Foot Guards.
Opening hours 10-4 daily except Fridays

WELLINGTON MUSEUM

(Apsley House, Horse Guards Avenu SW1 – ⊖ Hyde Park Corner – Tel: 01-499 5676)
The home of the first Duke c Wellington, the original address wa No. 1, London.
On display are many of the Duke trophies, uniforms, decorations, fir paintings and sculptures.
Open Monday to Saturday 10am to 5.50p Sunday 2.30pm to 5.50pm

Above: The Battle of Waterloo — the closing of the gates of Chateau Hougoumont — *(Guards Museum)*
Below: Richard the Lionheart kneels in fervent prayer before his victory at Acre — *(Royal Britain)*

ROYAL BRITAIN

(99 Aldersgate Street, EC2Y 8UY Tel. 01-588 5858 – ⊖ Barbican an Moorgate).
Opened in August 1988 it is permanent exhibition outlining 100 years of royal history from Edgar t Elizabeth II, using sophisticate audio-visual techniques. The exhibi tion which recreates the sights, sound and atmosphere of the lives of 5 monarchs is the work of top art an craft experts. The role of today Royal Family is examined, includin the pressure of being a 'Royal' in th 1980's.
Fast becoming one of London' popular spots.
Open 7 days a week 9am-5.30pm.

FREUD MUSEUM

20 Maresfield Gardens NW1 –
⊖ Finchley Road – Tel: 01-435 2002)
The centre-piece is Freud's famous
couch in which patients lay to search
their psyche. It was here that *Sigmund
Freud* lived and died after escaping
from the Nazis in Vienna (1938).
After his death (1939) his daughter
Anna lived on in the house, keeping
the main rooms as they had been in
his lifetime — packed with thousands
of classical Greek, Roman, Oriental
and Egyptian antiquities as well as
Freud's remarkable library.
Following extensive refurbishment, the
house is now open to the public *Wednesday to Sunday 12 noon – 5pm.*

SIR JOHN SOANE
MUSEUM

13 Lincoln's Inn Fields, WC2 –
⊖ Holborn or Chancery Lane –
Tel: 01-405 2107)
Former residence of Sir John Soane,
architect of the Bank of England. The
House contains thousands of archi-
tectural drawings, various antiquities
and works by Hogarth, Turner and
Watteau. It is a treasure trove in a
delightful and small setting.
Open Tuesday – Saturday 10am to 5pm.

DICKENS HOUSE
MUSEUM

48 Doughty Street, WC1N 2LF –
⊖ Chancery Lane or Holborn –
Tel: 01-405 2127).
Portions of Dicken's manuscripts,
letters, preliminary drawings by his
illustrators, first editions of his books,
including the original paper-wrapped
parts, the desk he used for public
readings of his works, the family
Bible, and many other exhibits,
including furniture, pictures, books
and memorabilia.

His drawing room has been reconstructed to reflect the period in which
he lived with carpet and wallpaper
and original furniture.
*Open Monday to Saturday 10am to 4.30pm
(Closed Sunday).*

KEATS HOUSE

*(Wentworth Place, Keats Grove, NW3
2RR – ⊖ Belsize Park –
Tel: 01-435 2062)*
Letters, manuscripts and relics of the
poet and his contemporaries can be
seen. Also new shop with Keat's
books and memorabilia, dolls in
period costume, stationery etc.
*Open Monday – Saturday 10am to 1pm
and 2pm to 6pm – Sunday 2pm to 5pm*

FLORENCE
NIGHTINGALE MUSEUM

*(Gassiot House, 2 Lambeth Palace
Road, SE1 7EU – Tel. 01-620 0374).*
Opened to the public on 7 February
1989, it is situated next to St.
Thomas' Hospital, where Florence
Nightingale established the first
school of nursing. The FNM will
provide an audio-visual interpretation
of nursing history, including Florence's memorabilia.

Florence Nightingale

CONRAN FOUNDATION DESIGN MUSEUM

(Studio 404, 45 Curlew Street, Docklands, London SE1 – Tel. 01-403 6933).
Opening on 19 July 1989, the Museum will house a permanent study collection of design, with space for temporary exhibitions.
Open 11.30am-6.30pm (except Mondays).

BANK OF ENGLAND MUSEUM

(Bartholomew Lane, EC2R 8AH – Tel. 01-601 5898)
Was officially opened in November 1988. It outlines the Bank's 300 year history and its work today. The Museum contains a reconstruction of the original bank stock office a video programme to cater both for people who know little about the Bank and advanced economics students. Also, an exhibition which includes the Bank's original charter, gold bars and banknotes.
Open Monday-Friday 10am-6pm.

THE RAGGED SCHOOL MUSEUM

(48-50 Copperfield Road, E3 – Tel. 01-232 2941)
Opened in 1989 it hosts displays and exhibits covering the history of the East End and the development of free education in Britain.
NB: Please phone for opening/closing hours.

Remember that with so much on offer, London has been rightly called the "Museum Capital of the World." While London will always be famous for its traditional attractions it is also a city of change and innovation, ensuring fresh appeal to visitors and locals alike.

To complete our section on Museums a few others deserve a mention:

BADEN-POWELL HOUSE *(Queen. Gate SW7 – ⊖ South Kensington o. Gloucester Road – Tel: 01-584 7030)*
This traces the life history of Baden Powell the founder of the **Scout** association. *Open daily 7am to 8pm.*

MUSEUM OF GARDEN HISTORY
(St. Mary-At-Lambeth, Lambeth Palace Road SE1 – ∅ Westminster – Tel 01-261 1891). A 17th century **Botanical Garden** with many rare plant. introduced into Britain by the Tradescants, both father and son.
The building retains its 14th century tower and was restored in 1851-52. Three generations of Tradescants, as well as William Bligh of Mutiny on the Bounty fame are buried in the churchyard. There has been a church on this site since 1062. The present building was saved from demolition in 1979 by the Tradescant Trust to establish the first Museum of Garden History.
Open Monday to Friday 11am to 3pm
Sunday 10.30am to 5pm
Closed from the 2nd Sunday of December to the 1st Sunday in March each year.

GEFFRYE MUSEUM *(Kingsland Road, E2 8EA – ⊖ Liverpool Street then bus 22 or 48 – Tel: 01-739 8365).*
It houses 18th century almshouses with a series of period rooms ranging from 1600 to 1939.
Open Tuesday to Saturday 10am to 5pm
Sunday 2pm to 5pm.

SHAKESPEARE GLOBE MUSEUM
(1 Bear Gardens SE1 ⊖London Bridge – Tel: 01-928 6342). It depicts Elizabethan theatre history from 1550 to 1642 with models and replicas of the *Globe and Cockpit* playhouses. A plaque on the wall marks the approximate site of the famous Globe Theatre where Shakespeare is said to have acted.

pen Tuesday to Saturday 10am to
30pm Sunday 2pm to 6pm (Ring bell for
admission)

or the future and at the same site
Bankside, London SE1 9EB – Tel. 01-
20 0202) plans are in progress to
omplete 'The International Shakes-
eare Globe Centre' by April 1992 to
nclude a permanent exhibition of
ondon's theatres, a shopping pre-
inct and piazza overlooking the
hames.

EWISH MUSEUM *(Woburn House,
Ipper Woburn Place WC1H 0EP – ⊖
uston – Tel: 01-388 4525).* Contains
collection of ritual objects and
ntiquities illustrating Jewish life and
vorship. Audio-visual programmes
xplain the Jewish faith and customs.
*pen Tuesday to Thursday (and Friday
uring the summer) 10am to 4pm.
unday (and Friday during the winter)
0am to 12.45pm
'LOSED, Monday & Saturday, Jewish
nd Public Holidays.*

MUSEUM OF METHODISM *(49
City Road EC1 – ⊖ Old Street – Tel:
1-253 2262).* This museum is housed
n the crypt of Wesley's chapel and
lustrates the development of Metho-
ism from the 18th century to the
resent day. John Wesley (1703-
791) was the founder of Methodism
nd here are exhibited many of his
ersonal belongings including the
lectrical machine invented by him
or treating illnesses.
Vesley is buried outside the chapel in
he forecourt of which is the bronze
tatue of Wesley with the celebrated
nscription. *"The World is my Parish".
Ipen Monday to Saturday 10am to 4pm
'unday 11am to 2pm.*

DR JOHNSON'S HOUSE *(17 Gough
Square EC4A 3DE – ⊖ Temple or
Chancery Lane – Tel: 01-353 3745)* is
vhere the celebrated diarist lived
from 1749-1759) and wrote his
amous dictionary — the first edition

of which is on display. The house is
decorated with articles of furniture
and objects from Johnson's period
and there is a large selection of
memorabilia about Johnson and his
circle.
*Open Monday to Saturday 11am to 5.30pm
(May-September) –
11am to 5.00pm (October-April).*

**The Thomas Coram Foundation for
Children** *(40 Brunswick Square, WC1N
1AZ – ⊖ Russell Square – Tel: 01-278
2424)* houses art treasures from the
old Foundling Hospital, including
works by Hogarth, Gainsborough
and Reynolds.
Open Monday to Friday 10am to 4pm.

**Percival David Foundation of Chinese
Art** *(53 Gordon Square, WC1H 0PD
· ⊖ Euston, Goodge Street, Russell
Square – Tel: 01-387 3909)*, houses a
unique collection of Chinese ceramics,
the majority of pieces dating to the
period 10th to 18th century.
*Open: Monday 2.00pm to 5.00pm.
Tuesday t o Friday 10.30am to 5.00pm
Saturday 10.30am to 1.00pm.*

Sir John Sloane Museum — see page 85.

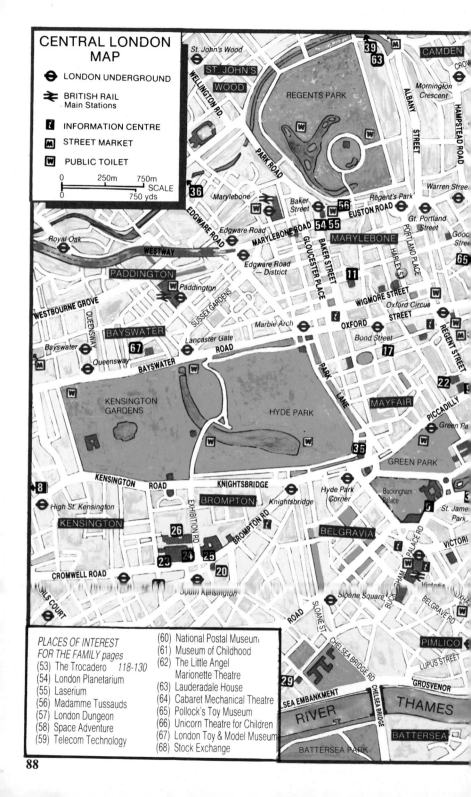

CENTRAL LONDON MAP

- ● LONDON UNDERGROUND
- ⇌ BRITISH RAIL Main Stations
- 🛈 INFORMATION CENTRE
- Ⓜ STREET MARKET
- Ⓦ PUBLIC TOILET

SCALE

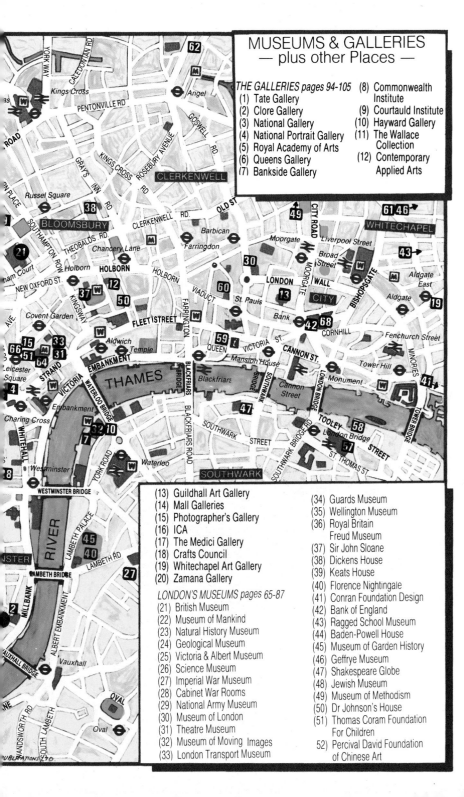

MUSEUMS & GALLERIES
— plus other Places —

THE GALLERIES pages 94-105
(1) Tate Gallery
(2) Clore Gallery
(3) National Gallery
(4) National Portrait Gallery
(5) Royal Academy of Arts
(6) Queens Gallery
(7) Bankside Gallery

(8) Commonwealth Institute
(9) Courtauld Institute
(10) Hayward Gallery
(11) The Wallace Collection
(12) Contemporary Applied Arts

(13) Guildhall Art Gallery
(14) Mall Galleries
(15) Photographer's Gallery
(16) ICA
(17) The Medici Gallery
(18) Crafts Council
(19) Whitechapel Art Gallery
(20) Zamana Gallery

LONDON'S MUSEUMS pages 65-87
(21) British Museum
(22) Museum of Mankind
(23) Natural History Museum
(24) Geological Museum
(25) Victoria & Albert Museum
(26) Science Museum
(27) Imperial War Museum
(28) Cabinet War Rooms
(29) National Army Museum
(30) Museum of London
(31) Theatre Museum
(32) Museum of Moving Images
(33) London Transport Museum

(34) Guards Museum
(35) Wellington Museum
(36) Royal Britain
     Freud Museum
(37) Sir John Sloane
(38) Dickens House
(39) Keats House
(40) Florence Nightingale
(41) Conran Foundation Design
(42) Bank of England
(43) Ragged School Museum
(44) Baden-Powell House
(45) Museum of Garden History
(46) Geffrye Museum
(47) Shakespeare Globe
(48) Jewish Museum
(49) Museum of Methodism
(50) Dr Johnson's House
(51) Thomas Coram Foundation
     For Children
(52) Percival David Foundation
     of Chinese Art

GREENWICH

In Britain, you are never far from the sea and never far from maritime history in London. **GREENWICH** in SE10 has been called, and rightly so *"the cradle of maritime history"*. Few places can claim a richer heritage of noble architecture and notable residents than Greenwich. Within its bounds were once 2 royal palaces, 2 royal dockyards, Wren's magnificent Royal Hospital for Seamen and the Royal Military Academy. It is now the home of the Royal Arsenal and the Royal Artillery in Woolwich and the Royal Naval College, the National Maritime Museum and the Royal Observatory in Greenwich. It has more Thames riverside than any of the other London boroughs (which has greatly affected its development), as well as many parks and open spaces offering a wide range of sport and leisure opportunities.

Historic Greenwich has much to offer.
NB: *See also chapter on "Outer London" and "Index".*

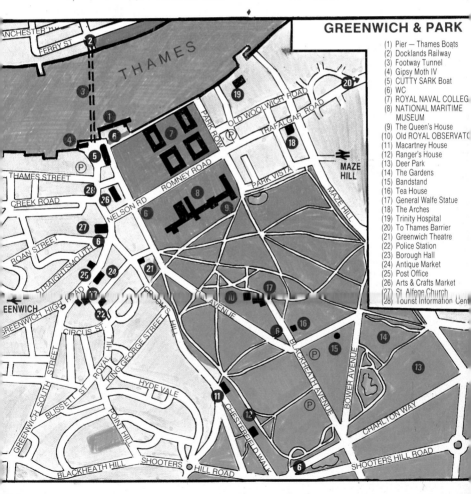

GREENWICH & PARK

(1) Pier — Thames Boats
(2) Docklands Railway
(3) Footway Tunnel
(4) Gipsy Moth IV
(5) CUTTY SARK Boat
(6) WC
(7) ROYAL NAVAL COLLEG
(8) NATIONAL MARITIME MUSEUM
(9) The Queen's House
(10) Old ROYAL OBSERVATO
(11) Macartney House
(12) Ranger's House
(13) Deer Park
(14) The Gardens
(15) Bandstand
(16) Tea House
(17) General Walfe Statue
(18) The Arches
(19) Trinity Hospital
(20) To Thames Barrier
(21) Greenwich Theatre
(22) Police Station
(23) Borough Hall
(24) Antique Market
(25) Post Office
(26) Arts & Crafts Market
(27) St. Alfege Church
(28) Tourist Information Cent

THE ROYAL NAVAL COLLEGE

(King William Walk SE10 – Tel: 01-858 2154)

This was once the Royal Hospital Greenwich. Originally it used to be the site of Greenwich Palace where Henry VIII; Mary I and Elizabeth I were born.

The famous Painted Hall and Chapel are especially magnificent and was here that Nelson's funeral was held in 1805.

Open daily (except Thursdays) 2.30pm to 5pm.

THE NATIONAL MARITIME MUSEUM

(Romney Road, Greenwich, SE10 9NF – Tel: 01-858 4422)

Opened in 1937 the National Maritime Museum is a *treasure house* of Britain's maritime heritage at peace and at war. It includes the *Queen's House* of 1616 by Inigo Jones (this was England's first house in the Palladian style and is linked to the two wings by colonnades built over the line of a former road running beneath the house), and the *Old Royal Observatory* centred around Christopher Wren's Flamsteed House of 1675.

Its new gallery *"Discovery and Seapower 1450-1700"* (opened in 1986), charts England's transition from economic obscurity to its position by the end of the 17th century as one of the great naval and commercial powers of Europe. Starting with the discoveries of the great explorers, the display traces the origins of the Royal Navy under Henry VIII and the exploits of the Elizabethan seamen, Drake and Hawkins.

The National Maritime Museum staged a new exhibition in 1988 about

National Maritime Museum and Old Royal Observatory *(National Maritime Museum)*

The Meridian Line, Old Royal Observatory *(National Maritime Museum)*

the defeat of the Spanish Armada — one of the most dramatic events in Britain's maritime history.

Open Monday – Saturday 10am to 6pm
Sunday 2pm to 6pm
(Winter): Monday – Friday 10am to 5pm
Saturday 10am to 5.30pm
Sunday 2pm to 5pm.

THE OLD ROYAL OBSERVATORY

(Greenwich Park, SE10 –
Tel: 01-858 1167)

Formerly *Flamsteed House,* the Old Royal Observatory is Britain's oldest scientific institution. Although built in 1675 new buildings were added in the 18th and 19th centuries.

In 1880 **Greenwich Mean Time (GMT),** dependant on accurate time-keeping, was made the Standard International Time and in 1884 the *Greenwich Meridian* was accepted as the O° line for the world.

Here you will find many astronomical, horological and navigational exhibits and a planetarium, also the largest refracting telescope in the U.K.

Open (Summer): Monday to Saturday
10am to 6pm – Sunday 12 noon to 6pm
(Winter): Monday to Friday 10am to 5pm
Saturday 10am to 5.30pm
Sunday 2pm to

Still in the vicinity we find other interesting but small museums:

THE ROTUNDA MUSEUM of ARTILLERY

(Repository Road, Woolwich, SE18 –
Tel: 01-856 5533 Ext. 385).

This Museum houses a fascinating display of the development of artillery since the 14th century.

The circular structure, designed by Nash for the reception of allied sovereigns after Napoleon's defeat, was re-erected here in 1819 as a military repository.

Open: (1 April-31 Oct.) Monday to Friday
12 noon to 5pm
Saturday & Sunday 1pm to 5pm
(1 Nov-31 March) Monday to Friday 12
noon to 4pm
Saturday & Sunday 1pm to 4pm.

ROYAL ARTILLERY REGIMENTAL MUSEUM

(Royal Military Academy – Academy Road, Woolwich, SE18 – Tel: 01-856 5533 Ext. 2523).
It is situated near the magnificent 18th century barracks.
The Museum outlines the Royal Regiment of Artillery's history and campaigns since its formation in 1716.

Open Monday-Friday 10am to 12 noon
2pm to 4pm

THE NORTH WOOLWICH OLD STATION MUSEUM

(Pier Road, E16 – Tel: 01-474 7244)
The Museum is a restored 1910 station and it houses displays of the Great Eastern Railway, including engines.

Open Monday to Saturday 10am to 5pm
Sunday 2pm to 5pm

GREENWICH BOROUGH MUSEUM

(Plumstead Library, Plumstead High Street, SE18 1JL – Tel: 01-855 3240)
Houses a local history gallery, covering times from the Stone Age to c.1900, and a natural history gallery. There are also temporary exhibitions. The Greenwich Borough Museum was opened in 1919.

Open Monday 2pm to 8pm
Tuesday, Thursday and Saturday 10am to 1pm and 2pm to 5pm.

ail Maker's Loft Neptune Hall *(National Maritime Museum)*

THE GALLERIES

To suit all tastes and fancies we describe below over 25 Galleries which could be visited. Some, like the Tate, the National Gallery and the Queen's Gallery are not only central but SHOULD be seen.

Max Beckman's
CARNIVAL
at the Tate
(Tate Gallery
Publications)

THE TATE GALLERY

(Millbank SW1P 4RG – ⊖ Pimlico – Tel: 01-821 1313 and 01-821 7128 for recorded information).

It was officially opened in 1897 by the Prince of Wales (afterwards King Edward VII). To make way for the Gallery, Millbank Prison was demolished in 1892 — it was started and financed by the sugar magnate (Sir) Henry Tate.

The TATE is London's premier modern art museum and it houses an important collection of British paintings from 1500 to the present day. It also traces the development of British and foreign art from the mid 1800's to the present day. All modern schools of painting and sculpture are superbly represented and because the Tate buys works almost before they are finished it is often many years ahead of general accepted tastes in art.

The Tate has announced a plan to develop the site adjoining it as a cluster of art museums, each with a separate collection and a distinct architectural character.

Above right: 'Piet Mondrian' Composition with Red, Yellow and Blue.
Below: Blake's — Nebuchadnezzar, *(Tate Gallery Publications)*

THE TATE GALLERY
— FLoor Plan —

(1) ENTRANCE
(2) Shop
(3) 16-18 Cent. Paintings
(4) Blake's Work
(5) Exotic &
    Subline Paintings
(6) British 19th Century
(7) British Watercolours
(8) Pre-Raphaelites
(9) Late Victorian
(10) Stairs to Lecture Room
(11) Modern Art since 1920
     — sculpture of 20th Cent.
(12) Stairs to Print Room
     Gallery
(13) Giacometti & Others
(14) Rothko
(15) Abstract Expressionism
     & General Art 1900-1940
(16) Dubuffet and others
(17) European Masters
     1940-1960
(18) Surrealistic
(20) Abstraction 1910-1940
(21) To CLORE GALLERY
(22) European Art 1910-1930
(23) British Art 1880-1920
(24) Cubism, Futurism,
     Votricism
(25) Impressionists &
     Post Impressionists

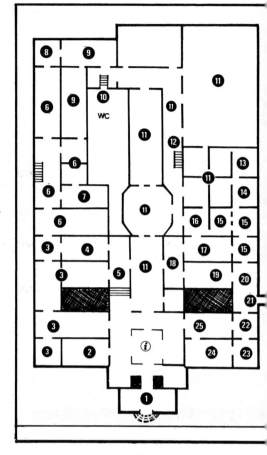

A Turner Painting — detail *(Tate Gallery Publications)*

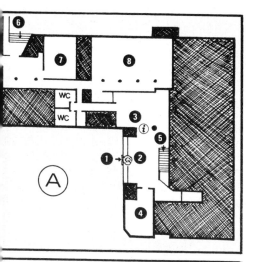

THE CLORE GALLERY
(Turner's Collection)
— Floor Plan —

A — ENTRANCE LEVEL

(1) Main Entrance (Millbank)
(2) Main Hall
(3) Shop
(4) Reading Room
(5) Stairs to Turner's Collection
(6) School Entrance from John Islip Street
(7) Classroom
(8) Auditorium

B — GALLERY LEVEL (TURNER)

(9) To Tate Gallery; Restaurant etc.
(10) Late Works
(11) Italy & Antiquity
(12) Petworth and East Gowes
(13) Studies & Projects
(14) Venice
(15) The Classical Ideal
(16) High Art & the Sublime
(17) England & Working Life
(18) Watercolours, Drawings etc.
(19) Up to Reserve Galleries
(20) Up to Reserve Galleries and Study Room
(21) Stairs down to main Hall

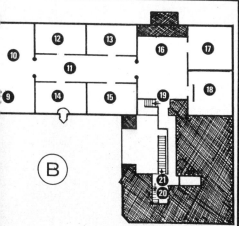

On 1 April 1987 the **CLORE GAL-LERY** was opened by the Queen. It is an L-shaped building on two floors — partly on the site of the former Queen Alexandra Military Hospital. The gallery now shows the **Turner Bequest** which has come together for the first time since Turner's death in 1851. It includes 300 oils and around 000 watercolours and drawings.

The Clore Gallery is only the first manifestation of a grand project for expanding the Tate in order to make its collections more easily available to the public. The second phase will include two new museums, one devoted to modern sculpture and another to new art i.e. the work of the last 10 years. A study centre will also be added.

THE NATIONAL GALLERY

(Trafalgar Square WC2 - ⊖ Charing Cross and Leicester Square – Tel: 839 3321)

Founded in 1824 and housed in this handsome classical-style building the National Gallery is a treasure house of European paintings with few equals. It contains more than 2,000 masterpieces and attracts over 3.5 million visitors a year. An extension to blend with the existing building (also overlooking the north side of Trafalgar Square), is planned for the very near future.

Displayed in 46 rooms (subject to periodic minor changes), the collection admirably covers all schools and periods of painting, but is especially notable for its examples of Rembrandt and Rubens and its representation of the Italian schools of the 15-16th centuries. The British school is only moderately represented since the national collections are shared with the Tate Gallery where also 20th century European paintings and sculptures will be found. Even so, works by John Constable, Thomas Gainsborough, J.M.W. Turner and others adequately present the British style. Apart from the impressive Italian masterpieces (much to be admired are works by Bellini, Fr. Angelico Alessandro Botticelli and Leonardo da Vinci), there are the superb collections of Rembrandt (Dutch) Rubens and Van Dyke (Flemish) and Goya and El Greco (Spanish). Netherlandish, French and German paintings are also very much in evidence.

General View of The National Gallery

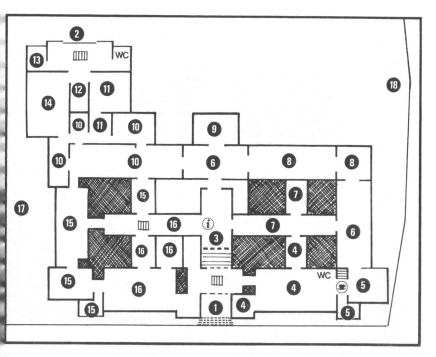

THE NATIONAL GALLERY
— Floor Plan

(1) ENTRANCE HALL
    (Trafalgar Sq.)
(2) Entrance (Orange St.)
(3) Shop
(4) French after 1800
    —Impressionists & Others
(5) Spanish School
(6) Italian after 1600
(7) British Painters
(8) French before 1800
(9) Italian 16th cent.
(10) Dutch School
(11) Early Northern
(12) Special Exhibits
(13) Theatre
(14) Flemish School
(15) 16th Century Italian
(16) Early Italian
(17) Site of New National
    Gallery Extension
    Under Construction
(18) Entrance to National
    Portrait Gallery

e view of the Gallery and Entrance from
Martin-in- the-Fields. The new extention is
der construction at the far end.

99

The National Portrait Gallery entrance which is to the northeast side of the main National Gallery building. It organises special exhibitions through the year.

THE NATIONAL PORTRAIT GALLERY

(St. Martin's Place WC2 – ⊖ Charing Cross and Leicester Square – Tel: 930 1556).

It adjoins the National Gallery on its northeast side and is today a major London attraction. The collection was founded in 1856 (thanks to the 5th Earl of Stanhope), with the object of illustrating British history, literature, arts and science by means of portraits of the most eminent men and women. The Italianate building was finally completed in 1896; an extension was added in 1933.

The collection now numbers over 8,000 paintings, sculptures, drawings, engravings and photographs. The exhibits on display are arranged chronologically — beginning with those of the late 15th century and ending with those of the 20th. Some are by great artists: Henry VII, Henry VIII and Sir Thomas. More are by Holbein; Gladstone and Disraeli by Millais, Sir Winston Churchill by Sickert. There are self-portraits by Hogarth and Gainsborough. Others are by unknown artists or by artists whose names are known but whose talents are minimal.

The rooms in the basement are usually reserved for recent acquisitions and special exhibitions.

Except in rare cases such as royalty portraits are added 10 years after the death of the subject.

ROYAL ACADEMY OF ARTS

Burlington House, Piccadilly W1 – ⊖
Piccadilly Circus and Green Park –
Tel: 734 9052).

Founded in 1768 by Sir Joshua Reynolds, the internationally-renowned RAAs is the oldest established society in Great Britain solely devoted to the fine arts. It also appears to be unique in the world as a self-supporting, self-governing body of artists which on its own premises, conducts art schools, holds open exhibitions of the works of living artists and organizes loan exhibitions of the arts of present and past periods.

Undoubtedly, it is through its exhibitions that the Academy has achieved its national and international reputation. Its Summer Exhibitions of contemporary paintings, drawings, engravings, sculpture and architecture has been held annually without a break for over 200 years. Some 10,000 works by 4,000 artists of whatever nationality or training are submitted and, of these, about 1300 are finally chosen. The artists are helped not only by direct sales but by their work being seen by many visitors. Centrally located and with such a high standing, the Academy is one of London's popular attractions. Wall and ceiling paintings by Sebastiano Ricci, Benjamin West, Angelica Kauffman and other eminent artists lavishly decorate old Burlington House and its annexe which was added to it in 1974.

The Entrance to The Royal Academy of Arts

South Bank Centre and Royal Festival Hall Building. Hayward Gallery is behind.

QUEEN'S GALLERY

(Buckingham Palace – Buckingham Palace Road SW1 – Tel: 930 3007).
Is a small gallery housing a frequently changing exhibition of items from the Royal Collection.

BARBICAN ART GALLERY

(Barbican Centre, Silk Street EC2 – ⊖ - Barbican and Moorgate – Tel: 638 4141)
Hosts a variety of exhibitions in a spacious gallery. The **"Image of London"** was its special feature for mid-1987 and it attracted a lot of visitors.

SOUTH BANK CENTRE

(Hungerford Railway Arches, Concert Hall Approach SE1 – Tel: 928 3002)
Comprising mainly the **Royal Festival Hall** and **National Theatre,** hosts regular exhibitions. Recent themes have included Beethoven and Maria Callas.

HAYWARD GALLERY

(South Bank SE1 – ⊖ Embankment –Tel: 928 3144 and for recorded information Tel: 261 0127)
Houses major art exhibitions organised by the Arts Council. The Hayward is a futuristic multi-level gallery in the South Bank entertainment complex.

BANKSIDE GALLERY

(48 Hopton Street SE1 – Tel: 928 7521) It is very near the South Bank Centre. In one of its recent exhibitions two works by the Prince of Wales were on show.

COMMONWEALTH INSTITUTE

(Kensington High Street W8 – ⊖High Street Kensington – Tel: 603 4535)
It is a permanent exhibition from the 49 member countries of the *Commonwealth* depicting their lifestyles, cultures, resources etc. An adjoining gallery regularly exhibits paintings.

COURTAULD INSTITUTE GALLERIES

(Woburn Square WC1 – ⊖ Goodge Street and Russell Square – Tel: 580 1015).
Most famous for its magnificent Impressionist and Post Impressionist Paintings.
Courtauld also contains an excellent collection of old Nash Drawings and Italian primitive paintings.

The impressive **SOMERSET HOUSE,** at the Aldwych by the River and, built in 1776-86, will become the permanent home of the Courtauld Institute paintings by the end of 1989.

THE WALLACE COLLECTION

(Hertford House Manchester Square W1 – ⊖Bond Street – Tel: 935 0687)
It was bequeathed to the nation by Lady Wallace in 1897, and was opened by the Prince of Wales on 22 June 1900 as a national museum. It is noted particularly for its fine display of French 17th and 18th century paintings, furniture, porcelain, arms and armour.
"The Laughing Cavalier" by Franz Hals is one of its best known paintings.

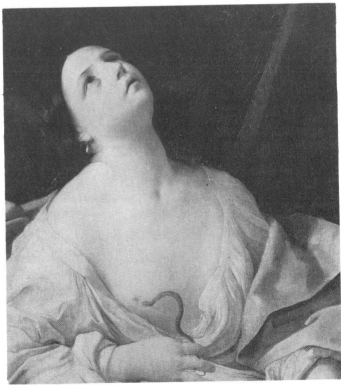

One of the exhibits at Queen's Gallery
(The Royal Collection)

CONTEMPORARY APPLIED ARTS

43 Earlham Street WC2 – ⊖ Holborn –Tel: 836 6993) includes interesting exhibitions. Lately it housed an exhibition of wooden sculptures by various artists who all use a figurative approach to carving.

GUILDHALL ART GALLERY

(King Street, Cheapside EC2 – Tel: 606 3030) has fascinating collections of pictures of London.

MALL GALLERIES *(17 Carlton House Terrace, The Mall SW1 – ⊖ Charing Cross – Tel: 930 6844)* houses various watercolours and portrait exhibitions.

PHOTOGRAPHER'S GALLERY *(5 & 8 Great Newport Street WC2 – ⊖ Leicester Square – Tel: 831 1772)* is a centre for exhibitions of work by modern and historical photographers.

ICA *(Nash House, The Mall, SW1 ⊖ Charing Cross – Tel: 930 3647)* is London's centre for contemporary art and artists.

THE MEDICI GALLERY *(7 Grafton Street, Bond Street, W1X 3LA – Tel: 629 5675)* also holds regular exhibitions — old prints, engravings etc.

CRAFTS COUNCIL GALLERY *(12 Waterloo Place SW1 – Tel. 930 4811)* Covering the whole span of the crafts, it hosts various unique exhibitions.

SERPENTINE GALLERY *(Kensington Gardens W2 – ⊖ Bayswater – Tel: 702 3079)* is set in the middle of the park. It is small but a very interesting gallery and holds exhibitions of contemporary art.

DULWICH COLLEGE PICTURE GALLERY

(College Road, SE21 – Tel: 693 5254). This is London's first public art gallery (and perhaps one of its most under-rated) with some fine paintings by *Rembrandt, Gainsborough, Van Dyck,* and others. *Closed Mondays.*

WHITECHAPEL ART GALLERY

(Whitechapel High Street, E1 – ⊖ Aldgate East, Tel: 377 5015) hosts a stimulating line-up of works by artists from the East End of London, an area which boasts the highest concentration of artists in the whole of Europe. Includes the whole spectrum of art being made today, with materials ranging from video to sculpture; content from figurative to conceptual.

THE ZAMANA GALLERY *(1 Cromwell Gardens SW1 – ⊖ South Kensington – Tel: 584 6612),* is a new exhibition centre dedicated to the art and culture of the Third World.

In the Greenwich (London South East) area, there are 3 places worth a visit.

WOODLANDS *(90 Mycenae Road, Blackheath, SE3 7SE – Tel: 858 4631)* was built in 1774 as a villa for J.J. Angerstein, a founder of Lloyds and patron of the arts. This fine Georgian House holds a varied collection of local topographical drawings and watercolours.

Outstanding exhibitions on a variety of visual arts are also shown, including a number of loans from national galleries.

TUDOR BARN *(Well Hall Pleasaunce, Well Hall Road, Eltham, SE9 – Tel: 850 2340),* is the only remaining building of *Well Hall,* which dates back to the Normans and was owned by Sir Thomas More's son-in-law; now houses an art gallery on the upper floor. Here are the original Tudor stone fireplace and oak beams — a delightful setting for the work of the area's artists and occasional exhibitions of local interest.

RANGER'S HOUSE *(Chesterfield Walk, Blackheath SE10 – Tel: 853 0035)* was the home of the 4th Earl of Chesterfield, a handsome red brick villa built in 1688. It now houses the Suffolk Collection of Jacobean, Elizabethan and Stuart portraits and the Dolmetsch collection of musical instruments. It also hosts chamber concerts and poetry readings.

The above selection (from the massive Tate and National Galleries to the much smaller Medici and Zamana Galleries) of London's galleries is certainly not a comprehensive one. Listed below are some which are worth a visit and are easily accessible from the capital's centre:

APSLEY HOUSE — W1 .... Tel: 499 5676
AFRICA CENTRE — WC2 ...... 836 1973
LISSON GALLERY — NW1 ..... 262 1539
IVEAGH BEQUEST — NW3 .... 348 1286
(Kenwood House)
KINGSGATE WORKSHOP
    GALLERY — NW6 .... 328 7878
JAPANESE GALLERY — W8 ... 229 2934
INSTITUT FRANÇAIS — SW7   589 6211
GOLDSMITH'S
    GALLERY — SE14 .... 692 7171
WOODLANDS ART
    GALLERY — SE3 .... 858 4631
BURY ST. GALLERY — SW1 ... 930 2902

There are also many *Commercial Galleries* which are worth a visit; many are located in busy shopping centres, but the biggest concentration is around the New Bond Street area.

N.B. Please check for opening and closing times. The *major* ones, like the Tate and the National Gallery are usually open 7 days a week from 10am to around 5.30pm but on Sunday from 2pm. Catering facilities in the major galleries are very good as are facilities for disabled people.

Also remember that London is considered by many to be the art capital of the world. It is a collector's haven with something to suit every taste and pocket. The list of fine galleries, shops and work centres specialising in art, craft and antiques is endless.

The monthly *"Galleries Magazine"* (a free publication found in hotel foyers and other tourist locations) is a must especially for those who wish to spend more time looking at London's Galleries.

een Park regular weekend open air exhibition — the other important one is at Bayswater Road.

St. Katharine's Dock provides something for everyone — a floating museum and a leisure centre.

CHAPTER SEVEN

MORE IMPORTANT LANDMARKS

BECAUSE LONDON has so much to offer, classification often becomes difficult. Below we will attempt to outline other star attractions which are worth seeing. Some can be visited in conjunction with other attractions listed elsewhere. *Please see our maps for further guidance.*

HISTORIC SHIPS

"THE CUTTY SARK" *(mentioned elsewhere)* in historic Greenwich (Tel: 858 3445 and 853 3589) is a star attraction.

This, the most famous of clipper ships, was launched in 1869 at Dumbarton on the Clyde (Scotland). She was designed for speed — for the highly competitive China tea trade. Her greatest days were, perhaps, as a wool clipper bringing the new season's clip from Sydney to London in record time year after year.

The Cutty Sark has been restored to her former glory as a tea clipper. Visitors can inspect the ship, several cabins are on view, and an exhibition on board tells her fascinating story. On the lower deck the **"Long John Silver"** collection of merchant ship's figureheads is on display. This is the most important collection in the country.

The Cutty Sark is seen by over $\frac{1}{2}$ million visitors a year.

THE GYPSY MOTH IV, close to the Cutty Sark was the first yacht to be raced single-handed round the world. In 1966, **Francis Chichester** set out to equal the times set by the wool clippers.

Visitors are welcome to see the accommodation and equipment on board used by Sir Francis Chichester.

Now that you have enjoyed the Cutty Sark and the Gypsy Moth there are other historic ships, the most interesting of which are on exhibition at St. Katharine's Dock.

ST. KATHARINE-by-the-TOWER *(St. Katharine's Way, E1).* This is a large leisure complex situated on the old **St. Katharine's Dock** which includes a yacht haven and a floating maritime museum. The *Maritime Trust* (founded by the Duke of Edinburgh in 1970), have now moved

107

several of their historic craft here from different parts of Britain. These include —

THE KATHLEEN and MAY, a three-masted double topsail schooner built in 1900. A new exhibition on board tells the story of Britain's coasting trade under sail. This was the last wooden trading schooner. Built in North Wales.

For details phone 403 3965.

The Thames barge **"CAMBRIA",** the last British ship to trade under sail alone;

"ROBIN", a traditional *"dirty British coaster with salt-caked smokestack".*

"LYDIA EVA", the last North Sea steam herring drifter.

"NORE", a typical lightship, and the **"CHALLENGE",** a steam tug.

There are other historic ships but do not forget **HMS BELFAST** which has been described elsewhere — see index.

Again on the Thames, one must not miss the **THAMES BARRIER** (Tel: 854 1373 in historic Greenwich), called the *"Eighth Wonder of the World"*. It is found at Unity Way, Woolwich SE18 5NJ.

This is situated between the Blackwall Tunnel and the Woolich Ferry. It is a magnificent structure spanning the Thames with huge shipping gates, which pivot through 90 degrees to close against potential flood tides. It's the world's largest moveable flood barrier.

The Barrier Visitors Centre is located some 300 yards downstream from the Barrier itself. There is a shop, exhibition, audio visual display, a pier, walkway and boat trips around the Barrier.

Open Daily 10.30am to 6pm – April to September
10.30am to 5pm – October to March.

FAMOUS SQUARES

London has many Squares *(Sloane, Grosvenor, Soho, Berkeley, Bloomsbury etc.)* steeped in tradition and history. We will only deal with two and then add Piccadilly Circus.

PARLIAMENT SQUARE *(SW1 – ⊖ Westminster)* was laid out by Sir Charles Barry in 1868 as a suitable approach to the Houses of Parliament. It contains some of the most prominent landmarks of London. The *Houses of Parliament, Westminster Abbey* and *St. Margaret's,* parish church since 1614 of the House of Commons, well known for its Elizabethan and Jacobean monuments. Raleigh, who introduced tobacco in England, is buried before the altar (but his head is interred at West Horsley, Surrey), while Samuel Pepys (1655) and Winston Churchill

(1908) were both buried here.

Flanked by some of London's best known buildings, the Square contains **statues** of many eminent statesmen *Field Marshal Smuts* (1870-1950) *Lord Palmerston* (1784-1865) *Lord Derby* (1799-1869), *Disraeli* (1804-1881), *Sir Robert Peel* (1788-1850) *Abraham Lincoln* (1809-1865), *George Cunning* (1770-1827) and *Sir W. Churchill* (1874-1965).

Near the **JEWEL TOWER** *(St. Margaret Street)* are the statues of *Oliver Cromwell* and of *Richard I* on horseback.

On the east side of the square is **Middlesex Crown Court** (formerly Middlesex Guildhall, used as a meeting place for exiled governments during the 2nd World War). Behind it is **Central Hall,** the headquarters of the Methodist Church, (the main hall

Trafalgar Square — an old photograph. The past and present blend together in and around this very popular Square.

can seat around 3000) where the first session of the United Nations Organisation was held in 1946.

Nearby is the new Government **Queen Elizabeth II Conference Centre** with facilities for high level international *"secure"* meetings.

Some of the principal *government offices* (e.g. **Treasury, Foreign and Commonwealth Office** etc.) are in Parliament Street, the continuation of Whitehall where the **CENOTAPH**, a Portland stone monument (to commemorate *"The Glorious Dead"*) is located. In nearby **Downing Street, No. 10** has been the official residence and office of the Prime Minister since 1735 (unfortunately the street is closed to visitors for security). Its most famous room is the *Cabinet Room* on the ground floor, with an 18th century wall panelling and Corinthian Columns. **No. 11** has been the residence of the *Chancellor of the Exchequer* (Minister of Finance) since 1805.

TRAFALGAR SQUARE *(WC2 ⊖ Charing Cross)* lies at the top end of Whitehall.

The Square was laid out at the suggestion of Nash to commemorate the great naval victory of Nelson who died in battle in 1805; it was completed around 1850.

THE NELSON MONUMENT stands at its centre, around 185 feet high with a statue of Lord Nelson at the top (facing south towards the River Thames in order to keep his good eye on his fleet). The base of the fluted granite column is surrounded by four lions modelled by Landseer and cast in bronze by Marochetti in 1867. The four bronze reliefs are cast from French cannons captured at naval bases. The fountains designed by Lutyens were added in 1948 and the sculptures are by Wheeler and McMillan.

The impressive church of St. Martin's. Little has changed from this old engraving

There are several important statues in the Square: *Sir Henry Havelock, Sir Charles J. Napier*, the equestrian statue of *George IV* by Chantrey, and bronze busts of *Lord Cunningham, Lord Jellicoe* and *Lord Beatty*.

Around the Square there are many important buildings. To the north is the **National Gallery** and just behind it the **National Portrait Gallery.**

ST. MARTIN-in-the-FIELDS (a neo-classical church) on the north east side of the Square was completed in 1724 and is the work of James Gibbs. The richly decorated ceiling by Artari and Bagutti is famous. The church has a long tradition of social service to the community — for many years housing the homeless. It is also the Parish Church of Buckingham Palace; Charles II was baptised and Nell Gwynne's (his mistress) burial is recorded here.

At the south east of the Square is

Charing Cross — the ancient road junction at the top of Whitehall which pre-dates Trafalgar Square by several centuries. Today most people associate Charing Cross with the area in front of Charing Cross Station. But it was at the top of Whitehall that Edward I had erected the last of a series of 13 crosses to mark the funeral procession of his wife Eleanor, to Westminster Abbey in 1291. The cross gave the junction its name Charing Cross, but it was destroyed in 1647 and the site has since been occupied by a fine equestrian statue of Charles I. London distances are measured from a bronze plaque by this spot.

Trafalgar Square is well known for its pigeons, political demonstrations, New Year's Eve revelry and the Christmas Tree erected here each December, donated by Norway in recognition of British assistance during the 2nd World War.

PICCADILLY CIRCUS (W1 ⊖ *Piccadilly Circus)* is the part at which Piccadilly, Regent Street, Shaftesbury Avenue and Coventry Street join.

At its centre is the famous **Fountain.** Known officially as the *Shaftesbury Memorial,* it was unveiled in 1893 in memory of Lord Shaftesbury (1801-1885), politician, philanthropist and social reformer.

The winged figure popularly known as **EROS** was intended by its sculptor (A. Gilbert) to represent an *"Angel of Christian Charity".* The advertisement lights of the Circus coalesce into a dynamic technicolour scene which in the imagination of millions epitomises the heart of the capital.

There are *plans* to develop the south side of Piccadilly — if approved by Westminster Council the works will take over 3 years to complete.

Above and Below: Two views of Piccadilly — A new and an old. The above shows London Pavillion after renovation in the late 1980's.

111

Some have already been pinpointed especially under *"famous squares"*.

ALBERT MEMORIAL *(Kensington Palace Gardens, W8).*

This is an elaborate memorial to the greatly loved consort of Queen Victoria. The Prince is depicted holding a catalogue of the Great Exhibition of 1881. On the steps are marble groups representing the four continents, and around the plinth are marble reliefs of the world's greatest artists and architects. The monument is under structural threat and work is undertaken at times which restricts visits.

QUEEN ALEXANDRA MEMORIAL *(Marlborough Gate, SW1).*

It was unveiled in 1932 by the Queen's son, George V. Behind the memorial, which includes a number of bronze allegorical figures on a red granite plinth, is a bronze screen with lamps in the top corners and below is a fountain.

QUEEN BOADICEA STATUE *(known as Queen Boudicca)* Victoria Embankment SW1, on the north side of Westminster Bridge).

It is a bronze group of the Queen and her daughters in a chariot. Made in the 1850's by Thomas Thornycroft and unveiled in 1902. Prince Albert lent horses as models.

CLEOPATRA'S NEEDLE *(Victoria Embankment, SW1).*

This granite obelisk (some 60 feet high) was originally erected circa 1500 BC with 2 others at Heliopolis — it then stood in front of the Temple of the Sun. It was brought from Egypt in 1878; another stands in Central Park, New York.

Queen Boadicea's statue.

112

GUARDS CRIMEA MEMORIAL

(Waterloo Place, SW1). It commemorates the 2162 officers, non-commissioned officers and privates of the three regiments of foot guards who fell in the Crimean War (1854-56). On the south side, guarding the memorial, are statues of Florence Nightingale, shown as the *'lady with the lamp'* and her associate and strong supporter Lord Sidney Herbert in peer's robes.

Other bronze reliefs associated with the war (characters, battles etc.) are also present.

MARBLE ARCH *(top end of Oxford Street W2),* was designed by Nash and erected in 1828 as an entrance to Buckingham Palace, and as a Memorial to the Napoleonic Wars. Proving to be too narrow for the State Coach it was moved to its present site as an entrance to Hyde Park in 1851.

In 1908 the park railings were moved back to allow the Arch to stand in isolation. Nearby, where Edgware Road intersects Bayswater Road, stood Tyburn Gallows, the scene of many executions.

QUEEN VICTORIA MEMORIAL

(outside Buckingham Palace) is surrounded by a stone balustrade at the centre of a circus in a very impressive fashion. The statue of Queen Victoria was sculptured by Thomas Brock in white marble and is crowned by a gilded bronze figure of Victory with Courage and Constancy at her feet. The monument designed by Sir Aston Webb, was erected in 1911.

THE MONUMENT *(Fish Street Hill, EC3)* and **NELSON'S COLUMN** *(Trafalgar Square)* have been noted elsewhere.

Marble Arch — an old engraving. Traffic is still as busy as it was then.
Below: Albert Memorial.

OTHER PLACES OF INTEREST

So far in this section we have discussed Historic Ships, Famous Squares and Monuments/Statues. Other attractions of special interest centrally located, are worth mentioning.

THE INNS OF COURT Lincoln's Inn, Middle Temple, Inner Temple and Gray's Inn — *(located mainly between the River and Fleet Street),* date from the 14th century and is believed that they came into existence for the purpose of teaching, controlling and protecting bodies of 'apprentices' i.e. students and barristers below the rank of Sergeant-at-Law. Each Inn is governed by Benchers (Masters of the Bench), and they alone have the power to call student's to the Bar i.e. to be able to appear in Courts of Law.

THE LAW COURTS *(Strand and Fleet Street, WC2 – Tel: 936 6000),* or **Royal Courts** were built here in the 19th century to concentrate in one convenient place all the superior courts concerned with *civil* ie non criminal cases. The building is brick (c.35 million) faced with Portland stone and contains more than 1000 rooms and some $3\frac{1}{2}$ miles of corridors. Over the main entrance are statues of *Christ* (centre) *King Solomon* (west) *King Alfred* (east), while *Moses* stands over the back door.

N.B. On the second Saturday in November the City of London Lord Mayor-elect rides in his coach in procession from the Guildhall to the courts to be sworn in by the Chief Justice.

General view of The Law Courts — from the Strand area.

114

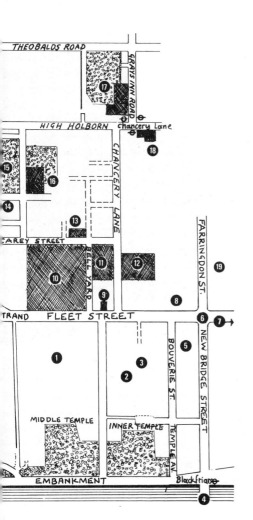

THE TEMPLES & INNS

— Area Map •not in scale —

(1) MIDDLE TEMPLE
(2) INNER TEMPLE
(3) Temple Church
(4) Blackfriars Bridge
(5) St. Bride's Church
(6) LUDGATE CIRCUS
(7) To St. Paul's
(8) Cheshire Cheese Pub
(9) St. Dunstan-in-the-West
(10) ROYAL COURTS OF JUSTICE
(11) THE LAW SOCIETY
(12) Public Records Office
(13) President's House
(14) Land Registry
(15) LINCOLN'S INN FIELDS
(16) LINCOLN'S INN
(17) GRAY'S INN
(18) Stable Inn
(19) CENTRAL CRIMINAL COURT

THE CENTRAL CRIMINAL COURT *(Old Bailey)* is located near St. Paul's Cathedral. The present building was completed in 1907 on the site of Newgate Prison. The lofty tower is surmounted by a bronze gilt figure of Justice.

N.B. During spectacular cases large crowds gather outside in the hope of gaining admission to the Public Galleries, which seat around 200

Old Bailey — an old engraving.

115

Above: Temple Church at the Inner Temple area.
Below: The London Diamond Centre at work.

LONDON DIAMOND CENTRE

(10 Hanover Street, W1R 9HF – ⊖ Oxford Circus – Tel: 629 5511), is a unique centre hosting exhibitions on diamonds where visitors can see diamond-polishers practising their crafts, a life-size, walk-in diamond mine and other aspects of the diamond craft and industry. The Centre (since 1977) is one of the largest diamond/jewellery showrooms in the world and visitors may make purchases a factory prices — certainly one c London's unusual but unique attrac tions.

Open Monday to Friday 9.30am to 5.30p Saturday 9.30am to 3.00pm (1.30p Winter)

HOUSE OF ST. BARNABAS-In SOHO *(1 Greek Street W1 ⊖ Totter ham Court Road – Tel: 437 1894).* Ha Georgian rooms and architectur with a garden and a Victorian copy c a 13th century French Gothic Chape.

Open Wednesdays 2.30pm to 4.15pm Thursdays 11am to 12.30pm

COLLECTOR'S CORNER *(Co burg Street NW1 –⊖ Euston or Eusto. Square – Tel: 922 6436).* Here yo may find all kinds of memorabili and ephemera connected with Britis Rail — everything from nameplate and signalling equipment to photo graphs, timetables, designs etc.

Open Monday to Friday 9am to 5pm Saturday 9am to 4.30pm

DAVID GODFREY'S HISTORI-CAL NEWSPAPER SHOP *(37 Kinnerton Street, SW1 – ⊖ Hyde Park Corner or Knightsbridge – Tel: 235 7788)* has a stock of antiquarian old newspapers from the year 1642, all in good condition, presented in plastic folders and covering major historical events (no reprints or replicas). Ideal to frame, collect, teach with, talk about or given as presents.

Open Monday to Friday 10am to 5pm
Saturday 11am to 4pm

OLD CURIOSITY SHOP "Dickens" *(13 Portsmouth Street, WC2 ⊖ Holborn – Tel: 405 9891).* Built in 1567 and immortalised by Charles Dickens it has two staircases and an original fireplace upstairs. Today the shop sells gifts and antiques.

Open April-October 9am to 5.30pm
5.00pm weekends)
November-March 9.30am to 5.30pm
5.00pm weekends)

PRINCE HENRY'S ROOM and SAMUEL PEPYS EXHIBITION *17 Fleet Street, EC4 – Tel: 353 7323),* hosts a collection of memorabilia of Pepys, the famous diarist, including an original letter to Charles II. The building dates from 1610 and the ceiling and wood panelling are inscribed with the initials "P.H." for Prince Henry who became Prince of Wales in 1610.

Open Monday to Friday 1.45pm to 5pm
Saturday 1.45pm to 4pm

GUILDHALL CLOCK MUSEUM *Guildhall, Aldermanbury EC2 –Tel: 606 3030 – ⊖ Bank/Mansion House),* holds one of the most important collections of clocks and watches bequeathed by the Clockmakers Company and dating from the 1600's) in the country.

Open Monday to Friday 9.30am to 4.45pm
November-March)

Monday to Saturday 10am to 5pm (April-October)
Sunday 2pm to 5pm

DESIGN CENTRE *(28 Haymarket SW1 – Tel: 839 8000 – ⊖ Piccadilly Circus),* has changing exhibitions of British design in the consumer, contract and engineering fields; also a shop with souvenirs designed and made in Britain.

Open Monday & Tuesday 10am to 6pm
Wednesday to Saturday 10am to 8pm
Sunday 1pm to 8pm

MUSEUM OF INSTRUMENTS (Royal College of Music) *(Prince Consort Road – South Kensington SW7) – Tel: 589 3643 – ⊖ South Kensington),* has almost 500 exhibits including the Donaldson Collection, string and wind instruments from the 16th-19th centuries with some instruments for Asia and Africa.

Open Monday and Wednesday (during term time) 11am to 4.30pm.

LEIGHTON HOUSE MUSEUM & ART GALLERY *(12 Holland Park Road, W14 – Tel: 602 3316 ⊖ High Street Kensington);* this House was designed by Lord Leighton in 1866 and it contains rooms furnished in period style and a permanent exhibition of Victorian Art. The *Arab Hall* — probably the most popular feature — is based on Moorish-Spanish design. The paintings, drawings and sculpture include works by Leighton, Burne-Jones and Millais.

Open Monday to Saturday 11am to 5pm (6pm during exhibitions).

CRICKET MEMORIAL GALLERY *(Lord's Ground NW8 – Tel: 289 1611 ⊖ St. John's Wood).* This gallery covers the history of cricket from its beginnings to the present day. It includes paintings, trophies and the Ashes.

Open Monday to Saturday 10.30am to 5pm on match days only – Appointment is required on other days. Please phone first.

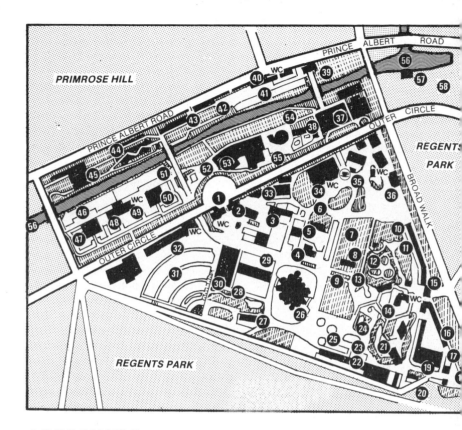

LONDON ZOO
— Location Area —

(1) MAIN ENTRANCE
(2) Giant Pandas
(3) Apes & Monkeys
(4) Shop
(5) Children's Playground
(6) Clock Tower
(7) Cockatoos
(8) Gibbons
(9) Rides
(10) Small Parrots
(11) Birds & Prey Avaries
(12) Three Island Pond
(13) Tigers
(14) Big Cats
(15) Party Gates & South Gate
(16) Wolf Wood
(17) Peafowl
(18) Tropical House for Humming Birds
(19) Bird House

(20) Pheasantry
(21) Lions
(22) Children's Zoo
(23) Penguins
(24) Water Birds
(25) Seals
(26) Elephant & Rhino Pavilion
(27) Sealions
(28) Southern Aviary
(29) Stork and Ostrich House
(30) Reptile House
(31) The Mappin Terraces
(32) Aquarium
(33) Eastern Aviary
(34) Members Lawn
(35) Flamingoes
(36) British Crows Aviary
(37) Meeting Room
(38) Insects

(39) British Owls
(40) North Gate
(41) Cranes & Geese
(42) Owls
(43) Pheasants
(44) Snowden Aviary
(45) Zoo Study Centre
(46) Deer
(47) Horses & Cattle
(48) Giraffes & Zebras
(49) The Cotton Terrace
(50) Camels & Llamas
(51) Antelopes
(52) Beavers
(53) Small Mammals & Moonlight World
(54) Great Apes Breeding Colony
(55) Otters
(56) Regents Canal
(57) Canal Enquiries
(58) Parking Area

CHAPTER EIGHT

PLACES OF INTEREST
FOR THE FAMILY

— Young People's and Children's London —

LONDON is expanding fast as the "fun capital for children." In recent years an abundance of treats have been packaged for youngsters and the process continues. Gone are the days when Londoner's vision of children enjoying themselves, was simply sailing on the Round Pond of **Kensington Gardens** or a visit to the **ZOO** in **Regents Park** — not that either should be missed.

LONDON ZOO

On the contrary the **ZOO** *(NW1 –Tel: 722 3333 – ⊖ Regents Park/Baker Street)*, is amongst other things presenting *"elephant workout"* with their friendly pair moving logs and *"meeting"* the public. New displays of birds and even venomous snakes are usually on show. The Zoo also runs a Young Zoologists Club for children 9-18 with free Zoo tickets and club magazine.

The London Zoo (covering an area of around 36 acres), is over 150 years old, with more than 5,000 species of animals, birds and reptiles and a world wide reputation for conservation and breeding.

Open daily 9am to 6pm (bank holidays to 7pm).

Three other Zoos worth mentioning are:

CHESSINGTON ZOO

(Leatherhead Road, Chessington, Surrey – Tel: 03727 27227 – BR Chessington South). Chessington is a complex around 13 miles from Central London. It comprises of a Zoo, bird garden, circus, picnic areas, reptile house. From 1987 themed amusement areas.

Open daily 10am-5pm — April to October 10am-4pm — November to March.

WHIPSNADE ZOO

(Dunstable, Bedfordshire – Tel: Dunstable 872 171), is worth a visit but it is some distance (approximately 37 miles) from Central London. Opened in 1931 it was turned into the first completely 'open' zoo in the world.

Open daily 10am to dusk (except Christmas Day).

WINDSOR SAFARI PARK

(Winxfield Road, Windsor – Tel. 0753 869841), is an exciting safari park which has killer whale, dolphin, sealion and parrot shows.

Open daily 10am to dusk (except Christmas day)

LONDON ZOO: *Above* Snowdon Aviary. *Below* Elephant bathing. *(Zoo Operations Ltd).*

CHILDREN can sail the world from the **Historic Ship Collection** at **ST. KATHARINES DOCK** near the **Tower** (housing the Crown Jewels) and they can open the mighty bascules of the century–old **TOWER BRIDGE** in a new control cabin simulation. The pristine Victorian engines used to provide power to raise the bridge up to 50 times a day. The exhibitions and overhead walkways can be visited any day. Keeping to the nautical theme children warm to the prospect of going aboard the 11,500 ton cruiser **HMS BELFAST** (the World War II Battleship), the last survivor of the Royal Navy's big ships — now a floating naval museum.

Very briefly, **HMS Belfast** was built by Harland Wolff in the city from which it took her name and launched on 17 March 1938 by Mrs Chamberlain (the Prime Minister's wife).

Her active career ended in 1963 when she was placed in reserve as an accommodation ship at Portsmouth.

In September 1971 she was moved to the Thames and opened to the public the following month.

Visitors may wander at will over many parts of the ship, which has been preserved as nearly as possible in her original state. Among the areas open to the public are the *Operations Room, Messdecks, Sick Bay, Boiler Room, Engine Room,* the *Captain's* and *Admiral's Bridges, Galley, Punishment Cells* and two of the four 6-inch *gun turrets.* In addition there are special displays devoted to *Mines,* the development of the Battleship, D-Day and many other naval subjects. Also a wide range of educational activities are available to schools and groups on board HMS Belfast.

London Pool, Morgans Lane, Tooley Street, SE1 – ⊖ London Bridge – Tel: 01-407 6434/ Daily 11am to 5.30pm.

Again in London's south-east we now move to **GREENWICH** SE10. Greenwich sits on the south bank of

un Fair at Battersea Park

the river Thames, 5 miles to the southeast of the City. It was strategically important to the Romans who used it to connect Dover and Canterbury with London. Its past is indeed exotic. Greenwich rose from humble origins as an ancient fishing village to embrace some of England's richest architecture and most noble history. Its name comes from the Anglo-Saxon "*Grenavic*" — green village.

Apart from its **Royal Naval College** and **NATIONAL MARITIME MUSEUM,** every youngster should know that the **Royal Observatory** (Greenwich Park — SE10, Tel: 858 1167), gives us *Greenwich Mean Time* (GMT). The Royal Observatory illustrates the history of the measurement of time and also includes astronomical exhibits. The buildings are now part of the National Maritime Museum.

In Greenwich too is the **CUTTY SARK,** the speedy 19th century clipper and **Gipsy Moth IV,** in which *Sir Francis Chichester* sailed solo around the world in 1966. It is 52 feet long and it was the first yacht to be raced single-handed round the world in 1966-67.

Downstream, the **THAMES BARRIER** looms with a series of massive silvery structures across the river, which can be visited close up by boat. Back at the visitor's centre, an audio-visual presentation explains why London is no longer at risk from surging tides.

A **foot tunnel** by the Cutty Sark under the river Thames (built for dock workers at the turn of the century) connects Greenwich with the **ISLE OF DOGS.** This is the low-lying north bank peninsula (not an island) created by the great bend in the Thames opposite Greenwich. The origin of the name has never been satisfactorily explained, though it is usually said that it was derived from the royal kennels which were once kept there. Now part of the Docklands regeneration programme.

Back to the heart of London, the TROCADERO houses anything you could want for a great day in town. The Trocadero is situated *(Coventry Street, W1V 7FE)* next to Piccadilly Circus tube station and is open from 10am to 10pm. Atmosphere on a multi-screen presentation with special effects (smoke and smog) is the stuff of **London Experience** *(Tel. 734 0555)* at the Trocadero. This brash, noisy and history — packed show (2,000 years of the capital) focuses on the Great Fire of London, the dark gloom in which Jack the Ripper did his evil deeds, the blitz and jollier everyday events.

At the **Guinness World of Records** (again in the Trocadero complex — Tel. 439 7331), measure yourself against the world's tallest man, walk though a whale's jawbone, see the deepest lake, the fastest runner and call up extra records at the touch of a button. Massive data banks are continually updated as new records are created providing the definitive reference for world achievements.

Enjoy all these, comfortable in all weathers, with a tempting choice of international and traditional food and atmosphere. Additional attractions planned for the interior include cinemas, DIY recording studios and possibly a Rock Museum. Linked to the Trocadero by an underground arcade is the *London Pavilion,* a retail/leisure centre opened in 1988. New developments for the autumn of 1989 include a theme restaurant and Madame Tussaud's Rock Circus Exhibition.

N.B. The original facade, which dates to 1885, has been retained.

Above: The Guinness World of Records section attracts many people — The Trocadero.
Below: Camden Canal (see also under markets) is an ideal place for young people.

Formerly at the Trocadero but now at 48 South Row, The Market, Covent Garden WC2, spend a few quieter moments amid treasingly 3-D holograms — fascinating to all ages. The futuristic **"Light Fantastic the Gallery of Holography"** *(Tel. 836 6423)*, is a unique and stunning visual experience. Holograms are 3 dimensional images recorded by Laser Light; they appear to float in space and are so lifelike that you feel you could reach out and take hold of them. See the toothy grin of the *Cheshire Cat* suspended in thin air and then, at a slightly changed angle, the cat aloft a branch.

Open daily from:
10-6 Monday, Tuesday & Wednesday
10-8 Thursday & Friday
10-7 Saturday
11-6 Sunday.

Mrs Thatcher the longest serving Prime Minister of the century.
(Madamme Tussauds)

As science has penetrated space, so opportunities to star gaze have grown. **"THE LONDON PLANETARIUM** *(Marylebone Road, NW1 – Tel: 486 1121 – adjacent to Baker Street tube)* keeps au fait with knowledge millions of light years away and entertains with shows. In fact the Zeiss projector takes you through time and space from the *Astronomer's Gallery* where special effects highlight the great men of science, to a comfortable seat beneath the dome for a new star show *"Universe"* which explores and explains the myths and mysteries of the cosmos. Thus, every hour on the hour visitors can see spectacular projections of the night sky and the stars. It gives way to the *Laserium* in the early evening.

Open daily 11.30am to 4.30pm — except Christmas Day.

The **LASERIUM** *(Marylebone Road NW1 – Tel. 486 2242, adjacent to Baker Street tube)*, has laser light concerts in the evening, blending rock music to weird and colourful laser beam displays. You will experience a spectacular feeling in sound and vision. Please phone for programme details.

Almost next door is **MADAMME TUSSAUDS** *(Tel. 935 6861)*. It contains wax figures of famous people from all walks of life including a *"Sleeping Beauty"* tableaux who breathes. New figures are added frequently — Fun for both adults and children.

Open 7 days to 5.30pm — except Christmas Day.

If you want to be panic-stricken, then visit the *Chamber of Horrors* at Madame Tussauds or the **LONDON DUNGEON** *(28-34 Tooley Street, SE1 – ⊖ London Bridge – Tel. 403 0606)*. It is situated under London Bridge Station and it houses a display

Joan Collins, famous British actress with other celebrities in The Conservatory — *(Madamme Tussauds)*

of past horrors — plague, hangings, tortures of every kind — recreated by means of dummies and tableaux. It is claimed to be the only medieval horror museum in the world — and it is quite frightening. It holds a peculiar fascination for older children but do not take young sensitive children.

Another must is **SPACE ADVENTURE** (64-66 Tooley Street, SE1 — Tel. 403 7417) which is a minutes walk from London Dungeon. Based on a simulated space trip and moon-walk, Space Adventure 3001 offers the experience of lift-off, orbit, inter-planetary travel, re-entry and landing. It was opened on 28 May 1988.

Open 7 days a week 10.30am-5.00pm

While in this part of London visit Tower Bridge and the Tower of London. Spend also a few hours at the **TELECOM TECHNOLOGY SHOWCASE** *(135 Queen Victoria Street, EC4 – ⊖ Blackfriars – Tel. 248 7444),* where you can see the history of around 200 years of communications told in an exhibition by British telecom. Early telegraphs, switchboards, ivory and gilt telephones, and Edwardian cable-carried entertainment service, prestel, telex, showscan TV digital fascimile, satellite communications and system X, are all there.

Open Monday to Friday 10am-5pm & Closed Bank Holidays.

Also in the vicinity is the **NATIONAL POSTAL MUSEUM** *(King Edward Street, EC1 – ⊖ St. Paul's – Tel. 432 3851),* which has a complete collection of British stamps and a large selection from other countries. Probably the most extensive exhibition in the world.

Open Monday to Friday 10am-4.30pm (4pm on Fridays).

While in the area, see the **MONUMENT** located in the northern approach to London Bridge in Monument Yard on the east side of Fish Street Hill EC4 (⊖ *Monument*). The Column made of Portland stone was designed by Wren to commemorate the Great Fire of London and it stands on the spot where the fire began in 1666. Completed in 1677 it originally carried an inscription, since erased, blaming the Roman Catholics for having started the fire.

It stands at 202 feet high, with a public gallery at 160 feet allowing a view across London in all directions. A spiral staircase of 311 steps leads to the top.

Opens April to September: Monday to Friday 9am to 6pm
Saturday & Sunday 2pm to 6pm
October to March: Monday to Saturday 9am to 2pm and 3pm to 4pm.

Further east is the Bethnal Green **MUSEUM OF CHILDHOOD** *(Cambridge Heath Road, E2 – ⊖ Bethnal Green – Tel. 980 2415)*, a nostalgic experience for adults and fine exhibitions to keep children amused. An offshoot of the Victoria & Albert Museum, it houses a famous collection of dolls houses, dolls, toys, puppets, childrens costumes and wedding dresses. There is a Saturday school for painting and other activities.

Open 10am to 6pm Monday to Saturday
2.30pm to 6pm Sunday
Closed Friday – Car parking space available.

In north London there is **THE LITTLE ANGEL MARIONETTE THEATRE** *(Dagmar Passage, Cross Street N1 – ⊖ Islington – Tel. 226 1787)*, which appeals to a lot of children. Opened in 1961 this is one of the very few theatres (seats 110) constructed for and devoted to the presentation of puppetry in all its forms. There is an adjacent workshop where marionettes, rod puppets and shadow puppets are designed and made.

At **LAUDERDALE HOUSE** *(Waterlow Park NW8 – ⊖ Archway, – Tel. 348 8716)*, there are school workshops for children including arts and crafts, drama and dance.

Please phone in advance for details.

Towards central London we come to **COVENT GARDEN.** On the site of the fruit, flower and vegetable market, the **Piazza** and **The Market** have shops and restaurants of all kinds. **The Royal Opera House** and St. **Paul's Church** (built by Inigo Jones) with memorials to famous actors are within the *'market'.*

Lunchtime (especially on a sunny day) is fun in Covent Garden for all ages. Year-round there is plenty of outside entertainment — clowns and conjurers — to occupy everyone. While in the area, pop up to the fashionable *Covent Garden General Store;* and more so there are interesting museums for all tastes and ages. **The London Transport Museum** *(Covent Garden Market, WC2E 7BB –Tel. 379 6344)*, is a must. Here horse driven and motor buses, trams, trolleybuses, steam and electric locomotives, models, posters and photographs tell the story of some 200 years of London's transport history. There are video displays and children's activity sheets and an opportunity for children to *'drive'* the various machines.

The **Cabaret Mechanical Theatre** *(33-34 The Market WC2 – Tel. 379 7961)* although created for adults the exhibits give much enjoyment to children. Opened in 1984 (it was previously in

Above: London Transport Museum — Visitors can operate controls of Trains. *(London Transport Museum)*
Below: The colourful Covent Garden.

Falmouth) it is a permanent exhibition of clockwork toys and other objects of interest. There is a cat that drinks milk, a skeleton that reveals a devil's kitchen, a barman serving drinks and a handshaking machine.

Open 7 days 10am-7pm.

Not far away is **POLLOCK'S TOY MUSEUM** *(1 Scala Street W1, ⊖ Goodge Street – Tel. 636 3452),* a fascinating little museum with a wonderful collection of toy theatres and peep shows with dolls, dolls houses and teddy bears. It also sells cut-out theatres and old-fashioned toys.

Open Monday to Saturday 10am to 5pm

The **UNICORN THEATRE FOR CHILDREN** *(Arts Theatre, Great Newport Street, WC2 – ⊖ Leicester Square – Tel. 836 3334),* was originally a touring company, but has been based here since 1960. It carries on the tradition of bringing the magic of live theatre to children in a form both enjoyable and informative.

Ring for details.

For **Childrens Theatre** etc. in central London (or in the vicinity) there is the:

Barbican Centre	Tel: 628 8795
Bloomsbury Theatre	388 5739
Lyric Theatre	741 2311
Longfield Hall	720 3530
Puppet Theatre Barge	249 6876
Tricycle Theatre	328 8626
Upstream Children's Theatre	633 9819
Wimbledon Theatre	540 0362

The **LONDON TOY & MODEL MUSEUM** *(October House, 21-23 Craven Hill, W2, ⊖ Lancaster Gate, Queensway, Bayswater, Paddington, Tel. 262 7905)* is privately-owned and probably houses Europe's finest collection of toy and model trains,

boats, cars, planes, dolls, bears etc It's certainly a treasure house — ful of wonderful things to look at and play with.

Open Tuesday to Saturday 10am to 5.30pm Sunday 11am to 5pm

Museums are the order of the day if you are visiting South Kensington The most popular is the **SCIENCE MUSEUM** in Exhibition Road. Small boys always seem to make for the *Exploration of Space* and *Launch Pad* — an area where they can let off steam — *(Tel. 589 6371).*

Next door is the **NATURAL HISTORY MUSEUM** which has collections relating to zoology, fossils, and botany. A detour could include the **GEOLOGICAL MUSEUM** which contains minerals and gems *"Treasures of the Earth"* with a mind-boggling library of maps and photographs.

The **COMMONWEALTH INSTITUTE** *(Kensington High Street, W8 ⊖ Kensington High Street – Tel. 603 0702),* has a strong educational bias providing an educational trip around the world based on links from Empire building days. In the main exhibition galleries visitors can see the *Gagalo* stiltman, a life size stilt dancer from Nigeria, discover facts about Singapore by using Singha, the computer, try out the Canadian skidoo, search for the black spider in Guyana or work the hand pump which brings fresh water to thousands of villages in the developing world.

Open Monday to Saturday 10am to 5.30pm Sunday 2pm to 5pm

THE **STOCK EXCHANGE** *(Old Broad Street, EC2N 1HP – Tel. 588 2355 ⊖ Bank),* is also worth an hour of your time. Visit the Gallery and see a film which explains the history of *'my word is my bond'* which should educate youngsters in money matters On the work front, the **POST OFFICE** at the Mount Pleasant Sorting Office *(EC1 – Tel. 239 2311)*, allows visitors in to learn about mechanization and the underground railway.

Also of special interest to youngsters are the **CABINET WAR ROOMS** (in basements off Whitehall) from where Winston Churchill ran his World War II operations and spoke on the hot line to President Roosevelt of the USA. It is a fascinating picture of war time London.

On a more lighter note try **BRASS RUBBING**. There are several such centres in Central London, with large collections of Medieval and Tudor brasses of knights, ladies, priests and children. Admission is free but a charge is made for the use of brasses and materials. The main centres are at:

The London Brass Rubbing Centre — *(St. James's Church, Piccadilly W1 –Tel. 437 6023).*

Westminster Abbey — *(SW1 – Tel. 222 2085*
St. Martins-in-the-Fields Church — *(Trafalgar Square, SW1 – Tel. 437 6023)*
All Hallows-by-the-Tower — *(EC3 – Tel. 481 2929)*

It is certainly fascinating to make your own unique souvenir of the visit.

All families enjoy seeing the **CHANGING OF THE GUARD** and the **Royal Mews.** The Guards are changed every day (during the summer) at 11.30am at **Buckingham Palace** and at **Horseguard's Parade** at 11am — *Mondays to Saturdays – 10am on Sundays.*

NB: The Guard Change is cancelled in very wet weather. The Royal Mews in Buckingham Palace Road SW1, has the exquisite **Coronation Coach** and Royal Horses.

he Commonwealth Institute where cultures from all the continents are on display — A very interesting lace for all ages. *(C.O.I.)*

More entertainment but of a different kind will be found if you visit **"THE HERITAGE COLLECTION** *(Syon Park, Brentford, Middlesex –Tel. 560 1378 – BR to Brentford)*. You will find here the largest display of British cars anywhere in the world, drawn mainly from the *British Leyland* collection. Over 90 vehicles are on show at any one time, arranged in tableaux to give an air of authenticity. Historically, the collection dates back to 1895.

Open 7 days a week, 10am to 5.30pm.

Not far away is the **KEW BRIDGE ENGINES TRUST** *(Kew Bridge Road, Brentford, Middlesex – Tel. 568 4757 –BR Kew Bridge)*. It houses historic steam engines from the Victorian age which were used for pumping water to the Metropolis. Many other items may be admired.

Open 7 days a week 11am to 5pm.

Young people relaxing at the highly popular Garden area.

Most museums and places of interest mentioned above have shops which sell many items. Listed below are others which are worth mentioning.

Hamleys in Regent Street is the temple of children's wordly play-things, but toys occupy space in most stores and **Harrods** in Knightsbridge also has a riveting pets department. **Oscar's Den** at NW6, SW1 and N1 specialises in selling party/carnival novelties, masks, balloons and party gifts for all ages and occasions. Children's entertainers can be arranged. **Circus Circus** in SW6 is called the *"One-Stop Children's Shop"* which sells new and nearly new clothes and equipment, bedroom and nursery furniture, party wear etc.

And for the handicapped children, the **National Library for the Handicapped Child** (Dickson Gallery — 20 Bedford Way, WC1H 0AL — Tel. 636 1500) is both centrally located and well equipped to serve children with reading handicaps. *Phone before arrival.*

London therefore offers so much for the family. The above is a summary but by no means a comprehensive list; nevertheless, it covers a lot for all tastes and fancies. And, we must not forget London's **Royal Parks**. There are summer music and puppet shows which have become part of young London as they were in the days of uniformed nannies.

NOTE:
> Some museums and other places of interest are discussed in greater detail under the relevant chapters/sections *(see index).*

For further information:- Use the **01** prefix if phoning from outside London.

LTBCB — 730 3450 & 730 3488.

CHAPTER NINE

THE GOLDEN SQUARE MILE

(The City of London)

THE CITY is in fact, slightly larger than a square mile. It covers an area of 677 acres and is $1\frac{1}{2}$ miles by $\frac{7}{8}$ of a mile at its widest points. Roman London, within the Walls, however, covered only 325 acres. The City is the **heart of the Metropolis** and historically, separates the distinctive cultures of the **East End** and the **West End.**

Traffic jams at the Bank; the heart of the city. *(An old photograph)*

The City stretches along the north bank of the Thames from Fleet Street in the west almost to the Tower of London in the east. In this small space are shops, parks, markets, homes, churches etc.

From Monday to Friday (on working days) some 300,000 people come into the City to work. In the evening they leave and only a few thousand residents (around 2.5%) remain, hence if you want to explore the City do it at the weekend or on a summer's evening.

Deep beneath the City's pavements lie the remains of the Romans, the City's first inhabitants. They arrived in 43 AD and stayed for four centuries, laying the foundations of this great capital city. They built the first **London Bridge** and a massive **Wall** — 2 miles long, 15 feet high and in parts 8 feet thick. Fragments of the wall remain — particularly around London Wall and the Tower of London. Roman pavement is preserved beneath *All Hallows Barking by-the-Tower* and, the remains of the

Above: City boundaries, entrance to Fleet Street.
Below: The new City Skyline as seen from Waterloo Bridge.

Roman Temple of **Mithras** can still be seen in *Queen Victoria Street,* one of the city's busiest thoroughfares. Once it was a shrine to Christianity's greatest rival; today commuters hurry past the altar where legionaires worshipped their pagan gods of courage. After the Romans left London it was settled by Saxons, sacked by Danes, rebuilt and sacked again. Then in 1066 **William the Conqueror** granted the citizens a charter, confirming their rights and privileges. The City's importance grew yet further, and by the 14th century merchants and craftsmen had formed themselves into powerful trade guilds. The City was thriving and very overcrowded. In 1655 the Great **Plague** ravaged its tight-packed streets killing around 1 in 3 Londoners and a year later the **Great Fire** of London destroyed $\frac{3}{5}$ of the City and old St. Paul's Cathedral. From the ashes of the fire the City was rebuilt but many made homeless did not return, yet London was growing fast. Two centuries later the railways brought the countryside closer to town and the City was left to concentrate on trade and commerce. Today, the **Bank of England,** Stock Exchange, Lloyds of London, the commodity exchanges, banks, insurance companies, accountants and lawyers, jostle for space in one of the richest square miles in the world.

At the heart of the City is **GUILDHALL,** seat of City government for nearly 1000 years. The present building, home of the *City of London Corporation,* who run the square mile, dates from the beginning of the 15th century — rebuilding began in 1411. As well as being the centre of

The Guildhall of London.

civic government where **Lord Mayors** and **Sheriffs** were elected and meetings of the *Court of Common Council* held (as they still are), Guildhall, as the largest hall in England after Westminster Hall, was also used for important trials such as those of Anne Askew for heresy in 1546 and the Earl of Surrey for treason in 1547. Tragic Lady Jane Grey, Queen for nine days was tried here with her husband Lord Guildford Dudley and sentenced to death in 1553. In 1606 the Jesuit, Henry Garnet was condemned for his part in the *Gunpowder Plot*.

Guildhall was and is a place of feasting. City banquets are legendary. Today banquets fare is more modest but the Lord Mayor of London still acts as host to guests of State and Crown, entertaining them with traditional pomp and ceremony from the City's private purse.

It is in Guildhall that the Lord Mayor of London, the capital's first citizen, is elected on *Michaelmas Day* (29 September). This is a chance to see the civic city in all its colourful splendour. There are gowned *Masters* and *Prime Wardens* of the City's livery companies, and *Ward Beadles* wearing tri-corn hats and carrying maces. The magnificently-robed Lord Mayor, Sheriffs, Aldermen and City High Officers carry nosegays of flowers believed in times gone by to ward off plagues and more practically to protect the nose from the stench of sewers and unwashed citizens.

The election ceremony has changed little since the middle ages and when it is over the newly-elected Lord Mayor emerges from Guildhall to be greeted by the fanfare of trumpets and peal of bells. He begins his busy year in November travelling in his gold coach to the Law Courts to

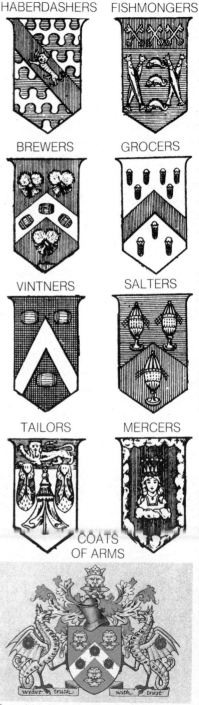

HABERDASHERS   FISHMONGERS

BREWERS   GROCERS

VINTNERS   SALTERS

TAILORS   MERCERS

COATS OF ARMS

Coat of Arms, Weavers Company

THE CITY OF LONDON
— Location Map —

(1) Western Boundaries
(2) ROYAL COURTS OF JUSTICE
(3) THE INNS
(4) St. Dunstan-in-the-West Church
(5) Dr. Johnson's House
(6) Daily Telegraph Building
(7) Daily Express Building
(8) Ludgate Circus
(9) ST. BRIDE'S CHURCH
(10) Prince Henry's Room
(11) Child's Bank
(12) Temple Church
(13) Inner Temple Hall
(14) Inner Temple Garden
(15) Middle Temple Hall
(16) Middle Temple Garden
(17) Floating Ships
(18) Sion College
(19) City of London School (site of)
(20) BLACKFRIARS BRIDGE
(21) Blackfriars Station
(22) Mermaid Theatre
(23) St. Benet's, Paul's Wharf Church
(24) St. Mary Somerset Church
(25) Painters' and Stainers' Hall
(26) St. Nicholas Cole Abbey
(27) College of Arms
(28) St. Andrew-by-the-
     Wardrobe Church
(29) Apothecaries' Hall
(30) St. Paul's Deanery Church
(31) ST. PAUL'S CATHEDRAL
(32) Tower of St. Augustine's
(33) St. Paul's Choir School
(34) St. Paul's Chapter House
(35) St. Martin Ludgate Church
(36) Stationers' Hall
(37) CENTRAL CRIMINAL COURT
(38) Holborn Viaduct Bridge
(39) St. Bartholomew-the-Less Church
     St. Bartholomew's Hospital
(40) Smithfield Meat Market
(41) Charterhouse
(42) St. Bartholomew-the-Great
     Church
(43) POSTAL MUSEUM
(44) St. Botolph Aldersgate Church
(45) MUSEUM OF LONDON
(46) Ironmongers' Hall
(47) THE BARBICAN
(48) St. Giles Cripplegate
(49) Chapel of Elsing Spital
(50) Whitbread's Brewery
(51) Barbican Art Centre
(52) Armourers' & Braziers' Hall
(53) CITY POLICE STATION
(54) Tower of St. Alban's
(55) Pewterers' Hall
(56) St. Anne & St. Agnes Church
(57) Haberdashers' Hall
(58) Goldsmiths' Hall
(59) St. Vedast's Church
(60) Sadlers' Hall
(61) Wax Chandlers' Hall

(62) St. Lawrence Jewry Church
(63) Gresham College
(64) Grocers' Hall
(65) Mercers' Hall
(66) St. Mary-le-Bow Church
(67) St. Mary Aldermary Church
(68) St. James' Garlickythe Church
(69) Vintners' Hall
(70) St. Michael Paternoster Royal Church
(71) Dyers' Hall
(72) CANNON ST. STATION
(73) SOUTHWARK BRIDGE
(74) Skinners' Hall
(75) Tallow Chandlers' Hall
(76) London Stone
(77) St. Mary Abchurch Church
(78) Rotherschilds'
(79) St. Mary Woolnoth Church
(80) MANSION HOUSE
(81) St. Stephen Walbrook Church
(82) Temple of Mithras (ruins)
(83) GUILDHALL
(84) St. Margaret Lothbury Church
(85) BANK OF ENGLAND
(86) ROYAL EXCHANGE
(87) STOCK EXCHANGE
(88) Drapers' Hall
(89) Finsbury Circus Gardens
(90) All Hallows London Hall
(91) LIVERPOOL ST. STATION
(92) PETTICOAT LANE MARKET
(93) Hoop & Grapes
(94) St. Botolph Aldgate Church
(95) Aldgate Pump
(96) St. Katherine Greek Church
(97) Spanish & Portuguese Synagogue
(98) Baltic Exchange
(99) St. Andrew Undershaft Church
(100) St. Ethelburga Bishopsgate
(101) Leathersellers' Hall
(102) St. Helen's Bishopsgate Church
(103) Merchant Taylors' Hall
(104) St. Peter Cornhill
(105) LLOYD'S BUILDING
(106) Leadenhall Market
(107) St. Michael Cornhill
(108) St. Edmund the King
(109) St. Clement Eastcheap
(110) MONUMENT
(111) Fishmongers' Hall
(112) LONDON BRIDGE
(113) St. Magnus Martyr Church
(114) Customs House
(115) Watermans' Hall
(116) St. Dunstan-in-the-East
(117) St. Mary-at-Hill Church
(118) St. Margaret Patteris
(119) Clothmakers' Hall
(120) Tower of All Hallows Staining
(121) Lloyd's Register of Shipping
(122) Trinity House
(123) Port of London Authority
(124) St. Olave's Hart Street
(125) Corn Exchange
(126) TOWER OF LONDON
(127) TOWER BRIDGE
(128) Fenchurch St. Station

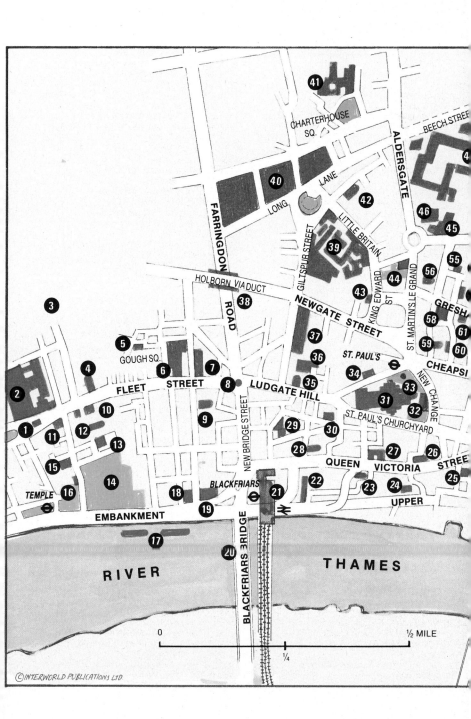

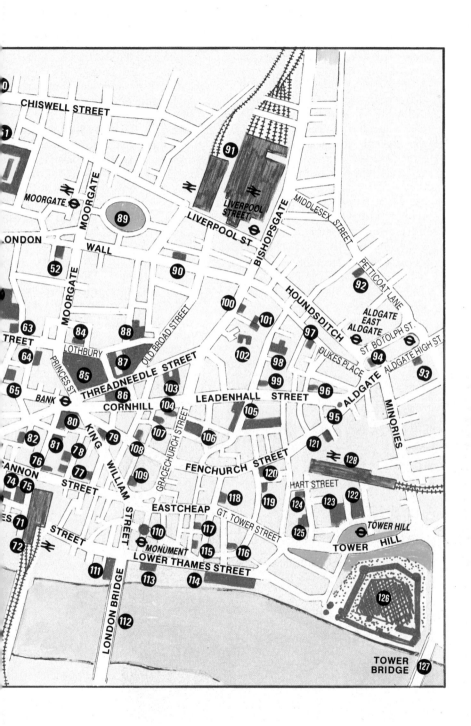

CHISWELL STREET

MOORGATE

LONDON WALL

MOORGATE

LOTHBURY

PRINCES ST

THREADNEEDLE STREET

BANK

CORNHILL

KING WILLIAM STREET

CANNON STREET

EASTCHEAP

STREET

LONDON BRIDGE

LOWER THAMES STREET

LIVERPOOL STREET

LIVERPOOL ST

BISHOPSGATE

MIDDLESEX STREET

HOUNDSDITCH

PETTICOAT LANE

ALDGATE EAST

ALDGATE

ST. BOTOLPH ST.

DUKES PLACE

ALDGATE HIGH ST

ALDGATE

MINORIES

OLD BROAD STREET

LEADENHALL STREET

GRACECHURCH STREET

FENCHURCH STREET

HART STREET

GT. TOWER STREET

MONUMENT

TOWER HILL

TOWER HILL

TOWER BRIDGE

52 63 64 65 84 85 86 87 88 89 90 91 92 93 94 95 96 97 98 99 100 101 102 103 104 105 106 107 108 109 110 111 112 113 114 115 116 117 118 119 120 121 122 123 124 125 126 127 128 80 81 82 76 77 78 79 74 75 71 72

137

make a formal declaration of office before the Lord Chief Justice. He is accompanied by his personal bodyguard of *Pikemen* and *Musketeers* dressed in 17th century uniform and a mile-long procession of bands, floats and armed services. Until the following November he will act as the City's leading diplomat and live in the elegant **Mansion House** (Bank Junction EC2), home of Lord Mayors since the mid 18th century. Probably the most precious possession of Mansion House is a set of 18th century armchairs presented to the Lord Mayor to commemorate Nelson's victory at the Battle of the Nile.

Liverymen who elect the Lord Mayor belong to companies whose origins date back to the medieval trade guilds. The *Weavers Company*, with a charter dating back to 1155, claims to be the oldest. Today around 20,000 liverymen belong to 97 companie some like the *Marketors* and *Chartere Accountants* formed only this centur; Some still have control over the trade — the Goldsmiths, hallma gold, silver and platinum, and th Fishmongers daily inspect fish sold i Billingsgate.

There are 38 livery halls in the Ci and most open on certain days t visitors. They range from the glitterir magnificence of the wealthy Fisl mongers with their ornate hall o London Bridge and the Goldsmitl with their fabulous treasures in Fost Lane, to the tiny 17th century Apoth caries Hall tucked away in Blackfria which still has its original fine carved staircase. Until the mediev: guilds had their own halls, they ofte met in churches, and religion playe an important part in their day-to-da life.

Mansion House

e Bank of England

Before the Great Fire of London 1666), the City was full of churches. There were nearly 100 parishes, each with a church. Even today it seems as though there is a church around every corner.

The oldest, parish church in London is **St. Bartholomew-the-Great** close to Smithfield Market. It was founded, together with nearby St. Bartholomew's Hospital in 1123 by a courtier *(called Rahere),* in thanksgiving for being cured for a fever, and the nave still has its massive Norman piers.

St. Ethelburga-the-Virgin in Bishopsgate, is 13th century and the tiniest church in the City; **St. Andrew Undershaft** in Leadenhall Street EC3, now dwarfed by modern buildings, is also pre 1666. It contains a monument to *John Stow,* London's first historian who died in 1605. Every year the Lord Mayor changes the quill pen in the effigy's hand at a special commemoration service.

When 86 churches were destroyed in the Great Fire, *Sir Christopher Wren* was given the task of rebuilding 51 of them. **ST. PAUL'S CATHEDRAL** was his greatest masterpiece, but other gems remain, although often rebuilt following damage in the blitz (1940-41).

There is **St. Bride's** (Fleet Street EC4) with its *"Wedding Cake"* spire, and the very beautiful **St. Stephen Walbrook** (founded probably before 1096), next to Mansion House, now being restored and described as "Wren's most accomplished church interior".

Then there is **St. Michael Paternoster Royal** (College Hill EC4), first mentioned in 1219 and rebuilt in 1689-94.

139

It is the burial place of *Dick Whittington,* London's most famous Lord Mayor; he is depicted with his legendary cat in one of the stained glass windows.

ALLEYS and COURTYARDS are a constantly recurring reminder of the City's past. The City's street pattern is medieval, and you should never resist the opportunity of driving or walking down a promising lane. Often dominated by lofty office buildings, fascinating tucked-away corners still remain. There is a maze of alleys off Cornhill with a **'secret' garden** behind *St. Michael Cornhill Church,* or **Wardrobe Court** (just south of St. Paul's Cathedral) which was the Royal Wardrobe of Edward III; or narrow **Cloth Fair** beside St.

Bartholomew's Church fronted by narrow 17th and 18th century houses A fascinating and rewarding detour is to wonder south of **Fleet Street** (EC4) into the **Temple,** founded by the *Knights Templar* in the 12th century and today the home of the legal profession.

Middle Temple Lane with its overhanging 17th century houses leads to Elizabethan Middle Temple Hall and some of the most peaceful courtyards lawns and gardens in London. In fact gardens and flowers are the city's special pride — there are some 180 open spaces, some only a few square yards, but each with a bench, a tub or flowers or a tree to provide a breathing space between office blocks

City street names remind us of the past and food is a recurring theme

Inner Temple

140

There is *Milk Street, Bread Street, Wood Street* and *Garlic Hill* — all reminders of medieval markets. The City still has its own markets. In **Leadenhall Market** (Gracechurch Street EC2), on the site of the old Roman basilica you can gaze into the eyes of gleaming fish, buy vegetables, fruit, flowers, pheasants, poultry and venison. It hums with activity from noon till 2pm when city workers are shopping. It takes its name from a mansion with a lead roof which belonged to the *Neville* family in the 14th century.

On the other side of the time scale, to see the wholesale meat market of **Smithfield** (EC1) at its best you must rise much earlier. Established during the 12th century, this ten acre market comes to life when London sleeps. Arrive there any time from 4am to 10am and you will find *"bummarees"* (kind of middlemen) and *"pitchers"* (vendors who occupy a pitch), and handcarts laden with giant carcasses being wheeled across sawdust strewn floors under a Victorian heaven of cast iron and glass.

Some of Smithfield's meat is destined for City restaurants — and even these have a place in history. Usually open for lunch only, they are often institutions in their own right. **Sweetings** in Queen Victoria Street EC4 is *London's oldest Fish Restaurant* famed for its oysters, and has its original Edwardian marble counters displayed in the window. Then there is **Simpson's** at No. 38½ Cornhill EC3 (note the number is not a mistake!) A former 18th century **Chophouse,** it still has the original tables and high backed stalls. Food is traditional English and *stewed cheese* is a must.

If you are in the City lunchtime you must sample a City **Pub.** They are packed between 12 noon and 3.00pm but many shut their doors soon after offices close in the evening and do not open weekends. In 1656 there were 1,153 (approximately) taverns in the City and today the concentration is greater than anywhere in the country. Names are magical — *Ye Olde Crutched Friars, The Magpie and Stump* and *Mother Bunch's Wine House.*

Ye Olde Cheshire Cheese in narrow Wine Office Court off Fleet Street, is reputedly one of London's oldest and most authentic taverns and a haunt of Dr. Johnson (an eminent 18th century scholar, whose statue gazes down Fleet Street) and other scholars and writers. Competing with it for age is **Ye Olde Watling** in Bow Lane EC4, rebuilt just a year after the Great Fire, and retaining its huge and blackened ceiling beams. Nearby is **Williamsons Tavern** in Grovelands Court with its flower baskets and

Cheshire Cheese famous sign

141

once the residence of Lord Mayors of London. And there is the **Old Jamaica Inn,** London's first coffee house, tucked away in St. Michael's Alley off Cornhill.

Everywhere you go in the City old rubs shoulders with the new. It is constantly changing and its *newest buildings* have a special exuberance and excitement. There is Britain's (and possibly Europe's) tallest building, the 600' 4" high **National Westminster Tower** in Bishopsgate EC2 whose 52 storeys cost £72 million; it was completed in 1980. It dominates the whole City. There is also the modern **West Wing of Guildhall** which contrasts yet blends so well with the older building. The latest is the ultra-modern **Lloyd's of London Building** in Lime Street EC3, in the heart of the financial district. Dreamed up by *Richard Rogers* of Pompidou Centre Fame (in Paris), it is designed "inside out"; its twelve storeys of glass and stainless steel pipework add an astonishing dimension to the City's streetscape. It has a viewing gallery on the 4th floor for visitors to watch the trading activities below and an exhibition to help explain it all.

Perhaps it is the **BARBICAN** which best encapsulates the City today. This *"gift to the nation"* by the City of London Corporation was built on 35 acres of land laid waste by the blitz. Now there are homes for around 6000 people, shops, gardens, lakes, two schools and an arts centre, **The Barbican Centre for Arts and Conferences** with 3 cinemas, a concert hall with a seating capacity of 2,026, a conference hall, library and art gallery and restaurants. The Barbican Hall is the home of the **London Symphony Orchestra** which plays up to 5 concerts a week over 3 four-week seasons a year and the **Royal Shakespeare Company** is resident in the Barbican Theatre which has been custom-built to the company's requirements. Members of both resident companies work closely with students of the adjacent Guildhall School of Music and Drama, one of the country's leading schools of the performing arts.

On a summer's day the **lakeside terraces** of the Barbican are packed with City office-workers. Striped umbrellas, fountains playing on the lake and buskers make it hard to believe that this is the heart of the teeming financial City. And one of the most exciting features of the Art Centre is the **Conservatory,** London's largest and most spectacular garden under glass. Built around the theatre's 100 foot fly tower, orchids, ferns and more than 200 varieties of fuschia are among the myriads of plants flourishing in this *"garden in the sky"*.

The Barbican, named after an outer fortification of the City possibly a watch-tower has within its boundaries the church of **St. Giles "without" Cripplegate** (Fore Street EC2), where Oliver Cromwell married Elizabeth Bourchier in 1620.

The Tudor-style **Ironmongers Company,** who date from the 15th century is tucked away on the southwest corner. And next door is the **Museum of London,** which traces London's history from prehistoric times to the present day in lively displays. (See under the Museums chapter).

When you visit the City, allow yourself plenty of time. There is always another side-street to explore another church to visit. And remember to **keep looking upwards;** for there you will see old facades above new shopfronts, hanging signs, clocks steeples, towers etc. etc.

ew of the Tower Bridge from Tower Hotel and St. Katharines Dock. The giant sundial is of interest to ny visitors.

he City is certainly the child of ansformation It has always adapted change and this is one of its rengths. More important, nowhere as there been such a concentration of xcellence in so many spheres — ommercial and charitable, profes-onal and voluntary, educational and ntrepreneurial and in civic adminis-ation. The City thus represents a nique matrix of tradition and innova-on. The City's motto **"O Lord, Guide s"** is certainly well merited.

N.B.(1) For other City landmarks e.g. the Museum of London, Bank of England, Stock Exchange, the Guildhall, (Chapel, Clock Museum and Library), St. Paul's etc., see index.

(2) The City Information Centre, St. Paul's Churchyard EC4 (Tel. 606 3030) offers a wide range of books and leaflets on the City of London.

(3) LTBCB — Tel. 730 3450/3488 for all events.

143

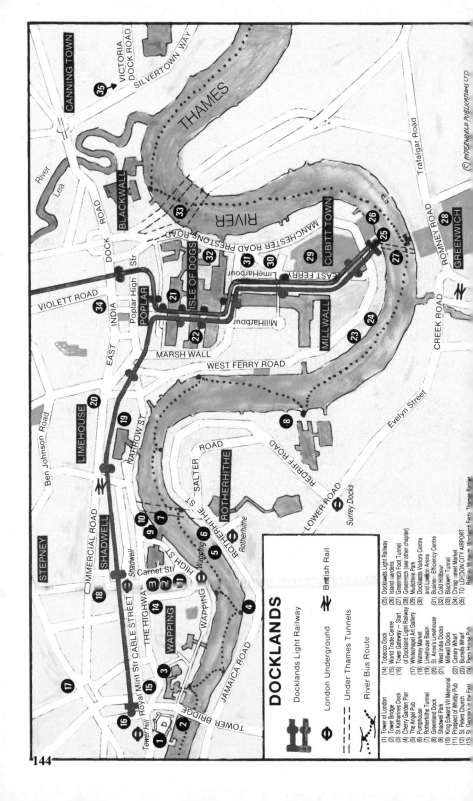

DOCKLANDS

•••• Docklands Light Railway

⊖ London Underground

- - - Under Thames Tunnels

River Bus Route

(1) Tower of London
(2) Tower Bridge
(3) St Katharines Dock
(4) Cherry Garden Pier
(5) The Angel Pub
(6) Pumphouse
(7) Rotherhithe Tunnel
(8) Greenland Dock
(9) Shadwell Park
(10) King Edward VII Memorial
(11) Prospect of Whitby Pub
(12) St. Peters Church
(13) St. George's in the East
(14) Tobacco Dock
(15) World Trade Centre
(16) Tower Gateway — Start
of Docklands Light Railway
(17) Whitechapel Art Gallery
(18) Watney Market
(19) Limehouse Basin
(20) St. Anne's Limehouse
(21) West India Docks
(22) Millwall Docks
(23) Canary Wharf
(24) Burrells Wharf
(25) Docklands Light Railway
(26) Island Gardens
(27) Greenwich Foot Tunnel
(28) Greenwich (see other chapter)
(29) Mudchute Park
(30) Docklands Visitors Centre
and London Arena
(31) Busine— Efficiency Centre
(32) Bold Hill Harbour
(33) Black—— Tunnel
(34) Crisp ——eet Market
(35) TO LO—DON CITY AIRPORT
Ro— x Museum, Woolwich Ferry, Thames Barrier

© INTERNFIELD PUBLICATIONS LTD

144

CHAPTER TEN

THE DOCKLANDS — LONDON'S 'NEW' CITY

A NEW LONDON is rising from the ruins of one of its oldest areas: its docks. New museums, shopping precincts, sport, leisure and entertainment complexes are being built to revitalise the neglected East End.

Docklands is a large area geographically (about 8½ square miles or 22 sq. kms. east of the City), spanning three London boroughs: Southwark (south of the river), Tower Hamlets and Newham. The districts in question are St. Katharine's, Wapping, Shadwell, Ratcliff, Limehouse, Poplar, Blackwall, Isle of Dogs, Rother-hithe, Bermondsey, Silvertown, North Woolwich and Beckton. The "London Docklands Development Committee" (LDDC), a government-appointed body, was set up on 2 July 1981 and charged with the task of regenerating 5,000 acres of land, Currently, many districts resemble a large building site as, among a sea of cranes, small armies of construction workers go about completing the largest and most exciting urban regeneration project in the world.

We may conveniently divide London's Docklands into 4 areas, each with its own particular character and offering its own exciting opportunities:

WAPPING and LIMEHOUSE

This historic area, within walking distance of the City, has attracted a lively community of creative businesses, while schemes such as Free Trade Wharf offer exciting locations. High quality housing developments and warehouse conversions in the area have proved very popular. **Tobacco Dock** "the alternative West End" and three times the size of Covent Garden, is a specialist shopping centre with a good selection of shops and restaurants under one roof. It's only minutes from the Tower and should soon be an irresistable tourist attraction. Two full size replica 18th century sailing ships are among its attractions. One will examine the history of piracy and the other will provide an audio-visual interpretation of R.L. Stevenson's 'Treasure Island'.

SURREY DOCKS — ROTHERHITHE
(South of the River Thames)

From London Bridge to Rotherhithe and the former Surrey Docks, major waterside developments are creating a thriving integrated community. Of special interest are:

Butler's Wharf, located on the south bank of the Thames just east of the Tower, is a leisure/shopping complex offering exciting opportunities. It also possesses nearly 100 beautiful apartments. The 'Conran Foundation Design Museum' will house a permanent study collection of design, with space for temporary exhibitions.

London Bridge City lying between London and Tower Bridges includes 60,000 square feet of retail space, a sports centre and a pub. 'The Hays Galleria', an attractive domed arcade in Tooley St. SE1, is the first part of the London Bridge Development to be completed — it was opened in early 1988. LBC is connected to London Bridge station by a pedestrian bridge link.

The new 'Daily Mail' site is also an imposing complex.

THE ISLE OF DOGS

Already a thriving and residential community, the pace of change has been remarkable particularly in the Enterprise Zone. Within it we find new developments:

Canary Wharf will provide 12.1 million sq. ft. of office space and retail accommodation, incorporating squares, water courts and waterside arcades on a scale not seen in the capital since the 19th century. The project's centrepiece will be the tallest building in Britain, an 800ft 'tower' providing over twice as much office space as any tower previously built in the UK. It is expected to be completed by 1990.

London Arena will be one of the largest sports, leisure and entertainments complexes in Britain, with a seating capacity of 12,615 and will cost an estimated £25 million to complete. The Arena will contain bars, eating places, hospitality suites, meeting rooms and a media centre. LA is situated near Crossharbour Station on the Docklands Light Railway (DLR) which has connections with the London tube at Tower Hill and Stratford.

ROYAL DOCKS

The massive Royal Docks are the "jewel in the Docklands crown", offering exceptional scope for imaginative scheme on a grand scale. Basic infrastructure work is already under way while housing developments and a shopping centre have been completed. **London City Airport** is located in the Royal Docks. Major development proposals encompassing housing, offices, shops, hotels and an exhibition centre are currently under review.

TRANSPORT

Dockland transport is undergoing dramatic changes — developments in transport systems play a central role in the success or failure of new attractions.

The Docklands Light Railway: The £77 million first phase, which has 16 stations, was officially opened on 30 July 1987 by HM the Queen. It runs from Tower Gateway in the east through Limehouse and Poplar to Island Gardens on the southern tip of the Isle of Dogs. There is also a northern arm which runs from Poplar to Stratford.

Red, white and blue trains run every 10 minutes and since the DLR is suspended above ground for much of its route, it gives passengers panoramic views of new developments.

Work has now begun on an underground western extension to Bank in the City and there are plans for an eastern extension running through the Royal Docks to Beckton.

There is a railway exhibition centre at Island Gardens open Monday to Friday 11am to 4pm; Saturday and Sunday from 11am to 5pm.

London City Airport *(Connaught Road, Silvertown E16 2PX–Tel: 01-474 5555).* Built on a quay between Royal Albert and King George V Docks, this £30 million airport for STOL (short take-off and landing) aircraft was opened by the Queen in November 1987.

Two airlines, Brymon Airways and Eurocity Express, currently operate there. There are services to Paris, Brussels, Plymouth, the Channel Islands and there are plans to schedule flights to other destinations in Europe.

Thames Line *(West India Dock Pier, E14 – Tel. 01-987 0311/941-5454)* started operating on 1 June 1988. Fast and reliable, Thames Line will call at regular 15 minute intervals at stops along the north and south banks of London's great river. There are plans to extend the service to Greenwich. Currently, Thames Line has 7 advanced 62-seater catamarans with airline style seats, capable of an excess of 25 mph.

A comfortable high-speed riverbus service designed to beat the capital's traffic jams.

Roads: A major new road network is being built that will bring vast improvements to the Docklands.

SUMMARY

Apart from the above there are **prehistoric churches** (e.g. All Hallows by the tower, is the oldest church in the City with over 1000 years of history), **museums** (e.g. HMS Belfast, Thames Barrier Visitors Centre and London Dungeon), **parks and open**

Rotherhithe Riverfront *(London Docklands)*

spaces (e.g. Shadwell Park also known as King Edward VII Memorial Park, St. Paul's Church Gardens, Mudchute Park, Island Gardens, Victoria Gardens and Russia Dock Woodland and Ecological Park which is Britain's largest man-made ecological park, built on site of filled-in docks and featuring a 65ft artificial hill, ponds, paths, woodland, scrub, grassland and wetland) and other *places of interest* which have combined to make London's Docklands "the greatest place in the world", certainly "a city of the 21st century".

NB:

For further information:

London Docklands Development Committee (LDDC) — Tel: 01-515 3000

London Tourist Board Convention Bureau — Tel: 01-730 3488

'Docklands Tours' (01-515 0960) is an interesting bus tour which takes in almost all of the Docklands.

'Cultural Heritage' (01-739 4853) is a guided walk mainly around St. Katharine's Dock and Wapping.

'Museum Docklands' (01-515 1162) provides an excellent service.

Above: Westminster Pier, an embarkation point for pleasure boats, an ideal way to explore the river Thames and the many bridges as described in this chapter.
Left: View of the River and Waterloo Bridge

CHAPTER ELEVEN

LONDON'S HISTORIC BRIDGES

THE ORIGIN

of the name is obscure but Ceasar called the River 'Thamesis'. It runs for around 216 miles (346 kms), is navigable for about 125 miles and it cuts London in half and is an essential part of the scene. The Thames termed the *"Father of the City"* was for centuries the main highway for Londoners. Monarchs in their gilded barges used the river which also saw the funeral procession of Nelson and Churchill.

There are many bridges and several tunnels serving pedestrian, road and rail traffic across and under the river. The great port of London extends eastwards down the estuary and the Pool of London lies between London Bridge and Tower Bridge.

Beyond the capital the Thames twists and winds its longway through pastoral green landscapes punctuated by villages, lovely estates, grand and old houses, medieval churches and marvellously well-tended gardens. In fact, the Thames is the principal river of England and it winds through six of the country's southern counties.

From Hampton Court to Tower Bridge there are numerous historic bridges. From west to southeast the 20 bridges are as follows:

HAMPTON COURT BRIDGE

The first Bridge on this site was built in 1753. An exotic seven-span timber bridge it was, despite its flimsy and undulating appearance, a road bridge 20 feet wide and the largest *Chinoiserie* bridge ever built.

Rebuilt in 1778 it was replaced by an iron one in 1865. The present structure was built in 1930-33 in reinforced concrete with stone and brickwork facing.

KINGSTON BRIDGE

There has been a bridge at this site since at least medieval times; in 1219 *William de Coventry* was appointed *Master of the Bridge*. In 1528 there was yet another grant of land for its maintenance and Henry VIII had his artillery brought over the river here rather than at London Bridge lest the latter be damaged by the weight.

It was freed from tolls in 1567 and made into a drawbridge in 1661. The present bridge of brick faced with stone was built in 1825-28 and was then freed from tolls in 1870. In 1914 it was widened on the upstream side.

RICHMOND BRIDGE

A five-span masonry bridge faced in Portland stone was built in 1774-77. Freed from tolls in 1859 it was widened in 1937.

TWICKENHAM BRIDGE

Built in 1933 this bridge, like Chiswick Bridge was constructed to take the *Great Chertsey Road* (A316) over the river. It was the first large-scale bridge in the country to use three-hinged reinforced concrete arches.

KEW BRIDGE

The first bridge on this low Surrey shore was built in 1758-59 with seven timber arches. Replaced by a stone bridge in 1784-89 it was formally opened free of tolls in 1873. The present bridge was erected in 1903.

CHISWICK BRIDGE

Built in 1933 with three concrete arches with Portland stone facing. Like the Twickenham Bridge it takes the Great Chertsey Road (A316) over the river.

It is the finishing point of the *University Boat Race*. Oxford (dark blues) and Cambridge (light blues) first raced each other from Hambleden Lock to Henley in 1829 —Oxford won. Since 1856 the race has become an annual event.

HAMMERSMITH BRIDGE

The first suspension bridge in London built in 1824-27 with a central span of 422 feet. Although replaced in 1883-87 by the present decorative suspension bridge, the old piers and abutments were reused. The deck girders were replaced in a major overhaul in 1973-76.

In outline and simplicity of style it is arguably the *"best looking bridge"* of its kind on the Thames. The traffic that crosses it daily has caused massive problems over the years.

PUTNEY or FULHAM BRIDGE

Thomas Phillips, a renowned master carpenter of the age built the first timber bridge in 1727-29. Until 1750, when Westminster Bridge opened, it was the only bridge across the river west of London. Its 26 spans, varying in size from 14 to 32 feet presented a serious obstruction to navigation and in 1870-72 the number of the spans was reduced by three to 23.

In 1882-86, the bridge was replaced by the present five-span granite bridge which was built upstream of the older structure.

WANDSWORTH BRIDGE

The first bridge on the site was built in 1870-73. It was a continuous *lattice-girder* bridge of five spans; in 1880 it was freed from tolls. In 1936-40 it was replaced by the present three-spanned bridge of steel-plate girder cantilever construction.

BATTERSEA BRIDGE

The first bridge was built of wood to the designs of *Henry Holland* in 1771-72, and it replaced the regular ferry between Chelsea and Battersea. Then the only bridge between Westminster and Putney, it transformed Chelsea from a village to a small town.

Demolished in 1881 it was replaced in 1886-90 by the present bridge with five cast-iron arches.

ALBERT BRIDGE

A quaint three-span bridge was constructed by R.M. Ordish on his *'straight-link suspension'* system in 1871-73. It was a hybrid-type of construction containing elements of both cantilever and suspension. In 1884 the suspension members were overhauled and in 1971-73 the deck was strengthened to take increased traffic loads.

CHELSEA BRIDGE

The first bridge, designed by *Thomas*

bove: Albert Bridge. *Below:* Chelsea Bridge.

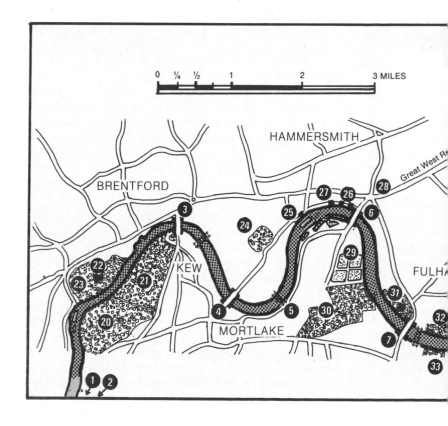

Page, was built in 1851-58. It was a suspension bridge with cast-iron towers. It is interesting to note that many human bones, Roman and British weapons were found during the digging of the foundations, indicating that a battle must have been fought here.

Freed from tolls in 1879, it was replaced by a suspension bridge in 1934.

VAUXHALL BRIDGE

The *'Regent's Bridge',* as it was first called, opened in 1816 and was the first iron bridge over the Thames in London. Freed from tolls in 1879, its two central piers were removed in 1881, converting therefore three of its nine arches into one to aid navigation. In 1895-1906, the structure was re-placed by the present bridge with five steel arches on granite piers.

LAMBETH BRIDGE

The first bridge on the site was built in 1861. It was a lattice-stiffened suspension bridge with three spans of 268 feet each designed by *P.W. Barlow.* In 1877 it was freed from tolls.

In 1929-32 it was replaced by the present five-span steel-arch bridge.

WESTMINSTER BRIDGE

For years there were suggestions for a bridge at Westminster but opposition from the City Corporation and the Thames watermen meant that nothing was done. However, the growth of the area in the 18th century urgently increased the need for a bridge.

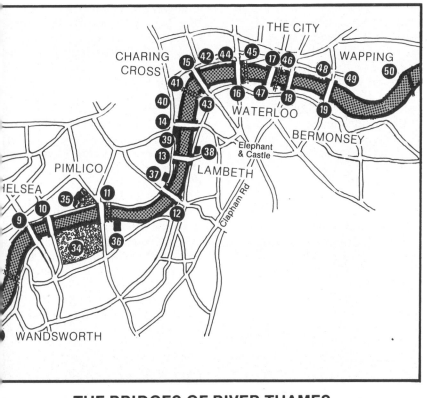

THE BRIDGES OF RIVER THAMES

(1) To RICHMOND Bridge
(2) To TWICKENHAM Bridge
(3) KEW Bridge
(4) CHISWICK Bridge
(5) Barnes Bridge (Rail)
(6) HAMMERSMITH Bridge
(7) PUTNEY Bridge
(8) WANDSWORTH Bridge
(9) BATTERSEA Bridge
(10) ALBERT Bridge
(11) CHELSEA Bridge
(12) VAUXHALL Bridge
(13) LAMBETH Bridge
(14) WESTMINSTER Bridge
(15) WATERLOO Bridge
(16) BLACKFRIARS Bridge
(17) SOUTHWARK Bridge
(18) LONDON Bridge
(19) TOWER Bridge

Some Important Landmarks
along the River Thames
(20) Old Deer Park
(21) Kew Gardens
(22) Syon House
(23) Syon Gardens
(24) Chiswick House
(25) Chiswick Mall
(26) Upper & Lower Mall
(27) Town Hall
(28) Hammersmith Flyover
(29) Reservoirs
(30) Putney Common
(31) Bishop's Park
(32) Hurlingham Park
(33) Wandsworth Park
(34) Battersea Park
     & Funfair
(35) Chelsea Hospital
(36) Battersea Power Station

(37) Tate Gallery
(38) Lambeth Palace
(39) Houses of Parliament
(40) Whitehall
(41) Victoria Embankment
(42) Somerset House
(43) Royal Festival Hall
(44) Temple Gardens
(45) St. Paul's
(46) Cannon Street Station
(47) Southwark Cathedral
(48) Tower of London
(49) St. Katharine's Dock
(50) Rotherhithe Tunnel
(51) West Indian Docks
(52) East Indian Docks
(53) Greenwich Pier
(54) Greenwich Park

153

Building began in 1738 and it was opened in November 1750. Westminster Bridge became the second masonry bridge over the Thames; its piers were founded in caissons — this was the first example of their use in Britain.

There were soon problems with the foundations and the present cast-iron bridge of seven arches was built in 1854-62 by *Thomas Page* with *Sir Charles Barry* as architectural consultant. Its width of 84 feet between the parapets was exceptional for the time.

The **Coade Stone Lion** of the South bank is by **W.F. Wordington** and the statue of **Queen Boudicca** on the north side is by **Thomas Thornycroft**.

WATERLOO BRIDGE

Designed by *John Rennie* the first bridge constructed on this site was in 1811-17 and opened by the Prince Regent on the second anniversary of the Battle of Waterloo in 18 June 1817.

Described as being the *"noblest bridge in the world"*, it was a granite bridge with nine elliptical arches and pairs of Doric columns at the piers. Originally it was known as the *"Strand Bridge"*, but in 1816 an Act of Parliament changed its name to Waterloo Bridge since,

"The said bridge when completed will be a work of great stability and magnificence, and such works are adapted to transmit to posterity the remembrance of great and glorious achievements".

In 1877 it was freed from tolls. In 1923 two of its piers settled alarmingly

Waterloo Bridge

Blackfriars Bridge

...nd a temporary bridge was built alongside. Despite strong protests, it was demolished in 1936 and in 1937-2 replaced by the present bridge of cantilevered reinforced concrete box girders.

BLACKFRIARS BRIDGE

The first bridge was built in 1760-69 and was constructed with nine semi-elliptical Portland stone arches. It was officially known as *"William Pitt Bridge"* but the public insisted on calling it Blackfriars.

In 1780 *Gordon Rioters* broke down the toll gates and took the money; five years later it was freed from tolls. It was replaced in 1860-69 by the present structure of five wrought-iron arches faced with cast iron on granite piers. In 1907-10 the bridge was widened on the west side from 70 feet to 105 feet.

SOUTHWARK BRIDGE

In 1814-19 *John Rennie* built a three-arch cast-iron bridge with a central span of 240 feet — the largest bridge ever constructed of this material. Robert Stephenson described the bridge as being,

> *"Unrivalled as regards its colossal proportions, its architectural effects and the general simplicity and massive character of its details".*

In 1912-21, it was replaced by the present five-span steel bridge.

LONDON BRIDGE

The first London bridge was probably built of wood between AD 100 and 400 during the Roman occupation. Around this wooden bridge a settlement grew up, a port and a meeting place of roads from every quarter. In a very real sense London exists because of London Bridge.

In 1014 *King Ethelred* and *King Olaf* of Norway burnt down the bridge to divide the Danish forces.

The first stone bridge was begun in

155

1176 by Peter, Chaplain of St. Mary Cole Church. The first mention of houses on the bridge was in 1201. It had 19 small arches and a drawbridge at the Southwark end.

Until 1750 when the first bridge at Westminster was completed, London Bridge was the only one spanning the Thames in London. In 1758-62 the houses were removed and the two central arches were replaced by a single navigation span. When this work was completed stones from demolished City gates were used to strengthen the arches.

Finally in 1823-1831 a new bridge *(replacing Old London Bridge which had stood for 622 years),* of five stone arches upstream of the old bridge was built by *Sir John Rennie* to his late father's design. The bridge was opened on 1 August 1831, by William IV and Queen Adelaide. The scene on the river as they came by water from Somerset House was one of extraordinary splendour.

The time taken to build New London Bridge (from driving of the first pile to the opening ceremony) was 7 years, 4 months and 16 days. Its length was 1,005 feet (including its two purposely-built approaches of King William Street and Moorgate, it was 2,350 feet) and its width was 56 feet. The height of the centre arch was $29\frac{1}{2}$ feet. In 1967-72 the present structure of pre-stressed concrete cantilevers forming three spans was built.

It must be explained that Rennie's bridge was sold and re-erected in the USA. Its new home, *Lake Havasu City,* Arizona (232 air-miles from Los Angeles) occupies a 26 square mile area bordered on one side by the Mahave Mountains and on the other by lake Havasu (an Indian name meaning "blue waters"), an artificial lake formed in the Colorado River by the construction of the Parker Dam. London Bridge was reconstructed on the neck of a large peninsula which

Sunset over the Thames

ower Bridge — Beyond is London Docklands with its new developments.

jutted out into lake Havasu. Through this neck an artificial water channel was cut, creating a new river, christened *"Little Thames"* for the old bridge to span and provide road access to the newly-formed island on which the City's airport stands.

TOWER BRIDGE

The first and only bridge below London Bridge. In 1884 it was decided to build a bascule bridge (in Gothic style) and John Wolfe-Barry was appointed engineer with Sir Horace Jones as architect.

The bridge was opened with great ceremony on 30 June 1894 by the Prince of Wales — later King Edward VII.

Its two bascules can open to allow ships to pass upstream to the Pool of London. Although ships seldom use the Pool these days, the mechanism is tested on Sunday mornings between 8.00 and 9.00 and is open to public view daily.

London's best known bridge, its towers are constructed with a steel frame clothed in stone in order to support the great weight of the bascules. They also contain lifts to convey pedestrians to the high level footbridge which was in use when the bridge was opened. The two side-spans are on the suspension principle, the decks being hung from curved lattice girders. The hydraulic machinery to raise and lower the bridge was preserved after electrification in 1976.

Some facts and figures about Tower Bridge:

★ The foundation stone was laid by The Prince of Wales on 21 June 1886; hence it took 8 years to complete.

157

★ It cost £1,184.000.

★ The bridge is maintained at no expense to the rate payer or tax payer by the *Bridge House Estates Trust* of the City of London.

★ In the construction of Tower Bridge the following materials were used:

36,857 tons of concrete		
27,260 ” ” brickwork		
30,000 ” ” masonry		
20,000 ” ” Portland cement		
11,300 ” ” iron and steel		
15,000 ” ” cast iron		

Tower Bridge — *(An old photograph)*

CHAPTER TWELVE

FAMOUS STREET and AREA NAMES
— Their Origin —

"THE STREETS OF LONDON",

it has been justly claimed, "whisper history". In this Royal metropolis there are streets where Shakespeare walked, houses where such literary giants as Dickens scribbled, places where Disraeli held court, spots where artists and powerful statesmen lived and worked — the list is beyond comparison.

It must be noted that the earliest city street names emerged from around the 10th century. We give here only a selection (around 60) and will be shown in alphabetical order.

ABBOTS LANE *(Bermondsey SE1).*
It was named in memory of the Medieval Abbots of Lewes, who stayed in their palatial mansion in Tooley Street when they came to Bermondsey on business. The Prior of Lewes supervised the foundation of the *Cluniac Abbey of Bermondsey* (at the bottom of Bermondsey Street — its main cloister is now Bermondsey Square), and Lewes Priory remained the head of the Cluniac order of England.

ABINGTON ROAD *(W8).*
The *Abbey of Abingdon* was left land here in 1109 by Geoffrey de Vere. The area was subsequently called Abbot's Kensington and the parish church, St. Mary Abbots.

ADELPHI TERRACE *(Strand WC2)*
The Adelphi area south of the Strand derives its name *"Adelphoi"* (from the Greek word meaning brothers),

from the famous Adam Brothers (Adam Street and Lower Adam Street) who in 1768 obtained a lease of the Durham House site. With skill and ingenuity they created an elegant residential district raised on high arches, with the Lower Streets underground at Thames level.

ALDGATE *(City EC3)*
Named after one of the four original gates in the city wall leading to the Roman Road to Colchester. The Saxon *"Aelgate"* means open to all, or a free gate.

BARBICAN *(Aldersgate Street, City EC1)*
A barbican was an extra fortification outside a medieval wall. The name is first found in London in 1279, referring to the watchtower just north of the city wall which guarded the road to the Aldersgate. It was part of a ring of defences, natural and

159

manmade, supplementing London Wall itself: on the south flowed the Thames, the east was guarded by the Tower, the west by the Fleet River and the Bailey (a rampart thrown up just outside the city wall), while the barbican and the swampy Moor Fields protected against invasion from the north.

BAYSWATER (W2)
The watering-place belonging to an Anglo-Norman called *Bayard* and situated where the river Westbourne crossed the Roman *Bayswater road.* There were several other springs and wells in the gravelly soil of this area.

BISHOPSGATE (City EC2)
It was a Roman road, entering the City through one of the gates of the north side. It gained its name from a tradition that the gate was restored in Saxon times by *Saint Erkenwald,* Bishop of London and Prince of East Anglia, who died in 693. Just inside its site stands the medieval church of *St. Ethelburga,* the only church in England dedicated to Erkenwald's sister.

BLACKFRIARS (City EC4)
Named after the great Dominican monastery of the *Black Friars* (a begging order of preachers) which stood here from c.1276 until Henry VIII's dissolution of the monasteries in 1538.

BLOOMSBURY (WC1)
Is the name given to a medieval manor which stretched from modern *Euston Road* to *High Holborn,* and west to east from *Tottenham Court Road* to *Southampton Row.* It is a corruption of Blemund's bury, the bury or manor house of *William de Blemund* who bought the land in 1201.

BOND STREET, NEW & OLD (W1)
Named after the speculative builder

Sir Thomas Bond of Peckham (a wealthy financier who arranged loans for Charles II and was Treasurer of the household of the Queen Mother Henrietta Maria) who developed the area between 1686 and 1716 where Clarendon House once stood.

CAMDEN (NW1)
The district now known as *Camden Town* was a prebend, a manor belonging to St. Paul's Cathedral, where the income supported a prebendary canon. By about 1670 *John Jeffreys* was farming the land on behalf of the Cathedral.

CANNON STREET (City EC4)
Shortened by the cockney dialect from its 12th century original "*Candlewrichstrete*" as it was then inhabited by the city's candlemakers and wick chandlers.

CATO STREET (Marylebone W1)
Like other local streets *(e.g.'s Homer Row and Virgil Place)* this has a classical name: *Marcus Porcius Cato* was a Roman statesman. In a room above a stable here the ringleaders of the '*Cato Street Conspiracy*' were trapped and arrested in 1820. The plot had aimed to murder Lord Castlereagh and Cabinet Ministers while they dined at Lord Harrowby's after which a new government was to be set up to relieve the prevailing misery following the Napoleonic Wars.

As a result of the scandal caused by the affair, the name was changed to *Horace Street,* after another Roman but the original name was restored in 1937.

CHEAPSIDE (City EC2)
Derived from the Anglo-Saxon '*ceap or market.* It was the City's central market for centuries and was also used for jousts and entertainments.

CHELSEA *(SW1)*

Was an Anglo-Saxon settlement. Originally referred to as *"Celehyth"* that is a hythe or landing place for chalk and lime. The name is also supposed to derive from *"Chesil"* a strand built up by sand and pebbles.

CLERKENWELL *(EC1)*

In the middle ages this was a pleasant village with an easy reach of London. The parish clerks of the City would gather once a year at the well, or spring, to put on a biblical play.

CORNHILL *(City EC3)*

Is one of the earliest names in the City, recorded even before the Norman Conquest of 1066. It is one of the twin hills of London facing Ludgate Hill. The City's corn market once stood here.

COVENT GARDEN *(WC2)*

Was the garden belonging to the Convent, or Abbey of Westminster. Owned by the monks from c.1222 it was confiscated by the crown at the Reformation and sold to the Earl of Bedford in 1552. A market began there in 1661.

DOWNING STREET *(Whitehall SW1)*

Was built by Sir George Downing.

An old engraving of Chelsea, showing the seat of the Duke of Beaufort.

He sat in both parliaments called by Cromwell but changed his allegiance when the Restoration was imminent and hurriedly assured Charles II of his support. The area now belongs to the Crown.

DRURY LANE *(WC2)*

An early medieval lane, originally called '*Via de Addwych*'. Named after Sir Robert Drury, a successful barrister from Suffolk, who bought some land here (circa 1500) so that he could build himself a fine town house.

EBURY STREET & SQUARE *(Westminster, SW1)*

The 430 acre Eubery farm stood here in Elizabeth I's time. The name is derived from the Saxon *"ey"* or water, and *"burgh"*, a fortified place.

ELY PLACE *(Holborn EC1)*

In 1290, John de Kirkeby, Bishop of Ely, bequeathed to his see Ely House, his home in Holborn famed for its gardens and vineyards stretching from Leather Lane to the River Fleet. Under Elizabeth I's reign Sir Christopher Hatton built a rival palatial mansion which encroached on Ely House. In 1772 it was finally demolished to make way for Ely Place and Court.

Until recently Ely Place was a detached part of the County of Cambridge and was rated as such. Even today it is shut off from the rest of London by heavy gates and a Patrolling Beadle and the Metropolitan Police appear to have no jurisdiction inside it.

FLEET STREET (EC4)

Originally the *Fleet Bridge Road* which carried traffic over the *River Fleet*. This river was named after its *'fleot'* (Anglo-Saxon for creek or tidal inlet) and rises at the Hampstead and Highgate ponds. Nowadays its course is through underground pipes.

GREEK STREET (Soho, W1)

Took its name from the Greek church which stood on the site of St. Martin's School of Art and the College for the Distributive Trades in Charing Cross Road and, probably had a back entrance in Greek Street. It was built for Greek refugees, who came to London during oppression by the Ottoman Turks and were granted permission in 1675 *'to build a church in any part of the City of London or Libertyes thereof, where they may freely exercise their Religion according to the Greek Church'*. Building began in 1677 but the Greeks abandoned the Church in 1681 as being *"too remote from the abodes of most of the Grecians – dwelling chiefly in the furthermost parts of the City"*.

HAYMARKET (SW1)

The site, until 1830, of the thrice-weekly market for hay and straw which was established early in the reign of Elizabeth I.

HOLBORN (EC1)

Named after the *"bourne in the hollow"* otherwise known as the River Fleet, which is now covered over by *Farringdon Street.*

HYDE PARK (W1, W2, SW1 and SW7)

Henry VIII enclosed it as a royal hunting park but James I opened it to the public. It was originally part of the manor of Ebury, consisting in the 13th century of one hide i.e., the amount of land which could be filled in a year by one plough, about 120 acres.

KENSINGTON (W8)

Derived from the name of the Saxon villa of *Chenesitum,* or *Cynesige's Farm,* which grew up near the Roman road — now the *High Street.*

KING'S ROAD (Chelsea & Fulham, SW3, SW10, SW6)

Is shown on the earliest maps of this district as a cart-track, used by the local farmers and gardeners. The Monarch who appropriated it was Charles II, officially as his route to Hampton Court, but according to local tradition, as a short-cut to *Nell Gwynn's* home in Fulham.

To protect his majesty from robbers lurking in the desolate fields through which King's Road passed *(the future Belgravia)* 29 royal guardsmen patrolled nightly to ensure that only the sovereign and his privileged guests approached the road. Passage was restricted to bearers of a special ticket marked with a crown on one side and *"The King's Private Road"* on the other. The road was opened to the public in 1830.

KNIGHTSBRIDGE (SW1, SW7)

The road from London to Hammersmith followed a bridge over the River Westbourne here. This is the stream which formed the *Serpentine* and still flows under Knightsbridge at Albert Gate, now buried deep in a sewer pipe. In the 11th century it was called *"Cnichtebrugge"*, the bridge of the young men. According to legend,

South Kensington, together with Kensington, Chelsea and Kings Road is very fashionable.

two knights once quarrelled and fought a duel on this bridge.

LEADENHALL MARKET (EC3)

Named after the hall with a leaded roof built by *Sir Hugh Nevill* in 1309. It was owned by Sir Richard *(Dick)* Whittington, Lord Mayor of London, in the early 15th century. After his death it was turned into a granary and poultry market. In 1730 it was rebuilt as a meat market and again rebuilt in 1881.

LEICESTER SQUARE (WC2)

The *Earl of Leicester* built his family mansion on the north side of the square, formerly Leicester Fields, in the mid 17th century whilst reserving the fields for the traditional use of the local peasants.

LITTLE BRITAIN (EC1)

The Norman Dukes of Brittany

established themselves here in the 13th century and its original name was *'Peti Bretane'*. Until the 18th century it was the centre of the City's book trade, housing many publishers and booksellers. John Milton's *'Paradise Lost'* was first published here.

LOMBARD STREET (EC3)

Named after the men from *Lombardy* in North Italy who took the places of Jewish moneylenders and bankers when the Jews were expelled from England in 1290. They worked under the heraldic sign of their native land, the *"Three Balls"*, the emblem of pawnbrokers ever since. Lombard Street is still the City's banking centre.

MAYFAIR (W1)

Named after the annual fair held during the first two weeks of May at *Brook Field* (now roughly Curzon

Street) on the bank of the river Tyburn. The original goods and cattle market, first held in 1688, soon degenerated into an excuse for an uninhibited good time — the refined residents of nearby Piccadilly were alarmed! The fair was banned in 1708, but continued furtively until Brook Field was built up in the 1750's.

NOTTING HILL GATE *(W11)*
Called *"Knottynghull"* in the 14th century the name was perhaps derived from the Saxon word *"cnott"* or hill. It was formerly the site of a turnpike gate where traffic tolls were gathered until 1864.

OLD JEWRY *(Cheapside, EC2)*
Was the central street of an extensive medieval ghetto. Prior to 1066 the land was Saxon royal domain which William the Conqueror transfered to the Jews to encourage them to settle in London and add to the City's wealth. The Jews were not constrained to live here by law, but probably chose to shelter there from the jealous rancour of the citizens. The name Old Jewry came into use after 1290.

OXFORD STREET *(W1)*
One of London's oldest roads, certainly Roman and possibly earlier. To the Anglo-Saxons it was the *"Broad Military Way"*, the route for armies marching westward. It was later called *Tyburn Way* but assumed its present name in the early 18th century.

PADDINGTON *(W1, W2)*
The farm or homestead (*'ton'*) of the Paeda family, an early Saxon family who settled in the area.

PALL MALL *(SW1)*
In Charles II's time (probably earlier)

Fleet Street. Although the glamour of the newspapers is over (they have all moved their offices), the fascination still remains.

Piccadilly Circus and Shaftesbury Avenue — *(An old photograph)*

his was a smooth grass alley set aside for the fashionable game of *"palemaille"* which the king introduced to England. It was similar in some ways to croquet. Later a new pall mall alley was built in St. Jame's Park which is now the processional avenue, *The Mall.*

PETTY FRANCE *(Westminster SW1)*

At the end of the 15th century this area was known as *"Petefraunce"* because it was the home of French wool merchants who came to trade at Westminster. Later, after the Edict of Nantes in 1685, many French refugees settled in this area.

PICCADILLY *(W1)*

This famous street takes its name from *"Pickadel Hall"* built by Robert Baker on the old road to Reading —during James I's reign. This in turn was named after some of the garments through which the young tailor made his money — the *"piccadil"*, which was a kind of ruff or collar and very fashionable at the time

PIMLICO *(SW1)*

In Tudor times Ben Pimlico was an inn-keeper whose beer was very famous. Then in the early 17th century an inn near Victoria was named after him and it was from this that the area took its name.

PORTOBELLO ROAD *(W10 & W11)*

Originally a cart-track which led to a farm house built by a local farmer called Adams in the early 18th century. He named it *Porto Bello Farm* after Admiral Vernon captured the town of Porto Bello in the Gulf of Mexico from the Spaniards in 1739. The area was urbanised in the 1860's.

PRINTING HOUSE SQUARE *(City EC4)*

After the Great Fire of London (1666) the King's Printing House was erected here. It was the official printing agency for all royal proclamations, speeches and Acts of Parliament until 1770 when it was moved. Then in 1785 John Walter founded a

165

paper called *"The Daily Universal Register"* which changed its name to *"The Times"* in 1788.

PUDDING LANE (EC4)

The *"pudding"* or *"offal"* from the butcher's shops in Eastcheap was sent down this lane on its way to the dung boats on the Thames. It was also the starting point of the Great Fire of London.

REGENT STREET (W1)

Designed by John Nash (as a *'Royal Mile'*) in the early 19th century for the Prince Regent — later George IV. It was part of a processional way from Carlton House, St. Jame's to the proposed Regent's Palace in what is now Regent's Park.

ROLLS PASSAGE (EC4)

Documents were once kept in rolls inside pipes housed in the buildings here. The *Rolls Office* has been rebuilt as the Public Records Office and contains documents ranging from the Domesday Book of 1086 to the present day. The P.R.O. is located in Chancery Lane (original building) but mainly in a modern building near Kew Bridge.

SAFFRON HILL (EC1)

One of the finest of the many gardens in medieval London was that of the *Bishops of Ely* just outside the City Wall. It was also an important source of saffron, which was originally grown in East Anglia and used in the Middle Ages as a golden dye, as some form of cure and in cooking.

ST. JAMES (SW1)

In the 11th century a leper asylum dedicated to St. James was founded here and run by 14 chaste maidens. This hospice continued in use until the dissolution of the monasteries in the 16th century when King Henry VIII built St. Jame's Palace there and annexed St. Jame's Park.

SAVOY PLACE & STREET (WC2)

The Manor or Liberty of the Savoy exists as a sort of a buffer state between the *"cities"* of London and Westminster. In 1246 it came into the hands of Peter, uncle of Queen Eleanor, one of the many kinsmen who followed Eleanor to England to see what profit could be made from her marriage to Henry III. When Peter became Count of Savoy in 126?, he left London for good, yet his name was to remain permanently attached to the Manor.

SHAFTESBURY AVENUE (W1 & WC2)

It was carved through a former slum area and opened in 1886 and was named after the late *7th Earl of Shaftesbury,* a famous 19th century philanthropist. At the end of the road, at the centre of Piccadilly Circus, stands a monument of Shaftesbury.

SLOANE STREET & SQUARE (SW1)

Named after the eminent physician and collector, *Sir Hans Sloane,* who bought the manor house in Chelsea in 1742 and later died there. His daughter married Lord Cadogan.

SOHO SQUARE (W1)

Before the Square was built in 1681 this was an area of open fields used for hunting. Its name derives from the medieval hunting cry *"So-ho"* — the English equivalent of the French *"tally-ho"*. This name was also probably given to a local inn popular with huntsmen.

THE STRAND (WC2)

A pre-Roman track, later Romanised. The name *"Stronde"* is found by 1185, at which date the road was probably literally the strand or shore of the Thames. Land had since been reclaimed by the church, the nobles

The busy area of Regent Street

and by the Tudors and Stuarts. In the 18th century the Adam brothers drove the river further back and finally the Victoria Embankment was made (1870) leaving the Strand several hundred feet from the water.

TEMPLE AVENUE, LANE & PLACE *(City EC4)*

This area was originally the London base of the *Knights Templars of Jerusalem,* a religious order of knights founded in 1119 who were pledged to protect pilgrims travelling the dangerous roads to the Holy Land. In the 14th century the land was leased to lawyers who were granted the freehold of the Inner and Middle Temple in 1608.

THREADNEEDLE STREET *(City EC2)*

The name is probably derived from a sign-board depicting *"three needles"*. The **Merchant Taylor's Hall** has stood here since the 14th century which may be the origin of the name. In the 18th century the street became the site of the Bank of England, often nicknamed *"the old lady of Threadneedle Street"*.

TOTTENHAM COURT ROAD *(W1)*

From before the 12th century this road led from the village of *St. Giles-in-the-Fields* to the court, or manor house, of **"Toten Hele"** which was mentioned in the Domesday Survey of 1086. Toten Hele was probably derived from *"tote hill"* or look-out hill. In the 18th century the manor was demolished to make way for the new road from Paddington, now the Euston Road.

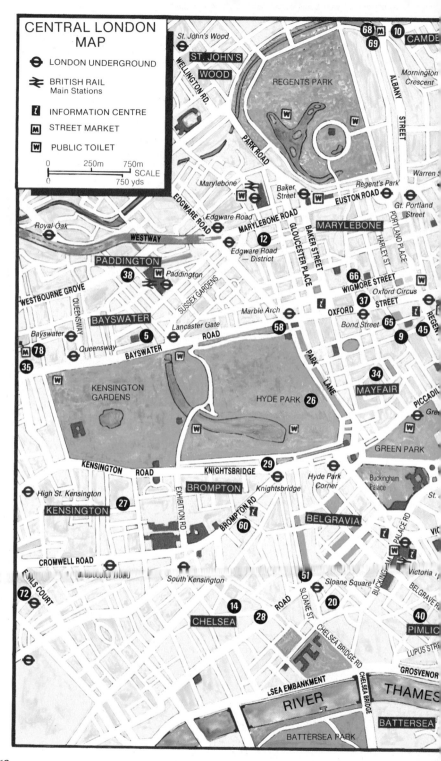

CENTRAL LONDON MAP

- 🚇 LONDON UNDERGROUND
- ⇌ BRITISH RAIL Main Stations
- 🛈 INFORMATION CENTRE
- Ⓜ STREET MARKET
- W PUBLIC TOILET

SCALE
0   250m   750m
0   750 yds

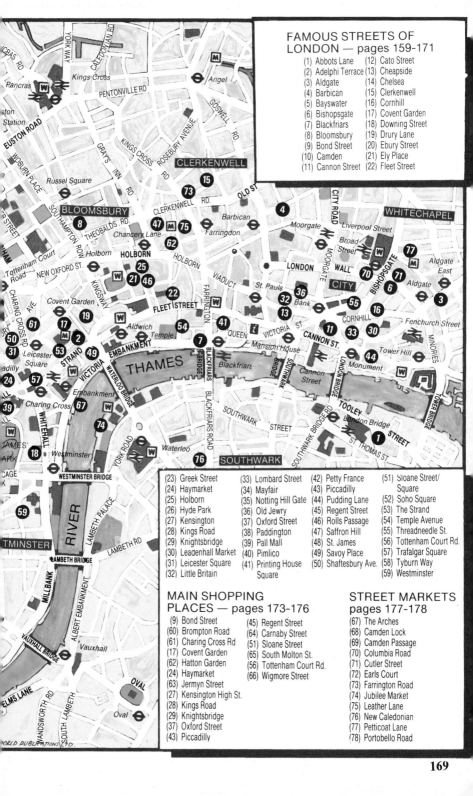

FAMOUS STREETS OF LONDON — pages 159-171

(1) Abbots Lane
(2) Adelphi Terrace
(3) Aldgate
(4) Barbican
(5) Bayswater
(6) Bishopsgate
(7) Blackfriars
(8) Bloomsbury
(9) Bond Street
(10) Camden
(11) Cannon Street
(12) Cato Street
(13) Cheapside
(14) Chelsea
(15) Clerkenwell
(16) Cornhill
(17) Covent Garden
(18) Downing Street
(19) Drury Lane
(20) Ebury Street
(21) Ely Place
(22) Fleet Street

(23) Greek Street
(24) Haymarket
(25) Holborn
(26) Hyde Park
(27) Kensington
(28) Kings Road
(29) Knightsbridge
(30) Leadenhall Market
(31) Leicester Square
(32) Little Britain
(33) Lombard Street
(34) Mayfair
(35) Notting Hill Gate
(36) Old Jewry
(37) Oxford Street
(38) Paddington
(39) Pall Mall
(40) Pimlico
(41) Printing House Square
(42) Petty France
(43) Piccadilly
(44) Pudding Lane
(45) Regent Street
(46) Rolls Passage
(47) Saffron Hill
(48) St. James
(49) Savoy Place
(50) Shaftesbury Ave.
(51) Sloane Street/ Square
(52) Soho Square
(53) The Strand
(54) Temple Avenue
(55) Threadneedle St.
(56) Tottenham Court Rd.
(57) Trafalgar Square
(58) Tyburn Way
(59) Westminster

MAIN SHOPPING PLACES — pages 173-176

(9) Bond Street
(60) Brompton Road
(61) Charing Cross Rd
(17) Covent Garden
(62) Hatton Garden
(24) Haymarket
(63) Jermyn Street
(27) Kensington High St.
(28) Kings Road
(29) Knightsbridge
(37) Oxford Street
(43) Piccadilly
(45) Regent Street
(64) Carnaby Street
(51) Sloane Street
(65) South Molton St.
(56) Tottenham Court Rd.
(66) Wigmore Street

STREET MARKETS pages 177-178

(67) The Arches
(68) Camden Lock
(69) Camden Passage
(70) Columbia Road
(71) Cutler Street
(72) Earls Court
(73) Farrington Road
(74) Jubilee Market
(75) Leather Lane
(76) New Caledonian
(77) Petticoat Lane
(78) Portobello Road

169

Westminster area, with Westminster Hall and Abbey on the lower part, left.
(An old illustration)

Tottenham Court Road, now the centre of Hi-Fi and electronic equipment shops. At the far end *(right)* is one of London's tallest buildings, The Centre Point.

TRAFALGAR SQUARE *(SW1, WC2)*

The national monument to Nelson's last victory. The Square was begun in 1829, 24 years after the battle of Trafalgar, and not finished until the 1840s. Around the base of Nelson's column, the focal point of the square, are 4 bronze reliefs showing scenes from the hero's life: *The Battle of the Nile, the bombardment of Copenhagen,* the *battle of St. Vincent,* and *death at Cape Trafalgar.*

TYBURN WAY *(W1)*

The site of the famous **Tyburn Gallows** is commemorated by a plaque on the road-island at *Marble Arch.* It stood at the junction of the Edgware Road and Tyburn Road (now Oxford Street) so-called because it bridged the river Tyburn *("boundary stream").* The 12 foot high triangular gallows were the site of many celebrated and crowd-pulling executions from the Middle Ages until 1783 when it hosted its last hanging.

WESTMINSTER *(SW1)*

Takes its name from its Abbey, the *"minster"* or monastery to the west of London, perhaps so-called to distinguish it from St. Paul's Cathedral in the east. There was a church here on *Thorney Island* by the 8th century. However the real founder of the abbey was Edward the Confessor who started to build his great edifice on the site of the present church in about 1050.

The famous Portobello Market

CHAPTER THIRTEEN

A BRIEF SHOPPING GUIDE and LONDON'S MARKETS

LONDON is an international shopping centre *par excellence,* able to provide any kind of merchandise. We will endeavour to give a brief account of the main shopping areas and then make some comments on street markets. London's West End (Oxford St., Regent St. and Bond St.) and the Kensington area, are very popular both with tourists and locals. Covent Garden, Edgware Road, Brent Cross, Wood Green and now the Docklands are also important shopping centres.

In alphabetical order here are some suggestions.

MAIN SHOPPING PLACES

BOND STREET *(W1 – ⊖ Bond Street).*
Has two parts: **New Bond Street** which abounds in high class fashion shops and **Old Bond Street** which has excellent beauty centres, art galleries etc.

BROMPTON ROAD *(SW1, SW3 ⊖ Knightsbridge).*
It is dominated by **Harrods,** a large store where one can purchase *"anything and everything":* many expensive items in evidence.

CHARING CROSS ROAD *(WC2 – ⊖ Tottenham Court Road).*
Famous for its bookshops like *Foyles, Collets* and *Waterstone.*

COVENT GARDEN *(WC2 – ⊖ Covent Garden).*
Originally the garden belonging to the Convent, or Abbey of Westminster; a market began there in 1661. By 1830 the place had become so crowded that permission was granted to erect a market, an articulated complex of neoclassical design with colonnades, arches and spacious balconies. This was in turn surrounded by other distinctive buildings such as the *Floral Hall* finished in 1860.

After the removal in 1974 of the vegetable market to Nine Elms SW8, the area was transformed, making good use of the existing structures. While the market was modernised to house boutiques, bookshops, gift and craftwork shops, restaurants and wine bars, the flower market was adapted to house the **London Transport Museum** — very popular with tourists.

Covent Garden is the place for shoppers who like pretty surroundings, bags of atmosphere, unusual shops, interesting places to eat and quite a lot of street theatre, from talented *buskers* to *Punch & Judy* shows, added to which is the advantage that many of the shops, particularly those under the main market roof stay open late, some until 8pm or so, during the week.

Part of its charm is the *Jubilee Market* which sells antiques on Mondays with hand-made crafts, jewellery and clothes the rest of the week.

HATTON GARDEN *(EC1 – ⊖ Chancery Lane).*

Arguably, the best known address for jewellery of all sizes and quantity.

HAYMARKET *(SW1 – ⊖ Piccadilly Circus).*

A market until 1830 it is now a road of sheer contrast. The *Royal Opera Arcade* was the first covered passage in London, 1818.

The main Covent Garden Central Hall — one of the most popular in London.

JERMYN STREET *(SW1 – ⊖ Piccadilly Circus).*

Famous for its perfume extracts and toiletries, soaps, cheeses (from all over the world), gift articles, smoker's requisites and footwear of exceptional quality.

KENSINGTON HIGH STREET *(W8, W14 – ⊖ High Street Kensington).*

Is the backbone of Kensington, one of the smartest districts in London. There are large departmental stores such as **Barkers,** and **Marks and Spencer** and the *Children's Book Centre,* said to be the largest in Europe with over 10,000 titles in stock.

KING'S ROAD *(SW3, SW6, SW10 – ⊖ Sloane Square).*

Chelsea's main artery, it extends from Sloane Square to Fulham. Full of restaurants, cafes and boutiques, a fashion-cult centre of *Swinging Sixties* with the *mini-skirt,* it is considered the ultimate showplace for outlandish clothes, thanks partly to those who throng its pavements in their fancy clothes.

Liberty's. One of the most famous departmental stores, off Regent Street.

KNIGHTSBRIDGE *(SW1, SW7 – ⊖ Knightsbridge).*

The road is bordered by luxury hotels, restaurants and large department stores and shops.

OXFORD STREET *(W1 - ⊖ Oxford Circus, Bond Street).*

Large departmental stores such as **DH Evans, Debenhams, John Lewis** and **Selfridges** offer a large variety of goods at competitive prices. Very popular with locals and tourists.

Just off Oxford Street is *Gray's Antique Market* **(Davies Street)** which has now spilled over around the corner to include *Gray's Mews Antique Market.* Here it is possible to buy a souvenir with a bit of history that is also easily portable such as a Victorian scent bottle.

PICCADILLY *(W1 – ⊖ Piccadilly Circus).*

Famous for its stores such as **Simpson's,** an international clothing store with every kind of garment for both sexes.

Close to Piccadilly Circus we find *Burlington Arcade (1819),* a covered passage in Regency style with some 40 shops selling everything from antiques to jewellery. *Piccadilly Arcade (1910)* specializes in china and giftware. The **Trocadero,** is London's newest and most exciting shopping complex. A must for all visitors and locals. The **London Pavilion** overlooking Piccadilly, and opened in 1988 is certainly worth a visit.

REGENT STREET *(W1, SW1 – ⊖ Oxford Circus, Piccadilly Circus).*

One can find everything from china to jewellery, motifs, toys, vintage wines, sporting gear and high quality clothes and antiques.

Adjacent to Regent Street is, **CARNABY STREET,** famous in the *"Swinging Sixties"* and now a pedestrian precinct with trendy clothes and souvenir shops; **Hanover Street** famous for its airline offices and the *London Diamond Centre;* and **Saville Row** is still one of the world's recognised centres of tailoring excellence.

SLOANE STREET *(SW1 – ⊖ Sloane Square).*

Here one can buy high quality British and foreign goods — everything from clothing to perfumes, china, furniture and antiques.

SOUTH MOLTON STREET *(W1 – ⊖ Bond Street).*

Is a pedestrian precinct full of beautiful shops selling clothes, shoes, knitwear and even hand painted silk shirts.

TOTTENHAM COURT ROAD *(W1 – ⊖ Tottenham Court Road).*

Everything from furniture, household items and trendy furnishings can be found here. The road is now littered with Hi-Fi shops; both visitors and locals come here to purchase such goods. Many bargains can be picked up.

WIGMORE STREET *(W1 – ⊖ Oxford Circus).*

Parallel to Oxford Street it has many fine shops. Off this road is **St. Christopher's Place** which has lately attracted some very good quality boutiques.

The Famous street of the 60's Carnaby Street, still attracts attention.

"The Arcade" at Albemarle Street, close to the other famous Burlington Arcade.

So much for departmental stores and specialist shops. What about **STREET MARKETS?** Almost every area of the capital has its own open air market with all kinds of articles on sale. A pick, of these, again in alphabetical order, are as follows:

THE ARCHES *(Villiers Street WC2 ⊖ Embankment).*
Weekdays, for coins, stamps, insignia and military medals.

CAMDEN LOCK *(Chalk Farm Road NW1 – ⊖ Camden Town).*
Also called *"Dingwall's Market".* Saturdays and Sundays, for antique objects and handcrafts. Exciting atmosphere.

CAMDEN PASSAGE *(Islington N1 – ⊖ Angel).*
Wednesday and Saturday, for prints, china, brass etc. Antiques here are usually of high quality.

CHURCH STREET *(NW8 – ⊖ Edgware Road).*
Saturday for antiques and collector's items. *"Alfie's"* celebrated its 10th anniversary recently by opening 70 more stands in its basement.

COLUMBIA ROAD *(E2 – ⊖ Liverpool Street).*
Sunday morning mainly for flowers and plants.

CUTLER STREET *(E1 – ⊖ Liverpool Street).*
Sunday morning for jewellery and coins.

EARLS COURT SUNDAY MARKET *(SW6 – ⊖ Earls Court).*
Sunday from 10am to 3pm. Has 1000's of bargains including leather ladies and gents fashions, footwear, basketware, silverware, fancy goods, fruit and vegetables. This famous market is probably unique because it

One of London's many colourful fruit and vegetable street markets.

caters for and serves the local population and tourists alike. Evidence of this can best be demonstrated by the fact that most traders are bilingual conversant in Arabic, Greek, German, Italian, French etc.

FARRINGTON ROAD *(EC1 - ⊖ Farrington).*

Monday to Saturday, small market for second hand books and prints.

JUBILEE MARKET *(Covent Garden WC2 - ⊖ Covent Garden).*

Monday to Saturday: For different items according to the day of the week. On Monday's there are usually displays of minor antiques.

KINGSLAND ROAD *(E2, E8 - ⊖ Liverpool Street – the buses).*

Saturday's only. Mainly for second hand goods. Often called *"Kingsland Waste Market"*.

LEATHER LANE *(EC1 – ⊖ Chancery Lane).*

Monday to Friday for general objects.

NEW CALEDONIAN *(Long Lane SE1 –⊖ Elephant and Castle).*

Friday mornings, for various antiques. This is used very much by dealers. As with other antique markets it must be visited early to get real bargains.

PETTICOAT LANE *(E1 ⊖ Aldgate East/Liverpool Street).*

The main market opens Sunday mornings from 9am to 2pm but there are also smaller markets which are open Monday to Friday. Articles of every kind are sold (from foodstuffs to clothing), and very large crowds are attracted. It is a huge, rambling market.

PORTOBELLO ROAD *(W10, W11 - ⊖ Notting Hill Gate).*

Established by the early 1870's, amongst its first dealers were gypsies who came to buy and sell horses at the nearby *Hippodrome* and to offer herbs in the market. For years there were problems as to whether the market should function in Portobello Road. In 1929 the first licence was officially granted and in 1948, after the closure of Caledonian Market, antique dealers came here in large numbers followed by bargain hunters. Today it is crowded with tourists. The main market is on Saturday and stretches the full length of Portobello Road. It is so picturesque that it is a must for all London visitors. You will experience a lively, bustling atmosphere.

N.B. Remember that the vast department stores (Harrods, Selfridges, Fortnum and Mason, Liberty, Peter Jones, John Lewis, Barkers, Marks and Spencer, Simpsons, Dickins and Jones, Debenhams etc.,) largely dominate the London shopping scene and provide a glittering array of goods in close proximity all under one roof. If someone somewhere makes an item then someone somewhere in London will sell it. The choice is endless.

Portobello Road Market offers all kinds of bargains.

Above: Portobello Market. *Below:* Covent Garden Market offers both Relaxation and Shopping excitement.

179

A recent production of the Musical CAN CAN in one of London's Theatres. *(Society of W.E. Theatres – Catherine Ashmore)*

CHAPTER FOURTEEN

EATING AND DRINKING OUT/
and Evening Entertainment

BY NIGHT London changes from being a showplace of history and pageantry into a glittering world of pleasure. Opportunities for a memorable evening out are endless — depending on your individual tastes and preferences.

As expected in a cosmopolitan centre like London there is a great profusion of restaurants with a large representation of national and ethnic cuisine. There is a large array of ethnic restaurants particularly Greek, Italian, Chinese and Indian centered around the Soho, West End, Covent Garden Edgware Road, Camden Town, Fulham Road, Kings Road, Hampstead, Greenwich, Camberwell and many other districts.

The visitor's choice is endless: traditional English food, foreign delicacies, international cuisine, vegetarian, seafood, health food, fast food and a great variety of take-away food.

There are cocktail bars, wine bars, hotel restaurants, tea rooms, all night places etc. scattered (often congested) all over London. You can even *Dine and Cruise.* Evening trips are a wonderful and memorable experience; combine your enjoyment with seeing London's major sites. All tastes and budgets are catered for. And don't miss out on **fish and chips.**

To blend in with the visitor's many experiences of this Royal Metropolis there is **traditional entertainment** at very reasonable prices.

For continuous **Medieval-type entertainment** by knights, minstrels etc. from England's past go to the *Bee-feater* (Tel. 408 1001) by the Tower of London, in historic vaults surrounded by the Thames and St. Katharine's yacht heaven.

For **Scottish-style fun** go to the *Caledonian* (Tel. 408 1001) in Hanover Street W1. For **traditional London Entertainment,** the *Cockney Cabaret* and *Music Hall* (Tel. 408 1001) in Charing Cross Road WC2 is ideal. At the *1520 AD Tudor Rooms* (Tel. 240 3979) in Swallow Street W1, one finds an amusing programme of items based on the year 1520 at the court of *Henry VIII. The Shakespeare's Feast* (Tel. 408 1001) in Blackfriars Lane EC4, offers a light-hearted tribute to England's famous playwright in an evening of excellent entertainment with Shakespearean characters, jugglers, jesters, magicians and duellists during a six-course feast.

Along the Victoria Embankment near Charing Cross there are several **Restaurant Ships** *('Wilfred', 'Hispaniola', 'Tattershall Castle'* and the *'Queenstern')* offering good food, wines and beers. The last-mentioned was built originally as a steamer in 1933. It now has two 90-cover restaurants, several bars, a private dining room for groups up to 50 and a small historical display area.

English Public Houses (probably around 6000 in London alone) are very popular with all classes of society and the *"local"* still dominates the tidal flow of the capital's drinking patterns. Some of the better known and traditional London pubs are as follows:

The Anchor (1 Bankside SE1 — Tel. 407 1577) is a historic riverside inn by the site of Shakespeare's Globe Theatre. Rebuilt in 1750 it has displays of Elizabethan objects found during renovation.

In the summer, life in the pubs extends to outside drinking.

Cittie of York (22 High Holborn WC1 — Tel. 242 7670) has probably the longest bar counter in Britain.

Clifton (96 Clifton Hill NW8 — Tel. 624 5233) has high ceilings, elegant wallpaper, stripped pine, bare boards, antique engravings and Art Nouveau metal work.

Dove Inn (19 Upper Mall W6 — Tel. 748 5405) is a 17th century pub with a fine terrace.

George Inn (off 77 Borough High Street SE1 — Tel. 407 2056) is the only surviving galleried pub in London. Rebuilt after the great Southwark fire of 1676. Dickens mentioned it in *"Little Dorrit"* and Shakespeare is said to have acted here.

Henry J. Bean's (195-197 King's Road SW3 — Tel. 352 9255) is now probably central London's best and most spacious terrace pub garden.

Hoop & Grapes (47 Aldgate High Street EC3 — Tel. 481 1375) is widely understood to be London's oldest pub.

A Thames Floating Pub

Ye Old Cheshire Cheese (Wine Office Court, off 145 Fleet Street EC4 — Tel. 353 6170) is famous with history going back to the 16th century. Its pudding is a famous speciality. Frequented by literary giants like Johnson and Dickens.

The Wells Tavern (Well Walk/Christchurch Hill NW3 — Tel. 794 5875) has armchairs, sofas, lots of Victorian engravings and cartoons, soft lighting and a relaxed atmosphere, thus making it extremely popular.

The Hampstead area (NW3) has 2 very interesting pubs associated with the famous highwayman — *Dick Turpin* - **Jack Straw's Castle** (Tel. 435 8885) and **Spaniard's Inn** (Tel. 455 3276).

Also in Hampstead is the **Old Bull & Bush** (Tel. 455 3685 & 458 4535) which dates from 1645. It is very popular with Londoners and Tourists and it has many film, TV and theatre stars as regulars.

Ye Olde Watling (29 Watling Street EC4 — Tel. 248 6235) was built in 1668 and then used as Wren's Office and hostel for builders during the construction of St. Paul's Cathedral.

Hence there is in London a wide variety of types and styles of pubs — riverside ones, pubs offering entertainment (eg. jazz), historic pubs, haunted pubs and pubs in hotels etc., pubs are seen everywhere and are ideal for visitors to mix with the locals.

London also has a great diversity of **night life** from jet set to smartly poor: *DISCOS* abound but some worth a special mention are the elegant and exclusive 'Tramps' (London SW1 — Tel. 734 3174) and '*Annabels*' (London W1 — Tel. 629 3558). '*Stringfellows*' (WC2 — Tel. 240 5534) and the '*Hippodrome*' (WC2 — Tel. 437 4311) are also well attended. The '*Cafe de Paris*' (W1 — Tel. 437 2036) with its live bands and the enormous disco at the *'Empire Ballroom'* (WC2 — Tel. 437 1446) are similarly very popular with Londoners and visitors. Also worth a mention are *'Samantha's'* (W1 — Tel. 734 6249), *'Maximus'* (WC2 — Tel. 734 4111) and *'Shaftesburys'* (W1 — Tel. 734 2017).

NIGHTCLUBS – The attraction of many night clubs is the cabaret or floor shows. Exciting nightspots, all centrally located, include the *'Stork Club'* (Tel. 734 3686), *'L'Hirondelle'* (Tel. 734 6666/1511), the *'Churchill'* (Tel. 408 0226), the *'Eve Club'* (Tel. 734 0879) and the *'Club De Luxe*' (Tel. 409 0822).

DINNER DANCE nightspots are also plentiful in London — and not just in the West End. Moreover, ethnic-type establishments catering for all tastes usually remain open to 3am. Superb evenings with good food and usually live music, at very reasonable prices, can be spent in places such as:

Barbarella's, 428 Fulham Road, SW6
Tel. 385 9434 and

47 Thurlow Street, SW7
Tel. 584 2000
Cleopatra, 146 Notting Hill Gate, W11
Tel. 229 7730
Concordia Notte, 29/31 Craven Road, W2
Tel. 402 4985
Costa Dorada, 47 & 55 Hanway Street, W1
Tel. 636 7139
Elysee, 13 Percy Street, W1
Tel. 636 4804
Gallipoli, Old Broad Street, EC2
Tel. 588 1922
Grecian, 27 Percy Street W1
Tel. 636 8913
Old Vienna, 94 New Bond Street, W1
Tel. 629 8716
Omar Khayyam, 177 Regent Street, W1
Tel. 437 3693
Rheingold Club, 361 Oxford Street, W1
Tel. 629 5343
Talk of London, Drury Lane, WC2
Tel. 491 7341
Villa dei Cesari, 135 Grosvenor Road, SW1
Tel. 828 7453
. . . the list is endless! . . .

TOPLESS, striptease clubs etc., for the more discerning individual are also provided by the capital. It has been rightly remarked that ". . . London by night may look dead but underneath the city is throbbing . . . lights are blazing and all tastes, pockets and fancies are fully catered for . . ."

For **THEATRE & CINEMA** lovers, London again claims to be at the top of the international list. The capital has enough of everything to satisfy the widest variety of tastes. In the West End alone (basically around Leicester Square) there are a fair number to choose from — most of them showing the latest releases. The West End again is the centre of the mainstream theatres with around 40 to choose from. Apart from their 6 evening performances every week (there are no shows on Sundays), the majority have matinees (afternoon ones) twice weekly. Full information about thea-

The Entrance to The London Palladium. By night the place becomes full of life and excitement. Plays and musicals are usually box office successes.

Above: Piccadilly is the centre of London's Night life. Nothing much has changed since the 60's when the photograph was taken.
Right: Soho by day: full of life and activity as this Soho Market shows. By night it all changes as the clubs with "sexy" shows would reveal!
Below: Dancers in one of London's famous nightspots (The Grecian Taverna).

185

Albert Hall where musical concerts, and many other events take place.

tres and productions can be found in the fortnightly and free 'London Theatre Guide'.

For **Classical Music** there are usually performances at the Barbican Hall, Royal Festival Hall, Wigmore Hall, Royal College of Music etc.

For **Opera** lovers there is the *'London Coliseum'* (St. Martin's Lane WC2 —Tel. 836 3131), the *Royal Opera House* (Covent Garden WC2 —Tel. 240 1066) and *Sadler's Well's* (Rosebery Avenue EC1 — Tel. 837 1672-3). There are other places but the above are centrally located and are well worth a visit.

There are also excellent facilities for **Rock Music** and **Jazz** lovers. The *Royal Albert Hall* (Tel. 589 8212) built in 1871, which holds over 5,000, hosts many **concerts.**

N.B.:

(1) Please book in advance for the more popular performances to avoid disappointment. Top of the bill for most visitors — and Londoners — are the glittering musicals and comedies. Top shows are booked well in advance. New film releases can also prove difficult to book.

(2) The easiest way to find **WHATS ON AND WHERE** from a very vast selection not only including all the above but also exhibitions, special events, festivals, lectures and night life, is to look in weekly magazines like *"What's On, "Where to Go", "City Limits", "This is London", "Time Out"* or in the national daily newspapers.

LONDON'S THEATRELAND

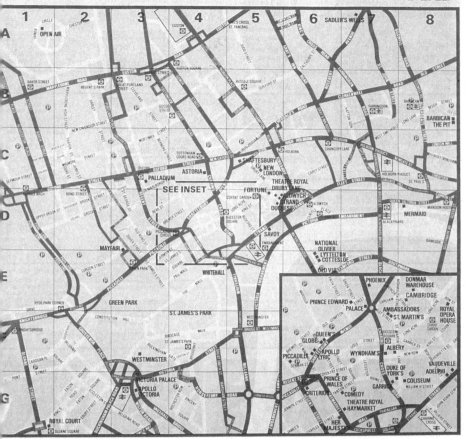

Above: Map of West End theatres. *Below left:* From the performance of Henceforward. *Below Right:* Theatre illuminated names. *(All Society of W.E. Theatres)*

St. Jame's Park

CHAPTER FIFTEEN

THE CAPITAL'S OPEN SPACES

DESPITE the fickleness of the British climate, Londoners have over the last few years, made a determined effort to turn the capital into an outdoor city, at least for the summer months. Visitors happily join in the throng at outdoor concerts, alternative entertainment in Covent Garden and at pavement cafes and pubs with open forecourts and gardens.

London's **PARKS** have always been recognised as one of its major assets. Through the year they provide an oasis of greenery and peace; in spring and summer they burst into colour. Five of London's nine spectacular and unique **ROYAL PARKS** are in the very heart of the capital and each has a special character of its own.

GREEN PARK is just to the north of Buckingham Palace and extends to Piccadilly. In 53 acres it features expanses of grass and trees. In Spring crocuses and daffodils abound. Queen's Walk opened in 1730, is named after Caroline, wife of George II, and is on the east side of the Park. In the days of Charles II the Park was often used for royal picnics.

ST. JAME'S PARK to the south of the Mall is larger with 93 acres of planted lawns and trees and an ornamental lake in the centre with a large number of water birds, including pelicans. The Park between the palaces of Whitehall and St. Jame's was laid out by Henry VIII in 1523 as a deer park and some of the trees date back to that time. In 1829 John Nash redesigned the park for George IV and incorporated the lake. This Park is one of the most attractive in London and the view of Westminster from the bridge over the lake is famous.

HYDE PARK was opened to the public in the early 1600s. The first football games, known as *"Hurling Matches"* were among the early pleasures of this open space, which soon became a fashionable haunt. Its most outstanding feature is undoubtedly the **Serpentine,** but it is the feeling of great space and freedom which characterises it. And, we must not forget **"SPEAKER'S CORNER"** at the Marble Arch end. This was the site of public hangings from c.1196 to c.1783, and is now a place where those with a message may exercise their right of free speech. Certainly well worth spending a few hours on a Sunday morning when large crowds usually gather to listen to "free expression".

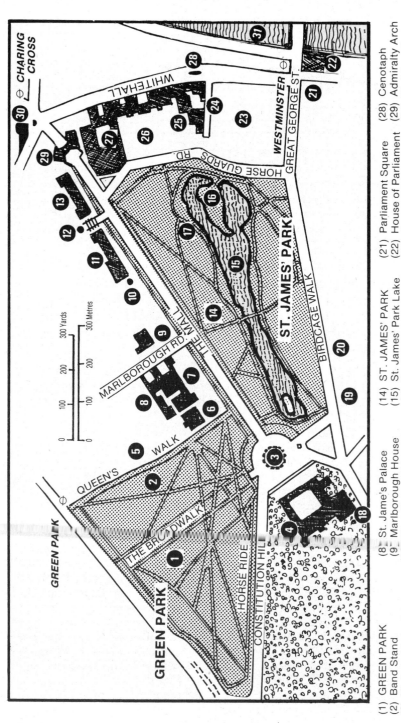

(1) GREEN PARK
(2) Band Stand
(3) Victoria Memorial
(4) BUCKINGHAM PALACE
(5) Spencer House
(6) Lancaster House
(7) Clarence House

(8) St. Jame's Palace
(9) Marlborough House
(10) King George Memorial
(11) Carlton House Terrace
(12) Duke of York Monument
(13) Mall Gallery & Institute
     of Contemporary Arts

(14) ST. JAMES' PARK
(15) St. James' Park Lake
(16) Duck Island
(17) The Cake House
(18) Green's Gallery
(19) Wellington's Barracks
(20) Guard's Chapel

(21) Parliament Square
(22) House of Parliament
(23) Government Offices
(24) Downing Street
(25) Treasury
(26) Horse Guards
(27) Admiralty

(28) Cenotaph
(29) Admiralty Arch
(30) Trafalgar Square
(31) River THAMES

KENSINGTON GARDENS
HYDE PARK

— Location Plan —

(1) MARBLE ARCH
(2) Speaker's Corner
(3) Victoria Gate
(4) Queen Anne's Alcove
(5) The Fountains
(6) Jenner Statue
(7) Lancaster Gate
(8) Spekes Monument
(9) Peter Pan Statue
(10) Statue of Physical Energy
(11) ROUND POND
(12) Elfin Oak
(13) Black Lion Gate
(14) Orme Square Gate
(15) Orangery
(16) Sunken Garden
(17) KENSINGTON PALACE
(18) William III Statue
(19) Band Stand
(20) Palace Gate
(21) Albert Memorial
(22) ALBERT HALL
(23) Alexandra Gate
(24) Surpentine Gallery
(25) The Temple
(26) Restaurant
(27) The Long Water
(28) Surpentine Bridge
(29) THE SURPENTINE
(30) Lido (Bathing Area)
(31) Prince of Wales Gate

(33) The Standing Dell Stone
(34) Boating House
(35) Royal Humane Society
(36) Ranger's Lodge
(37) POLICE STATION
(38) Hudson Memorial
(39) Bird Sanctuary
(40) Superintendent's Lodge
(41) The Ring Tea House
(42) Grosvenor Gate
(43) Curzon Gate
(44) Superintendent's Lodge
(45) Byron Statue
(46) Hyde Park Corner
(47) Wellington Museum
(48) Children's Playground

191

London's Parks are places of relaxation especially in sunny days.

KENSINGTON GARDENS date from the 17th century, when Kensington Palace was refurbished by William III. Kensington Gardens are separated from Hyde Park only by a road, but the difference in character is marked. It is more formal, more enclosed and gentle area than Hyde Park — it shares the Serpentine with it but here it is called the **"Long Water"**.

Amongst its other features are the **Albert Memorial**, designed by G. Scott and erected as a great monument to Queen Victoria's consort; the **"Flower Walk"** with its varied and colourful borders and **"Broad Walk"**, a handsome avenue of limes.

REGENT'S PARK, opened to the public in 1838, was named after the Prince Regent (Later George IV) who appointed J. Nash to design the layout, its approaches and a few houses within the Park itself. Regent's Park, is set apart from the other four Royal Parks in Central London and if the adjacent *Primrose Hill* is included in its area, it is, at 670 acres, the largest of the Central Parks.

Major landmarks of this Park are, a **large lake, Winfield House** (the home of the US Ambassador), the exotic **Queen Mary's Garden** (a lovely place of water, rock gardens, beautiful roses and overlapping trees) an **Open Air Theatre** (where performances of Shakespeare's plays are given in the summer); a **Mosque** (opened in 1977 is one of the largest outside Islamic countries and has a library and a school of calligraphy and a **Zoo**. The latter, the biggest in England was founded in 1829 and the complex includes an *Aquarium,* a *Pets Corner and Aviary,* an *Elephant House* and the open *Lion Terraces.* The Zoo is bounded on its far edge (north) by the **Regent's Canal.**

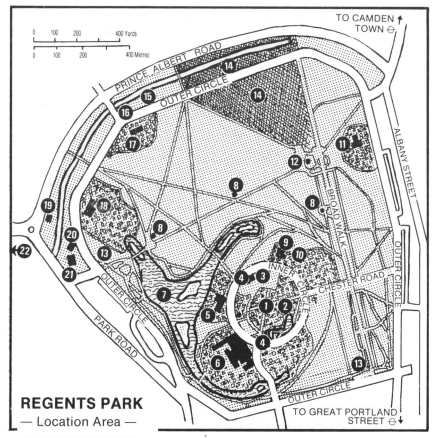

REGENTS PARK
— Location Area —

(1) MARY'S GARDENS
(2) Rose Gardens
(3) Open Air Theatre
(4) INNER CIRCLE
(5) The Holme
(6) Bedford College
    (University of London)
(7) Boating Lake
(8) Tea House
(9) St. John's Lodge
(10) Regents College
(11) St. Katherine's Lodge
(12) Bandstand
(13) Children's Playground
(14) LONDON ZOO
(15) Grand Union Canal
    (Regent's Canal)
(16) Macclesfield Bridge
(17) Regents Park College
(18) Winfield House
(19) Nuffield Foundations
(20) Hanover Lodge
(21) Mosque
(22) Lords Cricket House

at Regent's Park, Hyde Park, St. Jame's Park and in the **Embankment Gardens,** regular band concerts of the traditional kind are found at lunchtime or in the early evening, from June to August.

Battersea Park, on the south bank of the Thames is often used for major events (such as the *Easter Parade* which is a colourful display of scores of floats) and sports a glittering new *Japanese Pagoda.*

Holland Park, to the west, is a naturally wooded park with a local feel, a small collection of animals and its own theatre used for plays and music. But the best known of London's Open-Air Theatres is of course

193

at Regent's Park, where surrounded by tall trees, Shakespeare is on the programme from early June until late August.

Equally enchanting are the open-air concerts at **Kenwood Lake** on **Hampstead Heath**. English Heritage, which has taken over Kenwood from the Greater London Council (abolished 1986), is maintaining the concert programme which will run from June to August with jazz, pop and classical music. The National Trust are also planning a series of outdoor events in the summer at different venues. Phone the N.T. or Leisure Time for details *(see below)*.

Hampstead Heath with **Golders Hill, Parliament Hill** and **Kenwood,** forms a continuous stretch of more than 835 acres of park, woods and heath. There is a splendid view of parts of London from the *"Whitestone Pond"* on the north end of Heath Street which crosses the heath at its highest point.

TRADITIONAL Entertainment of a different kind is provided by London's *'buskers'* who can be seen in underground stations and at **Leicester Square.** They are at their very best in **Covent Garden** where there are regular performances at lunchtime and in the early evening, both under St. Paul's portico and in the Market itself. Even the City takes on an air of excitement during the *City of London Festival* when there is dancing in Paternoster Square (at other times as well), outside the Guildhall and at other locations.

Most London boroughs have their own festival or fair during the summer months — from Barnes to Lambeth and Southwark, Greenwich to Brent, there are local and ethnic festivities. Particularly interesting for visitors are the festivals at **Greenwich** (in June and August) with outdoor entertainment at the **Cutty Sark Gardens** and at **Richmond** with activities on the Green. The massive West Indian

Hampstead Heath, one of London's most popular parks.

Nottingham Hill Gate Carnival and the Greek & Cypriot Musical Festival, staged annually in Burgess Park, South London, are extremely interesting and for all the family.

A VISIT to London would not be complete without a **RIVER TRIP** at least from Westminster to the Tower. Upstream services to Kew, Richmond and Hampton Court operate through the summer (but check departures) and downstream services to Greenwich and the Thames Barrier operate frequently from Westminster, Charing Cross and Tower piers. In addition to the day time programme, there are evening cruises, with or without music or food.

London's **CANALS** can be explored on foot or with London Visitor and Convention Bureaus (LVCB's) handy guide *"Canal Walks"*, which includes six walks along the tow-paths in different parts of London. Canalboats offer a different view of these almost hidden waterways. For example, board at *Little Venice* or at *Camden Lock* and visit *London Zoo* at Regents Park with an inclusive ticket — i.e. admission to the Zoo plus your waterbus fare.

For further information: (use the **01** prefix if phoning from outside London)

LTBCB Information Service 730 3488/3450
National Trust 222 9251
English Heritage 734 6010

Part of Camden Lock waterway.

CHAPTER SIXTEEN

THE LONDON YEAR
Major Annual Events

This random selection includes events which are not in the London area and yet are an essential constituent of the Londoner's diary.

JANUARY

SALES — Usually prices are much lower in shops. Spend time and seek out the bargains which are found in all shops and departmental stores.

BOAT SHOW — held in Earls Court SW5. An international event for all boat enthusiasts.

FEBRUARY

CLOWN SERVICE — many clowns attend this service in full costume and traditional make-up. A free clown show is given.

GUN SALUTE — ACCESSION DAY — (6 February)

CHINESE NEW YEAR — Soho — W1 comes alive with decorations, streamers, and garlands (9 February).

MARCH

BOAT RACE — Cambridge and Oxford crews race from the University Stone. Putney, to Mortlake. An annual event since 1856.

CHELSEA ANTIQUES FAIR — Held at the Chelsea Old Town Hall SW3. A colourful event where bargain-seekers can be found.

APRIL

EASTER PARADE — a procession of around 80 floats, military bands, jazz bands and majorettes, Pearly Kings and Queens plus several well-known celebrities — Easter Weekend — Battersea Park SW11.

HARNESS HORSE PARADE — at the Inner Circle Regents Park NW1. Is a parade of London's working horses competing for prizes of rosettes, brass merit badges and prize cards.

GUN SALUTE — H.M. Queen's birthday (21 April) — Hyde Park.

MAY

CHELSEA FLOWER SHOW — held at The Royal Hospital, Chelsea SW3. Plants, flowers of all seasons, garden equipment, theme gardens and greenhouses are all on display.

F.A. CUP FINAL — Held at Wembley Stadium — A major and colourful sporting (soccer) event.

LONDON MARATHON — From Greenwich Park SE10 to Westminster Bridge SW1 — Annual 26-mile marathon through the streets of London — Attracts vast crowds.

JUNE

GUN SALUTE — Coronation Day (2 June) — Hyde Park

BEATING RETREAT — *Household Division* — Held at Horse Guards Parade SW1. It is a popular military display of marching and drilling bands with displays by mounted bands, trumpeters, massed bands pipes and drums. Some performances are given later in the evening by floodlight.

BEATING RETREAT — *Light (Royal) Division* — Held at Horse Guards Parade SW1 — Massed band display performed by a different Division each year, taking place a few days after the Household Division's Beating Retreat.

GUN SALUTE — *HRH The Duke of Edinburgh's Birthday* (10 June) — Hyde Park

TROOPING THE COLOUR — *The Queen's Birthday Parade.* This ceremony celebrates the Sovereign's official birthday. A very colourful event (see Royal Displays).

DERBY DAY — Held at Epsom, Surrey. A festival of racing featuring the Derby, one of the greatest horse races in the world for 3-year-old colts and fillies. A funfair also sets up on Epsom Downs for a week.

ROYAL ASCOT — Held at Ascot Racecourse, Berkshire. This famous race meeting, attracts the cream of "Society" especially on the famous *'Gold Cup'*. It is attended by the Queen and the Royal Family who drive from Windsor each day in open carriages. The Royal Procession goes down the course each day at 2pm before the first race at 2.30pm

ALL ENGLAND LAWN TENNIS CHAMPIONSHIPS (Wimbledon) — held at the All England Club, Wimbledon SW19. Start around the last week of June and finish during the first week of July. Top players from all over the world assemble here for these championships to try for what are perhaps the most coveted and prestigious titles of the tennis world.

HENLEY ROYAL REGATTA — Usually held end June/beginning July. This famous international rowing regatta has been held annually since 1839. It is rowed on a course upstream, against the current, running for 1 mile, 550 yards from Temple Island to just below Henley bridge.

Guards on parade, a rehearsal for the Trooping of The Colour.

THE ROYAL TOURNAMENT

— held at Earls Court Centre SW5. It is an action-packed spectacular (around 15 days) presented by the Armed Forces in aid of service Charities and the programme combines pomp, colour, pageantry and lots of excitement. H.M. The Queen and other senior members of the Royal Family are patrons of the Tournament and attend performances to take the Salute.

HENRY WOOD PROMENADE CONCERTS

— held from around the middle of July for 8 weeks, at the Royal Albert Hall SW7. The "PROMS" were founded in 1895 by Sir Henry Wood and are perhaps the most famous concert series in the world.

DOGGETT'S COAT & BADGE RACE

— From London Bridge to Chelsea, held in late July. This famous race for single sculls over a $4\frac{1}{2}$ mile course, was founded in 1714 by Thomas Doggett, a popular Irish comedian.

CITY OF LONDON FESTIVAL

— Usually for 3 weeks, is a colourful event. It captures the essence of tradition, history and entertainment with a dazzling selection of performers with music ranging from classical to jazz.

AUGUST

GUN SALUTE

— *Queen Mother's Birthday* (4 August) at Hyde Park.

LONDON RIDING HORSE PARADE

— held at Rotten Row, Hyde Park W2 at the beginning of the month. Commencing at 2pm this competition selects the best turned out horse and rider. The overall winner, the Supreme Champion, is awarded the much-coveted Moss Bros perpetual Challenge Cup, and each entrant reaching a satisfying standard is given an Award of Merit Rosette.

FAIRS

— Held in some parks around London. Lots of fun with games, machines to ride on, stalls of food etc.

NOTTING HILL CARNIVAL

— is held on August Bank Holiday, Sunday (end of the month) and Monday and continues into the early hours. Originally conceived as a children's carnival in 1965 it has become a popular West Indian event with carnival-goes dancing and singing together in the streets around Notting Hill and Ladbroke Grove W8.

SEPTEMBER

CHELSEA ANTIQUES FAIR

— held at the *Chelsea Old Town Hall SW3*. It is a major antiques fair with exhibits predating 1830.

HORSEMAN'S SUNDAY

— held at the Church of *St. John & St. Michael, Hyde Park Crescent W2*. Horses assemble from 11.30am at the church until the commencement of the Service at 12 noon, which is taken by a vicar on horseback. It lasts around 25 minutes and is followed by a procession of the horses singly and in pairs to receive commemorative rosettes, ending at 1pm. The horses then continue into Hyde Park for an outing on the $2\frac{1}{2}$ miles of riding tracks.

OCTOBER

PEARLY HARVEST FESTIVAL SERVICE

— held at *St. Martin-in-the-Fields WC2*. This is the best occasion to see Pearly Kings and Queens. The altar and pulpit are

During the Summer, London enjoys many open air activities and musical events. The picture shows open air music at the South Bank.

arranged with the fruit of the earth and a Pearly King reads one of the Lessons (service around 3pm) while the congregation sings the hymns of the harvest season.

HORSE OF THE YEAR SHOW
— held at the *Wembley Arena,* Wembley Middlesex. It is a popular horse show which features the best show jumpers from Europe and the UK.

TRAFALGAR DAY PARADE —
held fittingly at Trafalgar Square WC2/SW1 — the procession forms up on Horse Guards Parade at 10.15am and marches to the Square. Nelson's great sea victory at the *Battle of Trafalgar* on 21 October 1805 is celebrated by this colourful ceremony held on the Sunday nearest to the date. It ends with Nelson's Prayer and the National Anthem.

NOVEMBER

STATE OPENING OF PARLIAMENT (either late October or early November). It is a colourful procession of the Queen from Buckingham Palace to the Houses of Parliament.

REMEMBRANCE SUNDAY CEREMONY — held at the Cenotaph Memorial, Whitehall SW1. A memorial day for all 3 Services (RAF, NAVY and ARMY) and Allied Forces who gave their lives in the two World Wars. H.M. The Queen arrives at 10.59am; then a two minute silence at 11am is heralded and ended by a gun fired from Horse Guards Parade. The Queen, followed by others, then lays a wreath at the Cenotaph.

LORD MAYOR'S SHOW —The tradition of the Lord Mayor's Procession through the streets of the City of London dates from the 14th century and on this day he rides in the Lord Mayors Coach

Lord Mayor's Show — The most colourful in the "City" and one of the most popular in Greater London.

heading for the Law Courts for the final declaration of office (arriving at the Royal Courts of Justice at 11.45am; the trip taking exactly an hour). Many colourful floats and military bands take part in this famous event.

LONDON TO BRIGHTON VETE-RAN CAR RUN — Hyde Park to Madeira Drive, Brighton on the south coast. Enthusiasts from all over the world prime their veteran cars to take part in the gruelling run which starts between 8 and 9am to follow the A23 road to Brighton where they begin to arrive at around 10.45am. Usually takes place on the 1st Sunday of the month.

DECEMBER

WORLD TRAVEL MARKET — Usually held at Olympia W14. An excellent opportunity for everyone to see the world's beauty spots.

Regent Street Christmas Lights attract thousands of shoppers and visitors. The designs change every year.

Tour operators do their utmost over 5 days to explain what their respective countries have to offer — An exhibition held at the very beginning of December.

CHRISTMAS LIGHTS & TREES

— The traditional Christmas Lights are switched on in Oxford Street and Regent Street (mid-November) Christmas trees are erected at Bond Street, Covent Garden and Trafalgar Square, the latter being presented to the nation by the City of Oslo, Norway in mid-December. Carols are sung around the Tree in Trafalgar Square by groups in aid of many charities each evening until Christmas Eve.

Christmas illuminations normally continue until 6 January

For all the above and many other events you may telephone 01-730 3488 or 730 3450 for exact dates and times.

201

CHAPTER SEVENTEEN

OUTER LONDON
History
Attractions

FROM little known **Barking Abbey Ruins** in the East to famous **Hampton Court Palace** in the West and from the **RAF Museum** in the North to **Sutton's Whitehall** in the deep South, there are places to interest visitors in all London boroughs — a selection is listed below:

NORTH LONDON

BARNET lies to the north and north west, some 10 miles from central London and is one of the largest London boroughs. It is bounded on the west by the Edgware Road, the old Roman Watling Street. Roman finds indicate they had built settlements in the area. Worth noting is the fact that the *Battle of Barnet,* which was to be the turning point in the Wars of the Roses was fought in the **Hadley Highstone** area to the north of the borough in 1471.

In Barnet are located several quality museums. The **Barnet Museum** includes military artefacts and photographs of the area. The **Church Farm House Museum,** close to the Watford Way A41 and ⊖ Hendon Central, is a 17th century building set in a small garden. Regular exhibitions throughout the year on a variety of subjects are held there.

The **RAF Museum** illustrates the history of the RAF and its forerunners; *The Battle of Britain* Museum commemorates the battle of 1940-41; and the Bomber Command Museum is dedicated to the aircrew who died in the Second World War 1939-45. Under one roof (at Grahame Park Way — close to M1 & A41 ⊖ Colindale, Hendon NW9), they cover Britain's RAF and aviation history. Also in the borough is the **British Library Newspaper Collection** (Colindale NW9) which holds daily, weekly and provincial newspapers as well as foreign and Commonwealth ones; the daily collection dates back to 1801.

Nearby **ENFIELD** lies 11 miles to the north and north east of central London. Archaeological finds in the area provide evidence of Roman and Saxon settlements. The Domesday Survey, or simply "Domesday" (it is a record in two volumes of the great survey of England executed for William the Conqueror in 1086), records two manors, one in Enfield and the other at **Edmonton.** Until the 13th century Enfield was covered by large forests where the wealthy came to hunt.

Of special interest here are **Forty Hall and Park** — a fine example of Jacobean architecture. Now an art gallery and museum containing 17th and 18th century furniture, pictures, ceramics, glass, metalwork, maps, local history and temporary loan exhibitions. The Park consists of partly wooded grounds, with rose gardens and lakes. The Forty Hall estate runs into **Whitewebbs Park** covering 300 acres. It has an 18-hole public golf course.

Also of great interest is **Trent Park** with its 412 acres of park and woodland offering a nature trail, blind trail, pets enclosure and water garden. And, there is **Picketts Lock Centre** *(off Montague Road – north of the North Circular),* one of the largest leisure centres in south East England.

HARINGEY's major centres are **Wood Green, Tottenham, Hornsey, Muswell Hill, Highgate** and **Archway.** Wood Green is at the heart of the borough and boasts a large shopping centre *(⊖ Wood Green)* and the famous *Haringey Athletics Club (⊖ Finsbury Park).* Highgate derives its name from the *"tollgate"* which stood at the top of the hill.

Of special interest is the **Bruce Castle Museum** *(Nr Lordship Lane)* which houses exhibitions on postal and local history. The building also contains the *Middlesex Regimental Museum.* At the famous **Alexandra Palace and Park** *(⊖ Wood Green)* there are exhibitions, sports events and concerts. Park facilities include boating lake, children's playground, conservation area etc. There are Fairs at Bank Holidays and scores of exhibitions and conferences.

Tottenham is the centre of one of the top football teams **Tottenham Hotspurs.**

The London Borough of **ISLINGTON** borders on the City and the boroughs of Hackney, Haringey and Camden. Islington has many fine churches, memorials, squares and attractive canalside walks. It also has lively and colourful street markets.

It is interesting to record that the Domesday Day Book records Islington as a small settlement within the Great Forest of Middlesex. The area was largely rural

Famous people associated with the borough include radicals like Marx, Lenin and Garibaldi. Literary figures include Charles and Mary Lamb, George Orwell and Evelyn Waugh; the area has also Dickensian associations.

Historic Buildings abound in Islington: **Charterhouse** *(Charterhouse Square EC1 – ⊖ Barbican),* derives its name from Chartreuse in France where the Carthusian order of Monks was founded. The Clerkenwell Charterhouse was founded by *Sir Walter de Manny* in 1350 but from 1545-1611 the building became a palace. In 1611 Thomas Sutton purchased it and founded the modern Charterhouse as a hostel for elderly men and a school for boys (which moved to Godalming in Surrey in 1872). The original building dates mainly from the 16th century.

Clerk's Wells *(14-16 Farringdon Lane EC1 – ⊖ Farringdon),* is a medieval well, discovered in 1924 and believed to be over 1000 years old. It gives its name to **Clerkenwell.** The well has been restored and now has a viewing gallery and a small display of its history. **Marx Memorial Library** *(Marx House, 37A Clerkenwell Green EC1 – ⊖ Farringdon),* is housed in a building dating from the 1730's which was once a radical working man's club and the home of the 20th century press, the first socialist press in Britain. Lenin printed his journal *'Iskra'* here. The Library, founded in 1933, contains 1000's of books, pamphlets and periodicals relating to all aspects of socialism.

The Library and Museum of the **Order of St. John** *(St. John's Gate, St. John's Lane EC2 – ⊖ Farringdon),* housed in an early 16th century gatehouse, illustrates the history of the Order and its foundations.

Wesley's House and Chapel *(47 City Road EC1 – ⊖ Old Street)* is the original 18th century house in which *John Wesley* lived and died. His tomb is in the small garden behind the church. The **Museum of Methodism** housed in the crypt of Wesley's Chapel illustrates the development of Methodism from the 18th century to the present day.

Whittington Stone *(Highgate Hill N19 – ⊖ Archway)* marks the spot where *Dick Whittington* is supposed to have heard the Bow Bells calling him to *"turn again"*. He was Lord Mayor of London three times. The sculpture of Whittington's black cat was added in 1964.

Islington is also honoured to house the world-famous **Arsenal Football Club** *(Avenell Road N1 – ⊖ Arsenal).* The club originally based at Woolwich was formed by workers at the munitions factory there. The *"Gunners"* moved to Highbury in 1913 and are now London's most successful club — Cup Winners in 1987.

Close to central London is the borough of **CAMDEN,** boasting many of north London's key visitor attractions as it includes **Hampstead** and **Highgate.** Camden's cultural attractions include the world famous **British Museum** *(see Museums section),* several West End theatres and many cinemas. Among its major places of interest are: **The Freud Museum** which contains exhibits and restored rooms in *Sigmund Freud's* London home, furniture, extensive library and other antiquities.

Burgh House, a Grade I listed building

of the Queen Anne period housing the *Hampstead Museum* of local history. Art exhibitions, lectures, concerts and other events are held here.

Fenton House *(⊖ Hampstead),* a William and Mary style house is owned by the National Trust. It contains the Benton Fletcher collection of keyboard instruments and the Binning collection of porcelain and furniture. This collection is priceless.

Kenwood House, Iveagh Bequest *(Hampstead Lane),* has a fine collection of English and foreign paintings including works by Vermeer, Rembrandt, Gainsborough and Reynolds plus the Hull Grundy collection of jewellery. There are summer evening concerts by the lakeside and the grounds include gardens with a lime avenue and herbaceous borders.

Keats House *(between ⊖ Hampstead and ⊖ Belsize Park),* has a collection of letters, manuscripts and relics of Keats (he lived here from 1818 to 1820) and his contemporaries. It is the headquarters of the *Keats-Shelley Memorial Association.* Occasional poetry readings and musical evenings take place.

Lauderdale House is the old Manor House of Waterlow Park *(Highgate Hill)* and parts of the building date from 1580. Nell Gwynn is said to have stayed here. It is now used for exhibitions, concerts, art and craft demonstrations.

Hampstead Heath, 825 acres of heathland is a favourite leisure spot for Londoners. Within it are the grounds of Kenwood House. Facilities on the heath include fishing, model boat sailing, athletics track, horse-riding and swimming in three ponds. The Heath offers magnificent views over the city. Fairs are held there during Bank Holidays.

Waterlow Park *(Highgate Hill)* is a 27 acre park with three ponds, aviary and recreation facilities plus a scented section for the blind. **Highgate Cemetery** was founded in 1838 and is now a combination of burial ground and wildlife. The western section is maintained by the *"Friends of Highgate"*, and has a fascinating array of tombs and statues. The eastern section has a tomb of *Karl Marx* (a colossal statue sculptured by L. Bradshaw) and many other literary figures including George Eliot.

The Regent's Canal and its tow path are one of Camden's major attractions. The tow path, which in recent years has undergone many improvements, is open to walkers; it is now possible to walk for many miles along the canal passing some familiar as well as unfamiliar landmarks of a bygone age.

Camden Lock (⊖ *Camden Town)* is a unique centre for crafts, antiques, bric-a-brac and second hand clothing. Also a starting point for a Regent's Canal trip.

Art exhibitions are held regularly at the **Camden Arts Centre** and one of the major events in the borough is the annual *Camden Arts Festival* – a festival of dance, music, opera and jazz — held in early spring in various venues.

EAST LONDON

HACKNEY, covers an area which stretches from Liverpool Street in the south to Stamford Hill in the north and from the River Lea in the east to Finsbury Park in the west. Its proximity to the Roman City of London accounts for the Roman settlements in the borough. Traces of the Anglo-Saxon legacy survive in many of the borough's place names and in the 17th century the area became famous for its inns and many pleasure gardens.

In the borough, The **Geffrye Museum** named after Robert Geffrye Lord Mayor of London in 1685 *(Kingsland Road)* has a series of period rooms from 1600 to 1939 and costume galleries. The churches of **St. Augustine, St. Leonard's** and **St. Mary's Old Church** are interesting and should be mentioned. The former is said to have been built by the *Knights Templars,* the first known place of worship in Hackney. All that survives is the tower which dates from before 1292. St. Leonard's was founded in the 9th century. Rebuilt in 1740 it became known as the *"Actor's Church";* Shakespeare's friend James Burbage (d. 1597) and his son Richard (d. 1619), are buried here. In the churchyard, laid out as the garden, are the old stocks and whipping post. St. Mary's Old Church was rebuilt around 1563 and is a good example of an Elizabethan church.

To the east of central London lies **WALTHAM FOREST.** The borough is rich in history and evidence suggests that it was inhabited from prehistoric times. The Roman road from London crossed the **River Lea** at **Old Ford** and passed through **Leytonstone.** By the 18th century the area became a country retreat for London's wealthy. They built large mansions here but very few of these survive today. Of interest are **Queen Elizabeth's Hunting Lodge** *(Rangers Road – Epping Forest),* a timber framed hunting grandstand built for Henry VIII, now a museum holding displays of wildlife and history of Epping Forest; **The Vestry House Museum** *(*⊖ Walthamstow Central) containing a reconstructed Victorian parlour and police cell, the Bremer car and exhibits on local history —

domestic life, costume, crafts and industry; the **William Morris Gallery** *(Forest Road ⊖ Walthamstow Central)*, a mid-18th century house containing a collection of decorative art.

Two churches, those of **All Saints** and **St. Mary's,** were founded in the 12th century and since restored are fine examples of the early English style.

The 6,000 acre **Epping Forest** is now managed by the *City of London Corporation* for the enjoyment of the public and conservation of wildlife.

Within the borough of **TOWER HAMLETS** there are many historic churches and pubs, interesting museums, a rich industrial heritage and fine river and canal walks. Much of its *"cockney character"* thrives, even today, in many street markets.

Prehistoric settlements existed here, and much is known of the area's Roman history. Two former Roman roads traverse the borough, the **Roman Road** and the **Whitechapel Road.**

Places of interest include the **Bethnal Green Museum of Childhood** *(⊖ Bethnal Green)* which displays, in a handsome iron and glass building, a fine collection of dolls, toys, model theatres, children's costumes, wedding dresses, and a 19th century European decorative and Spitafields silks, which were at one time the main industry of the area.

The **Whitechapel Art Gallery,** founded in 1901 and recently renovated contains a wide range of temporary exhibitions of modern art.

The borough contains several parks as well — part of the Lee Valley Leisure Park, Mile End Park and the 217 acre Victoria Park. Tower Hamlets also has many urban farms which are worth a visit.

The area is also famous for its street markets which attract large crowds:

Columbia Road (for flowers and plants), **Petticoat Lane** (general goods and clothing), **Roman Road** (general goods) **Whitechapel Waste** (general goods) and **Billingsgate Market,** London's principal wholesale fish market.

Further east is **NEWHAM,** lying four miles to the east of the City of London. In pre-Roman times *"Hamme"* covered an area which almost corresponded to the present-day borough. The Domesday Book survey records three manors and nine water mills — commemorated today in some of the borough's street names.

By the 17th century important houses were being built here for wealthy city merchants. Although heavily bombed during the Second World War, the area still retains many of its historic churches, buildings and fine examples of industrial architecture.

Today, the docklands in Newham are undergoing major redevelopment and in October 1987, *Stolport* – an airport for short landing and take off aircraft — was opened at the Royal Docks.

Two Museums are worth a visit. The **Passmore Edwards Museum** contains a nice collection illustrating the local history, geology, archaeology and natural history of Essex. It also displays a collection of locally-produced Bow porcelain. The history of the *Great Eastern Railway,* with a reconstructed booking office and platform canopy can be wondered at the **North Woolwich Old Station Railway Museum.**

Apart from the churches that can be admired (such as **All Saints** which was built in the 12th century and **St. Mary Magdalene,** a Grade I listed building mainly Norman and without aisles), the area has several Mills. **Abbey Mills Pumping Station,** is a highly ornate Victorian pumping

Above Left: Highgate Cemetery. *Right:* The interior of Kenwood House which houses an Art collection. *Below left:* Usnisavijaya — Tibetan Goddess of Holy Life from the Horniman Museum & Library. *Right:* One of Outer London's summer ethnic events — Cypriot festival at Burgess Park.

station. *"Venetian Gothic"* in style, it has almost cathedral-like proportions complete with towers and cupolas. It was designed by Bazalgette and Cooper and built between 1865-68 to house 8 beam engines. N.B. Visits by arrangement with the Thames Water Authority (Tel. 01-534 6717).

Three Mills Conservation Area is one of the finest collections of waterside buildings in London set against an industrial backdrop and England's largest surviving tidal mills complex. Two of the mills remain. There are plans to develop it into a working museum.

Continuing eastwards is **BARKING** and **DAGENHAM.** The Roman road from London to Colchester crosses the borough at *Chadwell Heath.* Barking and Dagenham were amongst the earliest Anglo-Saxon settlements in Essex; it is from this that the borough takes its modern name.

Among the historic Houses are **Eastbury House,** the only surviving 16th century medium-sized manor house in Barking. The 3-storey red-brick building is owned by the National Trust and is the headquarters of *Barking Arts Council.* **The Valence House Museum** is a 17th century timber framed and plastered manor house on a partly moated site. It contains a small archaeological collection of human artefacts, local topographical paintings and maps and collections of the Fanshawe family portraits by Lely, Dobson, Kneller and others.

The Barking Abbey Ruins can also be seen. Its reputed founder was Erkenwald, afterwards bishop of London, who founded *Chertsey Abbey* for Monks, with himself as abbot, and Barking Abbey (circa 670) for nuns, with his sister Ethelberga as its first abbess. By the 10th century it had become a strict Benedictine Nunnery and one of the most important in the country. Following the dissolution in 1539 most of the Abbey buildings were destroyed. Remnants of the original structure can be seen in the grounds of the 13th century St. Margaret Parish Church; these include the Curfew or Fire Bell Gate rebuilt around 1460 (not open to the public), and the North-East Gate. St. Margaret Parish Church was built within the Abbey precincts. Some of the Norman masonry from the Abbey seems to have been re-used in the outer north aisle of the church itself. It was here that on 21 December 1762 Captain James Cook, the circumnavigator, married Elizabeth Batts of Barking.

SOUTH OF THE RIVER

In South-East London is the historic borough of **SOUTHWARK.** It stretches from the River Thames in the north to Dulwich in the south and includes within the boundaries **Bermondsey, Camberwell, Dulwich, Herne Hill, Peckham, Rotherhithe** and **Walworth.** Areas like Camberwell, Peckham and Dulwich developed as separate villages and hamlets which grew in the 19th century as they became fashionable with wealthy city merchants.

From early Roman times Southwark *(meaning specifically the settlement by London Bridge)* has played an important part in the capital's history. The area's strategic position on the River Thames made it a gateway between the city and ports and towns of Sussex and Kent across the Old London Bridge which was until 1750 the only bridge across the Thames in the city centre.

In the Middle Ages bishops and abbots resided here. Important monasteries were founded including **St. Mary Overie** and **Bermondsey Abbey.** St. Mary Overie survived the dissolution of the monasteries by becoming a parish church and later Southwark Cathedral in 1905. Nothing remains of Bermondsey Abbey. In Clink Street stood **Winchester House** built in 1109 as the London residence of the bishops of London. Today only the Rose Window of the great hall remains.

Southwark was also famous for its inns, which grew to serve the many travellers. In *"The Canterbury Tales"* Chaucer mentions the **"Tabard Inn"** as the starting point of the pilgrims journey to Canterbury. Among the historic inns which have survived are **The George** in Borough High Street, the last surviving galleried inn in London, rebuilt in 1676; **"The Anchor"** in Bankside which has associations with Samuel Johnson; and the **"Mayflower"** in Rotherhithe dating from the 17th century and said to have connections with the ship of the same name.

Apart from Samuel Johnson other celebrated literary figures have connections with the area e.g. *Charles Dickens,* who drew on his knowledge of the area as a, child in several works including *"Oliver Twist"* and *Little Dorrit".*

Places of interest in the borough include Museums, Historic Ships, Parks and Gardens, Cathedrals, Churches, Art Galleries, Markets etc. The **Brunel Engine House,** is a boiler and engine house used during the construction of the world's first underwater tunnel. The **Cumming Museum** *(Walworth Road)* houses Roman, medieval and post medieval finds, items associated with Dickens and Michael Faraday, old dairy equipment and the art work of George Timworth. Also objects illustrating superstitious beliefs from the turn of the century. The **Imperial War Museum** *(Lambeth Road, SE1 – ⊖ Lambeth North)* will be discussed in more detail under the section *"London's Museums".*

The **Livesey Museum** includes changing exhibitions of local and general interests. The **London Dungeon** *(28-34 Tooley St., SE1 – ⊖London Bridge)* is again discussed under another chapter — see index. The **Operating Theatre,** restored in 1822, is the only 19th century operating theatre in England. Exhibits on the history of surgery and herbal medicine.

The **Shakespeare Globe Museum,** exhibits Elizabethan theatre history from 1550-1643 with models and replicas of the Globe and Cockpit playhouses. Lectures and workshops for booked groups.

Historic ships include the World War II cruiser **HMS Belfast** and the **Kathleen and May** — the last remaining wooden three-masted topsail schooner. A National Maritime Museum exhibition on board the 86-year old ship covers all aspects of the coasting trade and the history of the ship. Important open-spaces in the borough include **Burgess Park** and **Dulwich Park.** The former *(Albany Road SE5 – Tel. 703 3911)* was planed to enhance a very urban area, and owes its prominence to *David Sadler MBE,* a world authority on flowers and plants. Burgess Park includes nature areas with wild flower mixtures, lake area with fishing, sailing and canoeing, greenhouse (giving information about indoor plants, window boxes etc)., concert area hosting a variety of local and ethnic events, adventure playground, childrens events, exhibitions, mobile zoo, sports facilities etc. Dulwich Park in London SE21 also has many recreational facilities; also a boating lake, aviary and a Tree Trail.

There are also two major cathedrals in Southwark. **St. Georges Cathedral** (Roman Catholic) in Westminster Bridge SE1, was designed by *A.W. Pugin* and consecrated in 1848. Bombed in 1941, sections of the original buildings have been incorporated the new one which was erected in 1958. **Southwark Cathedral** (Church of England) became a Cathedral in 1905. It is believed that a church has been standing on this site since 606. It was built by the Augustinians and the choir and retrochoir date from the 13th century. Although heavily restored in the 1830's some Norman work survives. Interesting monuments and tombs include a plaque to Shakespeare's brother Edmund. There is also the Harvard Memorial Chapel in memory of John Harvard the founder of the American University who was born in the parish.

There are also several art and picture galleries in the area. **Bankside Gallery** is the home of the Royal Society of Painters in Watercolours and The Royal Society of Painters — Etchers and Engravers. The **Dulwich Picture Gallery** has around 300 pictures on view in 13 rooms. It includes works by Rubens, Rembrant, Van Dyck and others. The **North Peckham Civic Centre Exhibition Gallery** has exhibitions by local artists, a library and a theatre. The **South London Art Gallery** houses around 9 temporary exhibitions per year and has collections of 19th and 20th century artists.

Southwark also hosts several markets: **Borough Market** is the oldest municipal fruit and vegetable and flower market in Britain. **East Street Market** (always crowded, in East St. Walworth), specialises in general goods, clothes, bric-a-brac, and plants. **The New Caledonian Antiques Market** deals with dealers only.

The borough of **LEWISHAM** lies 6 miles to the south east of Central London. Theatres in the area include the *Lewisham Theatre* in Catford and the *Albany Empire* fringe theatre in Deptford. Two museums are worth visiting: The **Horniman Museum and Library** *(London Road, Forest Hill, SE23)* is an ethnological museum dealing with the study of man and his environment. There is also a musical instrument collection. The **Local History Centre** is a fine 18th century manor house containing local archives. There are also regular exhibitions on aspects of local history.

The borough also has many open spaces. The **Beckenham Place Park** contains large areas of attractive woodland and also an 18th century mansion (with nature centre) soon to become the home of the Mander and Mitchensan Theatre collection. There is also an 18-hole public golf course.

The London Borough of **LAMBETH** stretches from the south bank of the Thames to the suburban area of **Streatham** and **Norwood**. Within the borough's boundaries are several attractions, the most historic being **Lambeth Palace** *(Lambeth Palace Road)* which has been the London Home of the Archbishop of Canterbury for seven centuries (the Palace is not open to the public). Also within Lambeth are the *South Bank Complex,* comprising The **National Theatre,** The **National Film Theatre,** The **Royal Festival Hall,** the **Museum of the Moving Image** and the **Hayward Gallery;** the **Oval Cricket Ground** and

County Hall, the former headquarters of the abolished Greater London Council.

Four museums are worth visiting; The **Imperial War Museum** will be dealt with under "Museums". The **London Taxi Museum** in Brixton Road SW9 is a small museum housing nine early examples of London taxi cabs from 1907. The Museum of **Garden History (St. Mary at Lambeth** — Lambeth Palace Road, SE1) is a 17th century botanical garden with many period and rare plants introduced into the country by the *Tradescants* father and son. John Tradescant (the father) was Charles I's gardener; the church is owned by the Tradescant Trust. It retains its 14th century tower and was restored in 1851-52. Three generations of Tradescants, as well as *William Bligh* (1817) of the Mutiny of the *"Bounty"* are buried in the churchyard. The **Soseki Museum** of London (80b The Chase SW4) is a private house now converted into a museum and devoted to *Soseki Natsume,* one of the distinguished Japanese novelists, who lived in 81 The Chase for two years.

BROMLEY lies some 15 miles from central London and is the largest of the London boroughs. It offers a blend of town and country and has many acres of parkland and open spaces. Settlements in the area date back to the Iron Age — finds were discovered at **Orpington** and **Keston Common.** The Romans also left their mark. And, many of the boroughs' ancient manor houses survived until the 17th century.

Places of interest include the following:

Chislehurst Caves, said to date from Roman times are 22 miles of caves *(chalk).* There are lamplight tours.

Bromley Museum houses archaeological exhibits from early stone age, Roman and Saxon sites, Victorian relics, geology and some ethnography.

Darwin Museum was the home of *Charles Darwin* for 40 years. Includes exhibits and Evolution Exhibition, gardens and *"Sandwalk".*

Bromley has over 120 parks, commons and open spaces. **Crystal Palace Park** provides a zoo, pony rides, boating lake, cafeteria, adventure playground, sports pitches, 1 o'clock club for children, manmade island (with models of giant prehistoric animals) and summer concerts. There are tours every second Sunday in the month of the Crystal Palace Foundation and Park. It also includes the *National Sports Centre,* an international stadium where many national and international events (e.g. swimming) are held.

BEXLEY, 13½ miles south-east from central London, has thousands of acres of open space, much of it in the Green Belt. This is a residential borough which developed between 1918 and 1940 to provide housing for the influx of workers to London. Earliest records of the name *Bexley* date back to 814, although archaeological discoveries suggest Stone Age, Bronze Age, Iron Age and Roman settlements.

Places of interest within the borough are the following:

The Silk Printing Works (since 1829) in Crayford, also mill shop selling silk items. **Erith Library** is a local museum illustrating the history of Erith and the development of its industry. **Hall Place** in *Bourne Road,* Bexley is a Tudor-Jacobean mansion, with museum and exhibitions of fine rose rock, herb and peat gardens and conservatory. There are occasional organ recitals on the historic "England" organ. The **Red House** was built in 1860 for *William Morris* who lived here for 5 years. It is a Gothic, two storey building retaining the original Morris decorations. **Lesnes Abbey Woods** contains the ruins of a 12th century Abbey and is a large wooded park with nature trail, orienteering course, geological site and a cafe. Two churches, **St. John** in Erith and **St. Paulinus** in Crayford date from the 12th century and **St. Mary the Virgin** from the 13th — the latter, although restored in the 19th century still retains its typically Kentish shingled spire.

GREENWICH, once known as the *"gateway"* to London, lies on the south bank of the Thames about 5 miles to the east from Trafalgar Square. The borough is rich in maritime history and has an outstanding architectural heritage with many fine parks and open spaces.

The range of attractions in Greenwich needs little introduction — all are discussed in other chapters. These include the **Royal Naval College,** the **National Maritime Museum,** the **Old Royal Observatory,** the **Royal Naval College,** the **Ranger's House** at Blackheath, the **Royal Artillery Regiment Museum** etc. Its most recent attraction is the **Thames Barrier** at Woolwich, opened in 1984. Also worth mentioning are **Macartney House** in Blackheath, described by General Edward Wolfe in the 1750's as "the prettiest situated house in England"; **Charlton House** in Charlton built c.1610; and **St. Luke's Church** also in Charlton and built in 1630. It is the burial place of Spencer Percival, the only British PM to be assassinated.

The outer borough of **SUTTON** is some 11 miles to the south west of Central London. The area has a rich historical past. Archaeological finds suggest that it was inhabited many thousands of years ago. The Saxons and the Romans also built settlements here.

Two Historic Houses are worth mentioning: **Little Holland House** was made and designed by *Frank Dickinson* (1874-1961) artist and craftsman and follower of the Arts and Crafts movement. **Whitehall** in Cheam is one of London's oldest timber-framed houses which has associations with Henry VIII's Nonsuch Palace, the Civil War and the Cheam School.

In Sutton there are nearly 1000 acres of parks and open spaces. **Beddington Park** was once the grounds of Carew Manor, a former extra Royal residence (now a school). Henry VIII visited here in 1531. Excavations near here in 1871 revealed the remains of a Roman villa. **Nonsuch Park** has 250 acres of wooded parkland and it was here that Henry VIII built *Nonsuch Palace* in 1538 (demolished in 1688) — three pillars mark the site.

SOUTH WEST

MERTON lies in southwest London and incorporates *Mitcham, Merton, Morden* and *Wimbledon.* The latter has the remains of what is believed to be an Iron Age Fort on **Wimbledon Common.** The Common was once notorious for duels, the last of which was fought here in 1840 when the *Earl of Cardigan* wounded captain *Harvey Tuckett.*

There are many places of interest. **Wandle Industrial Museum** illustrates the arts and crafts centered around the River Wandle from 1066 to the present day. The **Wimbledon Lawn Tennis Museum** *(Wimbledon Park)* includes exhibits of Victorian parlour, racket makers and workshops, costumes, trophies, equipment etc. The **Wimbledon Museum of Local History,** housed in a large upstairs room in the premises of the Wimbledon Village

Club, *Ridgway,* contains water colours, prints, maps, books and photographs of Wimbledon.

The **Wimbledon Windmill Museum** *(Wimbledon Common)* is housed in a windmill built in 1817. It depicts the history of windmills in pictures, tools and models.

Southside House is a former home of the *Pennington-Mellor* family, as well as of Swedish philanthropist *Axel Munthe.* Contains family treasures including paintings and furniture of the 17th to 19th centuries.

Two churches worth seeing are **St. Lawrence** *(London Rd, Merton),* rebuilt in 1636 it has 14th century windows and much 18th century work. **St. Mary the Virgin** *(Merton Park)* was built on 1115 foundations. The church has the pew of Lord Nelson. Nelson resided at Merton Place (now demolished) with Sir William and Lady Hamilton from 1801-1805.

For Sport there is **Canons Leisure Centre, Wimbledon FC,** the **All England Lawn Tennis** and **Croquet Club** and **Wimbledon Stadium** for all speedway, greyhound and stock car racing enthusiasts.

For children's entertainment there is the **Polka Children's Theatre** *(240 The Broadway SW19)* which provides theatre performances and puppet shows also exhibitions of *"puppets of the world"* and *"toys of Britain".*

KINGSTON-UPON-THAMES, is situated on the south-western outskirts of London. Within its boundaries are a section of Richmond Park and almost three miles of the River Thames.

The borough is close to three royal parks: **Richmond, Bushy Park** and **Hampton Court.** It is possible to follow riverside walks to Hampton Court, Teddington Lock and Richmond passing some of the more scenic stretches of the Thames.

Among the places to visit are: The **Kingston-upon-Thames Museum and Heritage centre** which houses local archaeological finds and a permanent exhibition. **Coronation Stone** is a slab of grey sandstone surrounded by a railing of Saxon design displayed beside the *Guildhall* in the centre of the town. This is traditionally the stone on which seven Saxon kings were crowned.

Chessington Zoo contains a bird garden, circus, reptile house and picnic areas etc.

WEST LONDON

RICHMOND-UPON-THAMES spans a delightful stretch of the River Thames from Hammersmith Bridge to Hampton Court. The borough takes its name from a palace rebuilt by Henry VII and renamed **Richmond Palace** after his Yorkshire earldom.

Among the Historic Houses are **Ham House** a 1610 country house containing an original collection of fine 17th century furniture and paintings plus a restored 17th century garden; **Hampton Court Palace** *(explained in an earlier chapter under Royal Homes),* described as the *"oldest Tudor Palace in England";* **Marble Hill House** which is a fine example of an English palladian villa built in 1724-29, with a collection of 18th century paintings and furniture; and the **Orleans House Gallery** situated on the riverside in a woodland setting housing a series of exhibitions throughout the year. For the history conscious the gallery derives its name from Orleans House, once the home of King Louis Philippe of France.

Historic Houses (to the date of

writing) open by appointment only are **Asgil House** (designed in 1765), **Kneller Hall** (houses museum of military musical instruments), **Pope's Grotto** (Alexander Pope lived here from 1719-1749) and **Strawberry Hill,** is Horace Walpole's famous *"Gothic Castle".*

There are many acres of open spaces, parks and gardens within the borough, as well as some fine riverside walks. **Richmond Park** is the largest of the royal parks covering 2500 acres, and was first enclosed by Charles I as a deer park. The park has some ancient oak trees and the superb *Woodland Garden* and *Isabella Plantation.* It also has several historic houses including the *King's Observatory,* the *White Lodge* built in 1727 as a hunting lodge for King George I — it now houses the Royal Ballet Junior School; *Thatched Lodge* is the home of Princess Alexandra and *Pembroke Lodge,* now a restaurant and cafeteria with a garden and terrace, was once the home of Lord John Russell and the childhood home of his philosopher grandson Bertrand Russel.

And there is the **Royal Botanical Gardens (Kew Gardens)** in Kew Richmond — (Tel. 940 1171. BR and ⊖ Kew Gardens). The superb R.B.Gs were begun more than 200 years ago by Princess Augusta, George III's mother. From the small 9-acre garden she planted, there are now 300 acres of landscaped gardens and the home for over 25,000 plant species from all over the world. **The Princess of Wales Conservatory,** opened on 20 July 1987 contains representative samples of Kew's immense tropical plant collections — from arid land plants of Africa and the Americas to the moist tropical displays which include pool and swamp habitats where the Giant Water Lily of the Amazon can

be seen. Distinctive buildings include the *Pagoda,* the *Orangery,* three *Temples* and many fine glass houses including the *Palm House* designed by Decimus Burton and completed in 1848 and the newly-renovated *Temperate House.* Also within the grounds are *Kew Palace* built in 1631 and later acquired by George III and Queen Charlotte's cottage built in 1772 and used by George III and his family for picnics in Kew Gardens.

Across the river is **Syon Park** with its many attractions as well as **Kew Bridge Engines Museum** and the **Musical Museum.**

HOUNSLOW, created in 1965, boasts several historic houses, museums and gardens. Hounslow's early history goes back to the Stone Age. Bronze and Iron age relics have also been found in the area and the Romans built roads and encampments here.

Gunnersbury Park Museum was a former Rothschild family mansion. Collections include items of local history, archaeology and transport. The **Heritage Motor Museum** in Syon Park, has a collection of British production cars from 1895 to the present day. **Hogarth's House,** was the country retreat of William Hogarth from 1749-64 but is now a museum displaying his paintings and engravings. **Kew Bridge Engines Trust** houses giant beam engines which operate under steam and are the largest of their kind in the world. Also possesses a working forge, traction engines and models, plus special events throughout the year. **The Musical Museum, British Piano Museum Trust** includes 10 reproducing piano systems working and 3 reproducing pipe organ systems; also street pianos, phonographs, musical boxes etc.

Also in the borough are **Boston Manor House** (built in 1623) **Chiswick House** designed as a *"Temple of the Arts"*, **Osterley Park House** (16th century mansion) and **Syon House** in Syon Park Gardens, was the London residence of the Duke of Northumberland. The gardens contain a lake, conservatory, aviary and aquarium. Also in the grounds of Syon Park is the **London Butterfly House,** containing species of butterflies from all over the world in tropical greenhouses.

NORTH WEST

BRENT, deriving its name from the *River Brent* lies in north-west London. Famous for its major sporting and musical events throughout the year. Brent has many acres of open parkland and several local parks.

For shopping enthusiasts the **Brent Cross Shopping Centre** (⊖ *Brent Cross)* should not be missed. For culture and history lovers the **Grange Museum of Local History** displays work, leisure, home life and transport of the area. Also Victorian parlour and an Edwardian draper's shop.

For sport enthusiasts there's **Wembley Stadium** (⊖ *Wembley Park).* The stadium was built for the British Empire Exhibition of 1924 and is now a major sports venue, including international soccer. Tours include a 15-minute audio visual presentation, Trophy Room, Royal Box, changing rooms kitted out for match day and the *"hallowed turf"*.

LEE VALLEY LEISURE PARK

The LVLP follows the course of the River Lea and stretches almost 23 miles from Ware in Hertfordshire to London's East End.

It is aimed to create a prime leisure and recreational complex. Many exciting events take place which attract very big crowds.

*For further information on each boroughs places of interest and activities, please telephone, as shown below: Use code **01-** in front if phoning from outside London.*

LTBCB	730 3488/3450
Barnet	202 8282
Enfield	366 6565
Hackney	986 3123 ext. 230
Waltham Forest	527 5544
Camden	278 4444 ext. 2165/2764
Tower Hamlets	980 3749
Newham	472 1430
Barking & Dagenham	592 4500 ext 2106
Southwark	703 6311
Lewisham	318 5421/2
Lambeth	274 7722
Bromley	464 3333
Bexley	303 7777
Greenwich	858 6376
Sutton	661 5000
Merton	543 2222
Kingston-Upon-Thames	546 5386
Richmond-Upon-Thames	940 9125
Hounslow	570 7728
Brent	904 1244
Haringey	881 3000
Islington	250 1039
Lee Valley Leisure Park	0992 717711 — No 01 required

NB. The Index/Glossary/Maps will help you to locate places of interest.

Kew Gardens. The Pagoda *(Royal Botanic Gardens — Kew)*

SCALE
0 1 2 3 4 miles
4 miles to 1 inch

CHAPTER EIGHTEEN

FACTFINDER — GENERAL INFORMATION

INFORMATION

British Travel Centre: 12 Regent Street, Piccadilly Circus SW1. Tel. 730 3400 for travel information, accommodation and bookings, bureau de change, gifts etc.
Monday to Saturday: 9am to 6.30pm
Sunday: 10am to 4pm.

Tourist Information Centre: Victoria station forecourt SW1.
Daily 9am to 8.30pm. Tel: 730 3488

London Tourist Board & Convention Bureau (LTBCB) — 26 Grosvenor Gardens SW1W 0DU (written enquiries)
Monday to Friday 9am to 5.30pm
Tel. 730 3488/730 3450 automatic queueing system.
Information centres in **Harrods** (4th floor) and **Selfridges** (ground floor), both open store hours; **Heathrow** Central Station daily from 9am to 6pm.

Apart from the LTBCB you may contact the —
British Tourist Authority/Board
Thames Tower, Blacks Road,
W6 9EL. Tel: 846 9000

National Trust
36 Queen Anne's Gate, SW1H 9AS
Tel: 222 9251

English Heritage
Fortress House
23 Saville Row, W1X 2HE
Tel: 734 6010

City of London Information Centre: St. Paul's Churchyard EC4.
Tel. 606 3030.
Monday to Friday 9.30am to 5pm
Saturday 10am to 12.30pm

London Regional Transport Information
(24 hour service)
Tel. 222 1234

Artsline: Information for disabled people on getting into theatres etc.

Camping: Tel. 730 3488 (LTBCB) for sites in and around London. There are a number of campsites. One popular centre is **Tent City** (providing excellent facilities), 6 miles west of London near east Acton tube and very handy for Heathrow Airport.

River Thames trips: Tel. 730 4812.

Driving Organisations: The Automobile Association's **(AA)** offices are at 5 New Coventry Street, Leicester Square, W1. Tel. 839 4355. The AA together with the Royal Automobile Club *(RAC)* Tel. 0923 33555 also help drivers and motorcyclists when they break down. They also provide information, publications and advice about driving and tours in Britain.
Their services can be used by members of many other driving organisations; contact one in your own country for information.

The Weather: British weather is unpredictable and often variable from region to region — some say "street to street". Come prepared for a mixture of all four seasons, all the time, anytime.
"Weatherline" for Greater London and south east England (up-dated several times a day).
Tel: 0898 500 480.

Mail: Post Offices are open from 9am to 5.30pm weekdays and 9am to 12.30 pm on Saturdays. They are identifiable by a red and yellow sign which can also be found outside many shops where sub post offices operate.

Voltage: Different to the USA and Europe, Britain operates on 240 volts AC, 50 cycles. Use a transformer.

HELP: There are lots of people who can help you in all kinds of ways. Two organisations are particularly useful because they deal with problems in general and can tell you how to get further help if needed.

(a) **Citizens Advice Bureaus** (CABs). They provide information and advice about problems with work, the law, shopping, local services, immigration — in fact, almost anything you can think of. CAB's are independent, and their service is FREE and CONFI-DENTIAL. In 1988 there were over 1,150 in the UK.

(b) **The Police** — An important part of the work of the Police in Britain is helping people. This may include anything from ·giving directions or looking after lost children to dealing with crime and accidents.

Telephone Directory information:-
Dial **142** for numbers in London.
Dial **172** for numbers outside London.
Dial **100** to call the Operator.
Timeline — Dial **123**.

"EMERGENCY"

Dial 999: for fire, police, ambulance, coastguard, care rescue and mountain rescue.

Doctor: 24 hours cover available — Tel. 900 0911 Ext. 13687; or any hospital out-patients department.

Dentist: Tel. 584 1008 for the name of the nearest dentist or try any hospital out-patients department.

Medical Express: Private treatment on a walk-in, no-wait basis. Monday to Friday around 8am to 8pm and Saturday 10am to 6pm, Chapel Place, W.1. Tel. 499 1991.

"MONEY"

Banks: Normally open Monday to Friday 9.30am to 3.30pm with 24-hour service at Heathrow and Gatwick airports.

Major hotels usually exchange foreign currency for residents. Bureau de Change (some provide a 24-hour service) make a charge (commission is much higher than banks) but please stick to those that display LTBCB plaques. Better still stick to the Banks.

American Express: 6 Haymarket SW1 — Tel. 930 4411. Open Monday to Friday 9am to 5pm and Saturday 9am to 12 noon. Cheques are cashed.

Cash Service: Open 24 hours at Trafalgar Square Post Office to Visa card-holders.

Tipping: Porters, commissionaires, hairdressers and taxi drivers expect tips of around 15%. In restaurants, if there is no service charge, add from 10-15%.

VAT: Value Added Tax, currently at 15%. This is included in the purchase price, but if it is added to your invoice, then ask for a *Customs Declaration Form* and it can be reclaimed if it is stamped at the airport of departure. If you are using the *Retail Export Scheme* to get back VAT you have paid, you will have to have the form with you to show to officials on your return journey.

"TRANSPORT"

London underground ⊖. The Underground or *"Tube"* (271-mile route network) as its universally known, is the fastest and easiest way to get around town — in central London you are never more than a few minutes walk from a station. Each line has a name but you will probably find the colours easier to remember (refer to map in the inside back cover). Destinations are always shown on the front of the train as well as on platform indicators. By using a free underground diagram to plan your journey, you will quickly be able to recognize which train you need.

London Buses: Probably the best way to see the sights of London is from the upper deck of the famous red buses —they pass almost all the capital's landmarks and all its famous shops.

A network of special *All Night Buses* run through central London serving Piccadilly Circus, Leicester Square, Victoria, Trafalgar Square, Hyde Park Corner, Marble Arch and many other parts convenient for theatres, cinemas, clubs and restaurants. Buses run every night and their stops have distinctive blue and yellow route numbers.

Tube and Buses — There are London Transport Travel and Information Centres in the following stations: Heathrow Central, Kings Cross, Euston, Charing Cross, Oxford Circus, Piccadilly Circus and St. Jame's Park. Also in Victoria B.R. station and Terminal 1 at Heathrow Airport. There is a 24-hour telephone information service — 222 1234.

British Rail: Travel Centres are located in major British Rail stations (Charing Cross, Euston, Paddington etc) and also at 12 Regent Street W1 and 407 Oxford Street W1. For Network South East dial 200 0200.

Thames Line Riverbus: Commercial operating in June 1988. It is a high speed riverbus service designed to beat London's traffic problems. At present the Thames Line has 7 advanced 62-seater catamarans with airline-style seats capable of an excess of 25 mph. Runs from Chelsea Harbour Pier to the West Indian Pier, stopping at several places. Tel: 01-987 0311.

TO HEATHROW AIRPORT

(a) By Underground ⊖ The Piccadilly Line runs from the centre of Heathrow direct to most of the popular hotel areas of London. The service is fast and frequent; trains run about every 5 minutes, 20 hours a day *(slightly less on Sunday)* and the journey is 40-45 minutes.

(b) By Airbus — Airbus is ideal if you have lots of luggage or want to see the sights along the way. You travel in fast comfortable double-deck buses right to your terminal. There are two Airbus routes (Route A1 leaves from Victoria Station and Route A2 leaves from Euston Station), running directly to all terminals at Heathrow, picking up at 13 points throughout the main hotel areas of central London.

Airbuses are fast, run daily from around 6.30am to 9.15pm, every 20-30 minutes.

Airbus A1 will take you to Terminal 4 in around 50 minutes and to Terminals 1, 2 and 3 in 60-70 minutes.

Airbus A2 will take you to Terminal 4 in 45-60 minutes and to Terminals 1, 2 and 3 in 60-85 minutes.

TO GATWICK AIRPORT

(a) By Rail – Gatwick is a mere 30 minutes from Victoria Station by British Rail's *Gatwick Express*. There are 4 fast, comfortable trains every hour from 5.30am to 9pm and an hourly service through the night.

(b) By Coach — *Flight Line 777* from Victoria Station from 5.40am and then every 10 and 40 minutes past each hour until 7.40pm then 8.40, 9.40 and 10.40pm.

(c) Jetlink: Coach service linking Gatwick and Heathrow airports, runs every 20 minutes. Tel. 668 7261.

Airports (Central & Outer London)
London Heathrow   Tel: 01-759 4321
London Gatwick 0293 28822
London City 01-474 5555
London Stanstead...........0279 502380
Luton 0582 405100

TAXIS

These are nearly always black and one size and may be hired in the streets when displaying lighted *"For Hire"* sign. Pay fare shown on the meter plus around 15% tip. There are over 13,000 licensed black cabs in London.

TOURS

Sightseeing Tours — London Transport's (LT) *"Sightseeing Tours"*, using a traditional double-deck bus, are probably the best way to see most of the capital. It is a great introduction to a magnificent city covering around 18 miles and lasting around $1\frac{1}{2}$ hours, passing most of London's landmarks including St. Paul's, Westminster Abbey, The Tower of London and Tower Bridge, Hyde Park, the Houses of Parliament and lots more.

All tours are guided (French and German commentary is available on certain departures from Baker Street) and there is also a special tour which includes direct entrance to Madame Tussaud's.

Guided Tours are also extremely worthwhile. This is a relaxing way to visit all the sights of London as well as many famous places throughout southern England. You travel in comfortable motorcoaches with panoramic viewing windows, accompanied by a fully qualified guide. London tours, County tours, even River tours; for one day or half a day to exciting destinations including Windsor, Hampton Court, Stratford-upon-Avon and Bath.

Guided Walks: These are extremely interesting and cheap. A Guided Walk is not only informative but it is sociable and above all great fun. After tasting the immense history of London from the top of a bus you must go down into the streets to savour its many flavours. Examples of such Walks include:

- *The London of Dickens and Shakespeare*
- *The Buried City*
- *Around the Old City Wall*
- *In the Footsteps of Sherlock Holmes*
- *London Theatre Walks*
- *Life in Medieval London*
- *London's Historic Docklands and The River Thames* etc.

In fact, you can discover the complete story of the capital from its Roman origins through the arrival of the Saxons and Vikings; learn about its people and events which have combined to make London a uniquely powerful and respected METROPOLIS.

If you are healthy and adventurous enough, try the Silver Jubilee Walkway, a 12 mile walk around London's famous places.

There are also **Personalised Tours,** in or around London, around the U.K. and even short trips abroad.

OPENING HOURS

Shops: Usually open Monday to Saturday from 9.30am to 5.30pm. There is late shopping on Wednesday in Knightsbridge and Thursday in the Oxford Street area.

Some supermarkets (selling mainly food and drink) are open much longer hours — some as late as 12 midnight and a few 24 hours.

PUBS: From 22 August 1988 licensed premises on weekdays can sell drink from 11am to 11pm — some pubs with music have extensions to well after midnight.

On Sundays an extra hour has been added to lunch-time drinking ie., from 12 to 3pm.

N.B. Not all pubs are open Saturday evenings and Sundays — certainly not those in the city.

Major *hotels* are usually licensed for residents to buy drinks 24 hours.

WORLD CLOCK:

When it is 12 noon Greenwich Mean Time (GMT) in London it is —

Amsterdam	13.00	Moscow	15.00
Athens	14.00	Munich	13.00
Bahrain	15.00	New York	07.00
Chicago	06.00	Singapore	19.00
Delhi	17.30	Sydney	22.00
Geneva	13.00	Tel Aviv	14.00
Hong Kong	20.00	Tokyo	21.00
Los Angeles	04.00	Toronto	07.00
Madrid	13.00	Vienna	13.00
Montreal	07.00	Zurich	13.00

*NB: * Having problems with a HOLIDAY BOOKING – Tel: 0898 400311.*

INDEX